CHINUA ACHEBE

Arrow of God

PENGUIN BOOKS

PENGUIN CLASSICS

Published by the Penguin Group
Penguin Books Ltd, 80 Strand, London WC2R 0RL, England
Penguin Group (USA) Inc., 375 Hudson Street, New York, New York 10014, USA
Penguin Group (Canada), 90 Eglinton Avenue East, Suite 700, Toronto, Ontario, Canada M4P 2Y3
(a division of Pearson Penguin Canada Inc.)
Penguin Ireland, 25 St Stephen's Green, Dublin 2, Ireland (a division of Penguin Books Ltd)
Penguin Group (Australia), 707 Collins Street, Melbourne, Victoria 3008, Australia
(a division of Pearson Australia Group Pty Ltd)
Penguin Books India Pvt Ltd, 11 Community Centre,
Panchsheel Park, New Delhi – 110 017, India
Penguin Group (NZ), 67 Apollo Drive, Rosedale, Auckland 0632, New Zealand
(a division of Pearson New Zealand Ltd)
Penguin Books (South Africa) (Pty) Ltd, Block D, Rosebank Office Park,
181 Jan Smuts Avenue, Parktown North, Gauteng 2193, South Africa

Penguin Books Ltd, Registered Offices: 80 Strand, London WC2R 0RL, England

www.penguin.com

First published in the African Writers Series 1965
Published in Penguin Classics 2010
011

Copyright © Chinua Achebe, 1964, 1974
All rights reserved

The moral right of the author has been asserted

Set in Dante MT Std 10.5/13pt
Typeset by Palimpsest Book Production Limited, Falkirk, Stirlingshire
Printed in Great Britain by Clays Ltd, St Ives plc

978-0-141-19156-0

www.greenpenguin.co.uk

MIX
Paper from
responsible sources
FSC™ C018179

Penguin Books is committed to a sustainable
future for our business, our readers and our planet.
This book is made from Forest Stewardship
Council™ certified paper.

To the memory of my father
ISAIAH OKAFOR ACHEBE

Preface to Second Edition

Whenever people have asked me which among my novels is my favourite I have always evaded a direct answer, being strongly of the mind that in sheer invidiousness that question is fully comparable to asking a man to list his children in the order in which he loves them. A paterfamilias worth his salt will, if he must, speak about the peculiar attractiveness of each child.

For *Arrow of God* that peculiar quality may lie in the fact that it is the novel which I am most likely to be caught sitting down to read again. On account of that I have also become aware of certain structural weaknesses in it which I now take the opportunity of a new edition to remove.

Arrow of God has ardent admirers as well as ardent detractors. To the latter nothing more need be said. To the others I can only express the hope that the changes I have made will meet with their approval. But in the nature of things there may well be some so steadfast in their original affection that they will see these changes as uncalled for or even unjustified. Perhaps changes are rarely called for or justified, and yet we keep making them. We should be ready at the very least to salute those who stand fast, the spiritual descendants of that magnificent man, Ezeulu, in the hope that they will forgive us. For had he been spared Ezeulu might have come to see his fate as perfectly consistent with his high historic destiny as victim, consecrating by his agony – thus raising to the stature of a ritual passage – the defection of his people. And he would gladly have forgiven them.

Chinua Achebe

Chapter One

This was the third nightfall since he began to look for signs of the new moon. He knew it would come today but he always began his watch three days early because he must not take a risk. In this season of the year his task was not too difficult; he did not have to peer and search the sky as he might do when the rains came. Then the new moon sometimes hid itself for days behind rain clouds so that when it finally came out it was already halfgrown. And while it played its game the Chief Priest sat up every evening waiting.

His *obi* was built differently from other men's huts. There was the usual, long threshold in front but also a shorter one on the right as you entered. The eaves on this additional entrance were cut back so that sitting on the floor Ezeulu could watch that part of the sky where the moon had its door. It was getting darker and he constantly blinked to clear his eyes of the water that formed from gazing so intently.

Ezeulu did not like to think that his sight was no longer as good as it used to be and that some day he would have to rely on someone else's eyes as his grandfather had done when his sight failed. Of course he had lived to such a great age that his blindness became like an ornament on him. If Ezeulu lived to be so old he too would accept such a loss. But for the present he was as good as any young man, or better because young men were no longer what they used to be. There was one game Ezeulu never tired of playing on them. Whenever they shook hands with him he tensed his arm and put all his power into the grip, and being unprepared for it they winced and recoiled with pain.

The moon he saw that day was as thin as an orphan fed grudgingly by a cruel foster-mother. He peered more closely to make sure he was not deceived by a feather of cloud. At the same time he reached nervously for his *ogene*. It was the same at every new moon. He was now an old man but the fear of the new moon which he felt as a little boy still hovered round him. It was true that when he became Chief Priest of Ulu the fear was often overpowered by the joy of his high office; but it was not killed. It lay on the ground in the grip of the joy.

He beat his *ogene* GOME GOME GOME GOME . . . and immediately children's voices took up the news on all sides. *Onwa atuo!* . . . *onwa atuo!* . . . *onwa atuo!* . . . He put the stick back into the iron gong and leaned it on the wall.

The little children in his compound joined the rest in welcoming the moon. Obiageli's tiny voice stood out like a small *ogene* among drums and flutes. He could also make out the voice of his youngest son, Nwafo. The women too were in the open, talking.

'Moon,' said the senior wife, Matefi, 'may your face meeting mine bring good fortune.'

'Where is it?' asked Ugoye, the younger wife. 'I don't see it. Or am I blind?'

'Don't you see beyond the top of the ukwa tree? Not there. Follow my finger.'

'Oho, I see it. Moon, may your face meeting mine bring good fortune. But how is it sitting? I don't like its posture.'

'Why?' asked Matefi.

'I think it sits awkwardly – like an evil moon.'

'No,' said Matefi. 'A bad moon does not leave anyone in doubt. Like the one under which Okuata died. Its legs were up in the air.'

'Does the moon kill people?' asked Obiageli, tugging at her mother's cloth.

'What have I done to this child? Do you want to strip me naked?'

'I said does the moon kill people?'

'It kills little girls,' said Nwafo, her brother.

'I did not ask you, ant-hill nose.'

'You will soon cry, long throat.'

The moon kills little boys

The moon kills ant-hill nose

The moon kills little boys . . . Obiageli turned everything into a song.

*

Ezeulu went into his barn and took down one yam from the bamboo platform built specially for the twelve sacred yams. There were eight left. He knew there would be eight; nevertheless he counted them carefully. He had already eaten three and had the fourth in his hand. He checked the remaining ones again and went back to his *obi*, shutting the door of the barn carefully after him.

His log fire was smouldering. He reached for a few sticks of firewood stacked in the corner, set them carefully on the fire and placed the yam, like a sacrifice, on top.

As he waited for it to roast he planned the coming event in his mind. It was Oye. Tomorrow would be Afo and the next day Nkwo, the day of the great market. The festival of the Pumpkin Leaves would fall on the third Nkwo from that day. Tomorrow he would send for his assistants and tell them to announce the day to the six villages of Umuaro.

Whenever Ezeulu considered the immensity of his power over the year and the crops and, therefore, over the people he wondered if it was real. It was true he named the day for the feast of the Pumpkin Leaves and for the New Yam feast; but he did not choose it. He was merely a watchman. His power was no more than the power of a child over a goat that was said to be his. As long as the goat was alive it could be his; he would find it food and take care of it. But the day it was slaughtered he would know soon enough who the real owner was. No! the Chief Priest of Ulu was more than that, must be more than that. If he should refuse to name the day there would be no festival – no planting and no reaping. But could he refuse? No Chief Priest had ever refused. So it could not be done. He would not dare.

Ezeulu was stung to anger by this as though his enemy had spoken it.

'Take away that word *dare*,' he replied to this enemy. 'Yes I say take it away. No man in all Umuaro can stand up and say that I dare not. The woman who will bear the man who will say it has not been born yet.'

But this rebuke brought only momentary satisfaction. His mind never content with shallow satisfactions crept again to the brink of knowing. What kind of power was it if it would never be used? Better

3

to say that it was not there, that it was no more than the power in the anus of the proud dog who sought to put out a furnace with his puny fart . . . He turned the yam with a stick.

His youngest son, Nwafo, now came into the *obi*, saluted Ezeulu by name and took his favourite position on the mud-bed at the far end, close to the shorter threshold. Although he was still only a child it looked as though the deity had already marked him out as his future Chief Priest. Even before he had learnt to speak more than a few words he had been strongly drawn to the god's ritual. It could almost be said that he already knew more about it than even the eldest. Nevertheless no one would be so rash as to say openly that Ulu would do this or do that. When the time came that Ezeulu was no longer found in his place Ulu might choose the least likely of his sons to succeed him. It had happened before.

Ezeulu attended the yam very closely, rolling it over with the stick again and again. His eldest son, Edogo, came in from his own hut.

'Ezeulu!' he saluted.

'E-e-i!'

Edogo passed through the hut into the inner compound to his sister Akueke's temporary home.

'Go and call Edogo,' said Ezeulu to Nwafo.

The two came back and sat down on the mud-bed. Ezeulu turned his yam once more before he spoke.

'Did I ever tell you anything about carving a deity?'

Edogo did not reply. Ezeulu looked in his direction but did not see him clearly because that part of the *obi* was in darkness. Edogo on his part saw his father's face lit up by the fire on which he was roasting the sacred yam.

'Is Edogo not there?'

'I am here.'

'I said what did I tell you about carving the image of gods? Perhaps you did not hear my first question; perhaps I spoke with water in my mouth.'

'You told me to avoid it.'

'I told you that, did I? What is this story I hear then – that you are carving an *alusi* for a man of Umuagu?'

'Who told you?'

'Who told me? Is it true or not is what I want to know, not who told me.'

'I want to know who told you because I don't think he can tell the difference between the face of a deity and the face of a Mask.'

'I see. You may go, my son. And if you like you may carve all the gods in Umuaro. If you hear me asking you about it again take my name and give it to a dog.'

'What I am carving for the man of Umuagu is not . . .'

'It is not me you are talking to. I have finished with you.'

Nwafo tried in vain to make sense out of these words. When his father's temper cooled he would ask. Then his sister, Obiageli, came in from the inner compound, saluted Ezeulu and made to sit on the mud-bed.

'Have you finished preparing the bitter-leaf?' asked Nwafo.

'Don't you know how to prepare bitter-leaf? Or are your fingers broken?'

'Keep quiet there, you two.' Ezeulu rolled the yam out of the fire with the stick and quickly felt it between his thumb and first finger, and was satisfied. He brought down a two-edged knife from the rafters and began to scrape off the coat of black on the roast yam. His hands were covered in soot when he had finished, and he clapped them together a few times to get them clean again. His wooden bowl was near at hand and he cut the yam into it and waited for it to cool.

When he began eating Obiageli started to sing quietly to herself. She should have known by now that her father never gave out even the smallest crumbs of the yam he ate without palm oil at every new moon. But she never ceased hoping.

He ate in silence. He had moved away from the fire and now sat with his back against the wall, looking outwards. As was usual with him on these occasions his mind seemed to be fixed on distant thoughts. Now and again he drank from a calabash of cold water which Nwafo had brought for him. As he took the last piece Obiageli returned to her mother's hut. Nwafo put away the wooden bowl and the calabash and stuck the knife again between two rafters.

Ezeulu rose from his goatskin and moved to the household shrine on a flat board behind the central dwarf wall at the entrance. His *ikenga*, about as tall as a man's forearm, its animal horn as long as the rest of its human body, jostled with faceless *okposi* of the ancestors black with the blood of sacrifice, and his short personal staff of *ofo*. Nwafo's eyes picked out the special *okposi* which belonged to him. It had been carved for him because of the convulsions he used to have at night. They told him to call it Namesake, and he did. Gradually the convulsions had left him.

Ezeulu took the *ofo* staff from the others and sat in front of the shrine, not astride in a man's fashion but with his legs stretched in front of him to one side of the shrine, like a woman. He held one end of the short staff in his right hand and with the other end hit the earth to punctuate his prayer:

Ulu, I thank you for making me see another new moon. May I see it again and again. This household may it be healthy and prosperous. As this is the moon of planting may the six villages plant with profit. May we escape danger in the farm – the bite of a snake or the sting of the scorpion, the mighty one of the scrubland. May we not cut our shinbone with the matchet or the hoe. And let our wives bear male children. May we increase in numbers at the next counting of the villages so that we shall sacrifice to you a cow, not a chicken as we did after the last New Yam feast. May children put their fathers into the earth and not fathers their children. May good meet the face of every man and every woman. Let it come to the land of the riverain folk and to the land of the forest peoples.

He put the *ofo* back among the *ikenga* and the *okposi*, wiped his mouth with the back of his hand and returned to his place. Every time he prayed for Umuaro bitterness rose into his mouth, a great smouldering anger for the division which had come to the six villages and which his enemies sought to lay on his head. And for what reason? Because he had spoken the truth before the white man. But how could a man who held the holy staff of Ulu know that a thing was a lie and speak it? How could he fail to tell the story as he had heard it from his own father? Even the white man, Wintabota, understood, though he came from a land no one knew. He had called Ezeulu the only witness of truth. That was what riled his enemies – that the white man whose father or mother no one knew should come to tell them the truth they knew but hated to hear. It was an augury of the world's ruin.

The voices of women returning from the stream broke into Ezeulu's thoughts. He could not see them because of the darkness outside. The new moon having shown itself had retired again. But the night bore marks of its visit. The darkness was not impenetrable as it had been lately, but open and airy like a forest from which the undergrowth had been cut. As the women called out 'Ezeulu' one after another he saw their vague forms and returned their greeting. They left the *obi* to their right and went into the inner compound through the only other entrance – a high, carved door in the red, earth walls.

'Are these not the people I saw going to the stream before the sun went down?'

'Yes,' said Nwafo. 'They went to Nwangene.'

'I see.' Ezeulu had forgotten temporarily that the nearer stream, Ota, had been abandoned since the oracle announced yesterday that the enormous boulder resting on two other rocks at its source was about to fall and would take a softer pillow for its head. Until the *alusi* who owned the stream and whose name it bore had been placated no one would go near it.

Still, Ezeulu thought, he would speak his mind to whoever brought him a late supper tonight. If they knew they had to go to Nwangene they should have set out earlier. He was tired of having his meal sent to him when other men had eaten and forgotten.

Obika's great, manly voice rose louder and louder into the night air as he approached home. Even his whistling carried farther than some men's voices. He sang and whistled alternately.

'Obika is returning,' said Nwafo.

'The night bird is early coming home today,' said Ezeulu, at the same time.

'One day soon he will see Eru again,' said Nwafo, referring to the apparition Obika had once seen at night. The story had been told so often that Nwafo imagined he was there.

'This time it will be Idemili or Ogwugwu,' said Ezeulu with a smile, and Nwafo was full of happiness.

★

About three years ago Obika had rushed into the *obi* one night and flung himself at his father shivering with terror. It was a dark night and rain was preparing to fall. Thunder rumbled with a deep, liquid voice and flash answered flash.

'What is it, my son?' Ezeulu asked again and again, but Obika trembled and said nothing.

'What is it, Obika?' asked his mother, Matefi, who had run into the *obi* and was now shaking worse than her son.

'Keep quiet there,' said Ezeulu. 'What did you see, Obika?'

When he had cooled a little Obika began to tell his father what he had seen at a flash of lightning near the ugili tree between their village, Umuachala, and Umunneora. As soon as he had mentioned the place Ezeulu had known what it was.

'What happened when you saw It?'

'I knew it was a spirit; my head swelled.'

'Did he not turn into the Bush That Ruined Little Birds? On the left?'

His father's confidence revived Obika. He nodded and Ezeulu nodded twice. The other women were now ranged round the door.

'What did he look like?'

'Taller than any man I know.' He swallowed a lump. 'His skin was very light . . . like . . . like . . .'

'Was he dressed like a poor man or was it like a man of great wealth?'

'He was dressed like a wealthy man. He had an eagle's feather in his red cap.'

His teeth began to knock together again.

'Hold yourself together. You are not a woman. Had he an elephant tusk?'

'Yes. He carried a big tusk across his shoulder.'

The rain had now begun to fall, at first in big drops that sounded like pebbles on the thatch.

'There is no cause to be afraid, my son. You have seen Eru, the Magnificent, the One that gives wealth to those who find favour with him. People sometimes see him at that place in this kind of weather. Perhaps he was returning home from a visit to Idemili or the other

deities. Eru only harms those who swear falsely before his shrine.'
Ezeulu was carried away by his praise of the god of wealth. The way
he spoke one would have thought he was the proud priest of Eru rather
than Ulu who stood above Eru and all the other deities. 'When he likes
a man wealth flows like a river into his house; his yams grow as big as
human beings, his goats produce threes and his hens hatch nines.'

Matefi's daughter, Ojiugo, brought in a bowl of foofoo and a bowl of
soup, saluted her father and set them before him. Then she turned to
Nwafo and said: 'Go to your mother's hut; she has finished cooking.'

'Leave the boy alone,' said Ezeulu who knew that Matefi and her
daughter resented his partiality for his other wife's son. 'Go and call
your mother for me.' He made no move to start eating and Ojiugo
knew there was going to be trouble. She went back to her mother's
hut and called her.

'I don't know how many times I have said in this house that I shall
not eat my supper when every other man in Umuaro is retiring to
sleep,' he said as soon as Matefi came in. 'But you will not listen. To
you whatever I say in this house is no more effective than the fart a
dog breaks to put out a fire . . .'

'I went all the way to Nwangene to fetch water and . . .'

'If you like you may go to Nkisa. What I am saying is that if you
want that madness of yours to be cured, bring my supper at this time
another day . . .'

When Ojiugo came to collect the bowls she found Nwafo polishing
off the soup. She waited for him to finish, full of anger. Then she
gathered the bowls and went to tell her mother about it. This was not
the first time or the second or third. It happened every day.

'Do you blame a vulture for perching over a carcass?' said Matefi.
'What do you expect a boy to do when his mother cooks soup with
locust beans for fish? She saves her money to buy ivory bracelets. But
Ezeulu will never see anything wrong in what she does. If it is me
then he knows what to say.'

Ojiugo was looking towards the other woman's hut which was
separated from theirs by the whole length of the compound. All she

could see was the yellowish glow of the palm oil lamp between the low eaves and the threshold. There was a third hut which formed a half moon with the other two. It had belonged to Ezeulu's first wife, Okuata, who died many years ago. Ojiugo hardly knew her; she only remembered she used to give a piece of fish and some locust beans to every child who went to her hut when she was making her soup. She was the mother of Adeze, Edogo and Akueke. After her death her children lived in the hut until the girls married. Then Edogo lived there alone until he married two years ago and built a small compound of his own besides his father's. Now Akueke had been living in the hut again since she left her husband's house. They said the man ill-treated her. But Ojiugo's mother said it was a lie and that Akueke was headstrong and proud, the kind of woman who carried her father's compound into the house of her husband.

Just when Ojiugo and her mother were about to begin their meal, Obika came home singing and whistling.

'Bring me his bowl,' said Matefi. 'He is early today.'

Obika stooped at the low eaves and came in hands first. He saluted his mother and she said '*Nno*' without any warmth. He sat down heavily on the mud-bed. Ojiugo had brought his soup bowl of fired clay and was now bringing down his foofoo from the bamboo ledge. Matefi blew into the soup bowl to remove dust and ash and ladled soup into it. Ojiugo set it before her brother and went outside to bring water in a gourd.

After the first swallow Obika tilted the bowl of soup towards the light and inspected it critically.

'What do you call this, soup or cocoyam porridge.'

The women ignored him and went on with their own interrupted meal. It was clear he had drunk too much palm wine again.

Obika was one of the handsomest young men in Umuaro and all the surrounding districts. His face was very finely cut and his nose stood *gem*, like the note of a gong. His skin was, like his father's, the colour of terracotta. People said of him (as they always did when they saw great comeliness) that he was not born for these parts among the Igbo people of the forests; that in his previous life he must have sojourned among the riverain folk whom the Igbo called Olu.

But two things spoilt Obika. He drank palm wine to excess, and he was given to sudden and fiery anger. And being as strong as rock he was always inflicting injury on others. His father who preferred him to Edogo, his quiet and brooding half-brother, nevertheless said to him often: 'It is praiseworthy to be brave and fearless, my son, but sometimes it is better to be a coward. We often stand in the compound of a coward to point at the ruins where a brave man used to live. The man who has never submitted to anything will soon submit to the burial mat.'

But for all that Ezeulu would rather have a sharp boy who broke utensils in his haste than a slow and careful snail.

Not very long ago Obika had come very close indeed to committing murder. His half-sister, Akueke, often came home to say that her husband had beaten her. One early morning she came again with her face all swollen. Without waiting to hear the rest of the story Obika set out for Umuogwugwu, the village of his brother-in-law. On the way he stopped to call his friend, Ofoedu, who was never absent from the scene of a fight. As they approached Umuogwugwu Obika explained to Ofoedu that he must not help in beating Akueke's husband.

'Why have you called me then?' asked the other, angrily. 'To carry your bag?'

'There may be work for you. If Umuogwugwu people are what I take them to be they will come out in force to defend their brother. Then there will be work for you.'

No one in Ezeulu's compound knew where Obika had gone until he returned a little before noon with Ofoedu. On their heads was Akueke's husband tied to a bed, almost dead. They set him down under the ukwa tree and dared anyone to move him. The women and the neighbours pleaded with Obika and showed him the threatening ripe fruit on the tree, as big as water pots.

'Yes. I put him there on purpose, to be crushed by the fruit – the beast.'

Eventually the commotion brought Ezeulu, who had gone into the near-by bush, hurrying home. When he saw what was happening he wailed a lament on the destruction Obika would bring to his house and ordered him to release his in-law.

For three markets Ibe could barely rise from his bed. Then one evening his kinsmen came to seek satisfaction from Ezeulu. Most of them had gone out to their farms when it had all happened. For three markets and more they had waited patiently for someone to explain why their kinsman should be beaten up and carried away.

'What is this story we hear about Ibe?' they asked.

Ezeulu tried to placate them without admitting that his son had done anything seriously wrong. He called his daughter, Akueke, to stand before them.

'You should have seen her the day she came home. Is this how you marry women in your place? If it is your way then I say you will not marry my daughter like that.'

The men agreed that Ibe had stretched his arm too far, and so no one could blame Obika for defending his sister.

'Why do we pray to Ulu and to our ancestors to increase our numbers if not for this thing?' said their leader. 'No one eats numbers. But if we are many nobody will dare molest us, and our daughters will hold their heads up in their husbands' houses. So we do not blame Obika too much. Do I speak well?' His companions answered yes and he continued.

'We cannot say that your son did wrong to fight for his sister. What we do not understand, however, is why a man with a penis between his legs should be carried away from his house and village. It is as if to say: You are nothing and your kinsmen can do nothing. This is the part we do not understand. We have not come with wisdom but with foolishness because a man does not go to his in-law with wisdom. We want you to say to us: You are wrong; this is how it is or that is how it is. And we shall be satisfied and go home. If someone says to us afterwards: Your kinsman was beaten up and carried away; we shall know what to reply. Our great in-law, I salute you.'

Ezeulu employed all his skill in speaking to pacify his in-laws. They went home happier than they came. But it was hardly likely that they would press Ibe to carry palm wine to Ezeulu and ask for his wife's return. It looked as if she would live in her father's compound for a long time.

*

When he finished his meal Obika joined the others in Ezeulu's hut. As usual Edogo spoke for all of them. As well as Obika, Oduche and Nwafo were there also.

'Tomorrow is Afo,' said Edogo, 'and we have come to find out what work you have for us.'

Ezeulu thought for a while as though he was unprepared for the proposal. Then he asked Obika how much of the work on his new homestead was still undone.

'Only the woman's barn,' he replied. 'But that could wait. There will be no cocoyam to put into it until harvest time.'

'Nothing will wait,' said Ezeulu. 'A new wife should not come into an unfinished homestead. I know such a thing does not trouble the present age. But as long as we are there we shall continue to point out the right way . . . Edogo, instead of working for me tomorrow take your brothers and the women to build the barn. If Obika has no shame, the rest of us have.'

'Father, I have a word to say.' It was Oduche.

'I am listening.'

Oduche cleared his throat as if he was afraid to begin.

'Perhaps they are forbidden to help their brothers build a barn,' said Obika thickly.

'You are always talking like a fool,' Edogo snapped at him. 'Has Oduche not worked as hard as yourself on your homestead? I should say harder.'

'It is Oduche I am waiting to hear,' said Ezeulu, 'not you two jealous wives.'

'I am one of those they have chosen to go to Okperi tomorrow and bring the loads of our new teacher.'

'Oduche!'

'Father!'

'Listen to what I shall say now. When a handshake goes beyond the elbow we know it has turned to another thing. It was I who sent you to join those people because of my friendship to the white man, Wintabota. He asked me to send one of my children to learn the ways of his people and I agreed to send you. I did not send you so that you might leave your duty in my household. Do you hear me? Go and tell the people who chose you to go to Okperi that I said no. Tell them that tomorrow is the day on which my sons and my wives and my son's wife work for me. Your people should know the custom of this land; if they don't you must tell them. Do you hear me?'

'I hear you.'

'Go and call your mother for me. I think it is her turn to cook tomorrow.'

Chapter Two

Ezeulu often said that the dead fathers of Umuaro looking at the world from Ani-Mmo must be utterly bewildered by the ways of the new age. At no other time but now could Umuaro have taken war to Okperi in the circumstances in which they did. Who would have imagined that Umuaro would go to war so sorely divided? Who would have thought that they would disregard the warning of the priest of Ulu who originally brought the six villages together and made them what they were? But Umuaro had grown wise and strong in its own conceit and had become like the little bird, nza, who ate and drank and challenged his personal god to single combat. Umuaro challenged the deity which laid the foundation of their villages. And – what did they expect? – he thrashed them, thrashed them enough for today and for tomorrow!

In the very distant past, when lizards were still few and far between, the six villages – Umuachala, Umunneora, Umuagu, Umuezeani, Umuogwugwu and Umuisiuzo – lived as different peoples, and each worshipped its own deity. Then the hired soldiers of Abam used to strike in the dead of night, set fire to the houses and carry men, women and children into slavery. Things were so bad for the six villages that their leaders came together to save themselves. They hired a strong team of medicine-men to install a common deity for them. This deity which the fathers of the six villages made was called Ulu. Half of the medicine was buried at a place which became Nkwo market and the other half thrown into the stream which became Mili Ulu. The six villages then took the name of Umuaro, and the priest of Ulu became their Chief Priest. From that day they were never again beaten by an enemy. How could such a people disregard the god who founded their town and protected it? Ezeulu saw it as the ruin of the world.

On the day, five years ago, when the leaders of Umuaro decided to send an emissary to Okperi with white clay for peace or new palm frond for war, Ezeulu spoke in vain. He told the men of Umuaro that Ulu would not fight an unjust war.

'I know,' he told them, 'my father said this to me that when our village first came here to live the land belonged to Okperi. It was Okperi who gave us a piece of their land to live in. They also gave us their deities – their Udo and their Ogwugwu. But they said to our ancestors – mark my words – the people of Okperi said to our fathers: We give you our Udo and our Ogwugwu; but you must call the deity we give you not Udo but the son of Udo, and not Ogwugwu but the son of Ogwugwu. This is the story as I heard it from my father. If you choose to fight a man for a piece of farmland that belongs to him I shall have no hand in it.'

But Nwaka had carried the day. He was one of the three people in all the six villages who had taken the highest title in the land, Eru, which was called after the lord of wealth himself. Nwaka came from a long line of prosperous men and from a village which called itself first in Umuaro. They said that when the six villages first came together they offered the priesthood of Ulu to the weakest among them to ensure that none in the alliance became too powerful.

'Umuaro kwenu!' Nwaka roared.

'Hem!' replied the men of Umuaro.

'Kwenu!'

'Hem!'

'Kwezuenu!'

'Hem!'

He began to speak almost softly in the silence he had created with his salutation.

'Wisdom is like a goatskin bag; every man carries his own. Knowledge of the land is also like that. Ezeulu has told us what his father told him about the olden days. We know that a father does not speak falsely to his son. But we also know that the lore of the land is beyond the knowledge of many fathers. If Ezeulu had spoken about the great deity of Umuaro which he carries and which his fathers carried before him I would have paid attention to his voice. But he speaks about events which are older than Umuaro itself. I shall not be afraid to say that neither Ezeulu nor any other in this village can tell us about these events.' There were murmurs of approval and of disapproval but more of approval from the assembly of elders and men of title. Nwaka walked forward and back as he spoke; the eagle feather in his red cap and bronze band on his ankle marked him out as one of the lords of the land – a man favoured by Eru, the god of riches.

'My father told me a different story. He told me that Okperi people were wanderers. He told me three or four different places where they sojourned for a while and moved on again. They were driven away by Umuofia, then by Abame and Aninta. Would they go today and claim all those sites? Would they have laid claim on our farmland in the days before the white man turned us upside down? Elders and Ndichie of Umuaro, let everyone return to his house if we have no heart in the fight. We shall not be the first people who abandoned their farmland or even their homestead to avoid war. But let us not tell ourselves or our children that we did it because the land belonged to other people. Let us rather tell them that their fathers did not choose to fight. Let us tell them also that we marry the daughters of Okperi and their men marry our daughters, and that where there is this mingling men often lose the heart to fight. Umuaro Kwenu!'

'Hem!'

'Kwezuenu!'

'Hem!'

'I salute you all.'

The long uproar that followed was largely of approbation. Nwaka had totally destroyed Ezeulu's speech. The last glancing blow which killed it was the hint that the Chief Priest's mother had been a daughter of Okperi. The assembly broke up into numerous little groups of people talking to those who sat nearest to them. One man said that Ezeulu had forgotten whether it was his father or his mother who told him about the farmland. Speaker after speaker rose and spoke to the assembly until it was clear that all the six villages stood behind Nwaka. Ezeulu was not the only man of Umuaro whose mother had come from Okperi. But none of the others dared go to his support. In fact one of them, Akukalia, whose language never wandered far from 'kill and despoil', was so fiery that he was chosen to carry the white clay and the new palm frond to his motherland, Okperi.

The last man to speak that day was the oldest man from Akukalia's village. His voice was now shaky but his salute to the assembly was heard clearly in all corners of the Nkwo market place. The men of Umuaro responded to his great effort with the loudest Hem! of the day. He said quietly that he must rest to recover his breath, and those who heard laughed.

'I want to speak to the man we are sending to Okperi. It is now a long time since we fought a war and many of you may not remember the custom. I am not saying that Akukalia needs to be reminded. But I am an old man, and an old man is there to talk. If the lizard of the homestead should neglect to do the things for which its kind is known, it will be mistaken for the lizard of the farmland.

'From the way Akukalia spoke I saw that he was in great anger. It is right that he should feel like that. But we are not sending him to his motherland to fight. We are sending you, Akukalia, to place the choice of war or peace before them. Do I speak for Umuaro?' They gave him power to carry on.

'We do not want Okperi to choose war; nobody eats war. If they choose peace we shall rejoice. But whatever they say you are not to dispute with them. Your duty is to bring word back to us. We all know you are a fearless man but while you are there put your fearlessness in your bag. If the young men who will go with you talk with too loud a voice it shall be your duty to cover their fault. I have in my younger days gone on such errands and know the temptations too well. I salute you.'

Ezeulu who had taken in everything with a sad smile now sprang to his feet like one stung in the buttocks by a black ant.

'Umuaro Kwenu!' he cried.

'Hem!'

'I salute you all.' It was like the salute of an enraged Mask. 'When an adult is in the house the she-goat is not left to suffer the pains of parturition on its tether. That is what our ancestors have said. But what have we seen here today? We have seen people speak because they are afraid to be called cowards. Others have spoken the way they spoke because they are hungry for war. Let us leave all that aside. If in truth the farmland is ours, Ulu will fight on our side. But if it is not we shall know soon enough. I would not have spoken again today if I had not seen adults in the house neglecting their duty. Ogbuefi Egonwanne, as one of the three oldest men in Umuaro, should have reminded us that our fathers did not fight a war of blame. But instead of that he wants to teach our emissary how to carry fire and water in the same mouth. Have we not heard that a boy sent by his father to steal does not go stealthily but breaks the door with his feet? Why does Egonwanne trouble himself about small things when big ones are overlooked? We want war. How Akukalia speaks to his mother's people is a small thing. He can spit into their face if he likes. When we hear a house has fallen do we ask if the ceiling fell with it? I salute you all.'

Akukalia and his two companions set out for Okperi at cock-crow on the following day. In his goatskin bag he carried a lump of white chalk and a few yellow palm fronds cut from the summit of the tree before they had unfurled to the sun. Each man also carried a sheathed matchet.

The day was Eke, and before long Akukalia and his companions began to pass women from all the neighbouring villages on their way to the famous Eke Okperi market. They were mostly women from Elumelu and Abame who made the best pots in all the surrounding country. Everyone carried a towering load of five or six or even more big water pots held together with a net of ropes on a long basket, and seemed in the half light like a spirit with a fantastic head.

As the men of Umuaro passed company after company of these market women they talked about the great Eke market in Okperi to which folk from every part of Igbo and Olu went.

'It is the result of an ancient medicine,' Akukalia explained. 'My mother's people are great medicine-men.' There was pride in his voice. 'At first Eke was a very small market. Other markets in the neighbourhood were drawing it dry. Then one day the men of Okperi made a powerful deity and placed their market in its care. From that day Eke grew and grew until it became the biggest market in these parts. This deity which is called Nwanyieke is an old woman. Every Eke day before cock-crow she appears in the market place with a broom in her right hand and dances round the vast open space beckoning with her broom in all directions of the earth and drawing folk from every land. That is why people will not come near the market before cock-crow; if they did they would see the ancient lady in her task.'

'They tell the same story of the Nkwo market beside the great river at Umuru,' said one of Akukalia's companions. 'There the medicine has worked so well that the market no longer assembles only on Nkwo days.'

'Umuru is no match for my mother's people in medicine,' said Akukalia. 'Their market has grown because the white man took his merchandise there.'

'Why did he take his merchandise there,' asked the other man, 'if not because of their medicine? The old woman of the market has swept the world with her broom, even the land of the white men where they say the sun never shines.'

'Is it true that one of their women in Umuru went outside without the white hat and melted like sleeping palm oil in the sun?' asked the other companion.

'I have also heard it,' said Akukalia. 'But many lies are told about the white man. It was once said that he had no toes.'

As the sun rose the men came to the disputed farmland. It had not been cultivated for many years and was thick with browned spear grass.

'I remember coming with my father to this very place to cut grass for our thatches,' said Akukalia. 'It is a thing of surprise to me that my mother's people are claiming it today.'

'It is all due to the white man who says, like an elder to two fighting children: You will not fight while I am around. And so the younger and weaker of the two begins to swell himself up and to boast.'

'You have spoken the truth,' said Akukalia. 'Things like this would never have happened when I was a young man, to say nothing of the days of my father. I remember all this very well,' he waved over the land. 'That ebenebe tree over there was once hit by thunder, and people cutting thatch under it were hurled away in every direction.'

'What you should ask them,' said the other companion who had spoken very little since they set out, 'what they should tell us is why, if the land was indeed theirs, why they let us farm it and cut thatch from it for generation after generation, until the white man came and reminded them.'

'It is not our mission to ask them any question, except the one question which Umuaro wants them to answer,' said Akukalia. 'And I think I should remind you again to hold your tongues in your hand when we get there and leave the talking to me. They are very difficult people; my mother was no exception. But I know what they know. If a man of Okperi says to you come, he means run away with all your strength. If you are not used to their ways you may sit with them from cock-crow until roosting-time and join in their talk and their food, but all the while you will be floating on the surface of the water. So leave them to me because when a man of cunning dies a man of cunning buries him.'

The three emissaries entered Okperi about the time when most people finished their morning meal. They made straight for the compound of Uduezue, the nearest living relation to Akukalia's mother. Perhaps it was the men's unsmiling faces that told Uduezue, or maybe Okperi was not altogether unprepared for the mission from Umuaro. Nevertheless Uduezue asked them about their people at home.

'They are well,' replied Akukalia impatiently. 'We have an urgent message which we must give to the rulers of Okperi at once.'

'True?' asked Uduezue. 'I was saying to myself: What could bring my son and his people all this way so early? If my sister, your mother, were still alive, I would have thought that something had happened to her.' He paused for a very little while. 'An important mission; yes. We have a saying that a toad does not run in the day unless something is after it. I do not want to delay your mission, but I must offer you a piece of kolanut.' He made to rise.

'Do not worry yourself. Perhaps we shall return after our mission.

It is a big load on our head, and until we put it down we cannot understand anything we are told.'

'I know what it is like. Here is a piece of white clay then. Let me agree with you and leave the kolanut until you return.'

But the men declined even to draw lines on the floor with the clay. After that there was nothing else to say. They had rebuffed the token of goodwill between host and guest, their mission must indeed be grave.

Uduezue went into his inner compound and soon returned with his goatskin bag and sheathed matchet. 'I shall take you to the man who will receive your message,' he said.

He led the way and the others followed silently. They passed an ever-thickening crowd of market people. As the planting season was near many of them carried long baskets of seed-yams. Some of the men carried goats also in long baskets. But now and again there was a man clutching a fowl; such a man never trod the earth firmly, especially when he was a man who had known better times. Many of the women talked boisterously as they went; the silent ones were those who had come from far away and had exhausted themselves. Akukalia thought he recognized some of the towering headloads of water pots they had left behind on their way.

Akukalia had not visited his mother's land for about three years and he now felt strangely tender towards it. When as a little boy he had first come here with his mother he had wondered why the earth and sand looked white instead of red-brown as in Umuaro. His mother had told him the reason was that in Okperi people washed every day and were clean while in Umuaro they never touched water for the whole four days of the week. His mother was very harsh to him and very quarrelsome, but now Akukalia felt tender even towards her.

Uduezue took his three visitors to the house of Otikpo, the town-crier of Okperi. He was in his *obi* preparing seed-yams for the market. He rose to greet his visitors. He called Uduezue by his name and title and called Akukalia *Son of our Daughter*. He merely shook hands with the other two whom he did not know. Otikpo was very tall and of spare frame. He still looked like the great runner he had been in his youth.

He went into an inner room and returned with a rolled mat which he spread on the mud-bed for his visitors. A little girl came in from the inner compound calling, 'Father, Father.'

'Go away, Ogbanje,' he said. 'Don't you see I have strangers?'

'Nweke slapped me.'

'I shall whip him later. Go and tell him I shall whip him.'

'Otikpo, let us go outside and whisper together,' said Uduezue.

They did not stay very long. When they came back Otikpo brought a kolanut in a wooden bowl. Akukalia thanked him but said that he and his companions carried such heavy loads on their heads that they could neither eat nor drink until the burden was set down.

'True?' asked Otikpo. 'Can this burden you speak of come down before me and Uduezue, or does it require the elders of Okperi?'

'It requires the elders.'

'Then you have come at a bad time. Everybody in Igboland knows that Okperi people do not have other business on their Eke day. You should have come yesterday or the day before, or tomorrow or the day after. *Son of our Daughter*, you should know our habits.'

'Your habits are not different from the habits of other people,' said Akukalia. 'But our mission could not wait.'

'True?' Otikpo went outside and raising his voice called his neighbour, Ebo, and came in again.

'The mission could not wait. What shall we do now? I think you should sleep in Okperi today and see the elders tomorrow.'

Ebo came in and saluted generally. He was surprised to see so many people, and was temporarily at a loss. Then he began to shake hands all round, but when Akukalia's turn came he refused to take Ebo's hand.

'Sit down, Ebo,' said Otikpo. 'Akukalia has a message for Okperi which forbids him to eat kolanut or shake hands. He wants to see the elders and I have told him it is not possible today.'

'Why did they choose today to bring their message? Have they no market where they come from? If that is all you are calling me for I must go back and prepare for market.'

'Our message cannot wait, I have said that before.'

'I have not yet heard of a message that could not wait. Or have you brought us news that Chukwu, the high god, is about to remove the foot that holds the world? If not then you must know that Eke Okperi does not break up because three men have come to town. If you listen carefully even now you can hear its voice; and it is not even half full yet. When it is full you can hear it from Umuda. Do you think a market like that will stop to hear your message?' He sat down for a while; nobody else spoke.

'You can now see, *Son of our Daughter*, that we cannot get our elders together before tomorrow,' said Otikpo.

'If war came suddenly to your town how do you call your men together, *Father of my Mother*? Do you wait till tomorrow? Do you not beat your *ikolo*?'

Ebo and Otikpo burst into laughter. The three men from Umuaro exchanged glances. Akukalia's face began to look dangerous. Uduezue sat as he had done since they first came in, his chin in his left hand.

'Different people have different customs,' said Otikpo after his laugh. 'In Okperi it is not our custom to welcome strangers to our market with the *ikolo*.'

'Are you telling us, *Father of my Mother*, that you regard us as market women? I have borne your insults patiently. Let me remind you that my name is Okeke Akukalia of Umuaro.'

'Ooh, of Umuaro,' said Ebo, still smarting from the rebuffed handshake. 'I am happy you have said of Umuaro. The name of this town is Okperi.'

'Go back to your house,' shouted Akukalia, 'or I will make you eat shit.'

'If you want to shout like a castrated bull you must wait until you return to Umuaro. I have told you this place is called Okperi.'

Perhaps it was deliberate, perhaps accidental. But Ebo had just said the one thing that nobody should ever have told Akukalia who was impotent and whose two wives were secretly given to other men to bear his children.

The ensuing fight was grim. Ebo was no match for Akukalia and soon had a broken head, streaming with blood. Maddened by pain and shame he made for his house to get a matchet. Women and children from all the near-by compounds were now out, some of them screaming with fright. Passers-by also rushed in, making futile motions of intervention.

What happened next was the work of Ekwensu, the bringer of evil. Akukalia rushed after Ebo, went into the *obi*, took the *ikenga* from his shrine, rushed outside again and, while everyone stood aghast, split it in two.

Ebo was last to see the abomination. He had been struggling with Otikpo who wanted to take the matchet from him and so prevent bloodshed. But when the crowd saw what Akukalia had done they called on Otikpo to leave the man alone. The two men came out of the hut together. Ebo rushed towards Akukalia and then seeing what he had done stopped dead. He did not know, for one brief moment, whether he was awake or dreaming. He rubbed his eyes with the back of his left hand. Akukalia stood in front of him. The two pieces of his *ikenga* lay where their violator had kicked them in the dust.

'Move another step if you call yourself a man. Yes I did it. What can you do?'

So it was true. Still Ebo turned round and went into his *obi*. At his shrine he knelt down to have a close look. Yes, the gap where his *ikenga*, the strength of his right arm, had stood stared back at him – an empty patch, without dust, on the wooden board. 'Nna doh! Nna doh!' he wept, calling on his dead father to come to his aid. Then he got up and went into his sleeping-room. He was there a little while before Otikpo, thinking he might be doing violence to himself, rushed into the room to see. But it was too late. Ebo pushed him aside and came into the *obi* with his loaded gun. At the threshold he knelt down and aimed. Akukalia, seeing the danger, dashed forward. Although the bullet had caught him in the chest he continued running with his matchet held high until he fell at the threshold, his face hitting the low thatch before he went down.

When the body was brought home to Umuaro everyone was stunned. It had never happened before that an emissary of Umuaro was killed abroad. But after the first shock people began to say that their clansman had done an unforgivable thing.

'Let us put ourselves in the place of the man he made a corpse before his own eyes,' they said. 'Who would bear such a thing? What propitiation or sacrifice would atone for such sacrilege? How would the victim set about putting himself right again with his fathers unless he could say to them: Rest, for the man that did it has paid with his head? Nothing short of that would have been adequate.'

Umuaro might have left the matter there, and perhaps the whole land dispute with it as Ekwensu seemed to have taken a hand in it. But one small thing worried them. It was small but at the same time it was very great. Why had Okperi not deigned to send a message to Umuaro to say this was what happened and that was what happened? Everyone agreed that the man who killed Akukalia had been sorely provoked. It was also true that Akukalia was not only a son of Umuaro; he was also the son of a daughter of Okperi, and what had happened might be likened to he-goat's head dropping into he-goat's bag. Yet when a man was killed something had to be said, some explanation given. That Okperi had not cared to say anything beyond returning the corpse was a mark of the contempt in which they now held Umuaro. And that could not be overlooked. Four days after Akukalia's death criers went through the six villages at nightfall.

The assembly in the morning was very solemn. Almost everyone who spoke said that although it was not right to blame a corpse it must be admitted that their kinsman did a great wrong. Many of them, especially the older men, asked Umuaro to let the matter drop. But there were others who, as the saying was, pulled out their hair and chewed it. They swore that they would not live and see Umuaro spat upon. They were, as before, led by Nwaka. He spoke with his usual eloquence and stirred many hearts.

Ezeulu did not speak until the last. He saluted Umuaro quietly and with great sadness.

'Umuaro kwenu!'

'Hem!'

'Umuaro obodonesi kwenu!'

'Hem!'

'Kwezuenu!'

'Hem!'

'The reed we were blowing is now crushed. When I spoke two markets ago in this very place I used the proverb of the she-goat. I was then talking to Ogbuefi Egonwanne who was the adult in the house. I told him that he should have spoken up against what we were planning, instead of which he put a piece of live coal into the child's palm and asked him to carry it with care. We all have seen with what care he carried it. I was not then talking to Egonwanne alone but to all the elders here who left what they should have done and did another, who were in the house and yet the she-goat suffered in her parturition.

'Once there was a great wrestler whose back had never known the ground. He wrestled from village to village until he had thrown every man in the world. Then he decided that he must go and wrestle in the land of the spirits, and become champion there as well. He went, and beat every spirit that came forward. Some had seven heads, some ten; but he beat them all. His companion who sang his praise on the flute begged him to come away, but he would not, his blood was roused, his ear nailed up. Rather than heed the call to go home he gave a challenge to the spirits to bring out their best and strongest wrestler. So they sent him his personal god, a little wiry spirit who seized him with one hand and smashed him on the stony earth.

'Men of Umuaro, why do you think our fathers told us this story? They told it because they wanted to teach us that no matter how strong or great a man was he should never challenge his *chi*. This is what our kinsman did – he challenged his *chi*. We were his flute player, but we did not plead with him to come away from death. Where is he today? The fly that has no one to advise it follows the corpse into the grave. But let us leave Akukalia aside; he has gone the way his *chi* ordained.

'But let the slave who sees another cast into a shallow grave know that he will be buried in the same way when his day comes. Umuaro is today challenging its *chi*. Is there any man or woman in Umuaro who does not know Ulu, the deity that destroys a man when his life is sweetest to him? Some people are still talking of carrying war to Okperi. Do they think that Ulu will fight in blame? Today the world is spoilt and there is no longer head or tail in anything that is done. But Ulu is not spoilt with it. If you go to war to avenge a man who passed shit on the head of his mother's father, Ulu will not follow you to be soiled in the corruption. Umuaro, I salute you.'

The meeting ended in confusion. Umuaro was divided in two.

Many people gathered round Ezeulu and said they stood with him. But there were others who went with Nwaka. That night he held another meeting with them in his compound and they agreed that three or four Okperi heads must fall to settle the matter.

Nwaka ensured that no one came to that night meeting from Ezeulu's village, Umuachala. He held up his palm-oil lamp against the face of any who came to see him clearly. Altogether he sent fifteen people away.

Nwaka began by telling the assembly that Umuaro must not allow itself to be led by the Chief Priest of Ulu. 'My father did not tell me that before Umuaro went to war it took leave from the priest of Ulu,' he said. 'The man who carries a deity is not a king. He is there to perform his god's ritual and to carry sacrifice to him. But I have been watching this Ezeulu for many years. He is a man of ambition; he wants to be king, priest, diviner, all. His father, they said, was like that too. But Umuaro showed him that Igbo people knew no kings. The time has come to tell his son also.

'We have no quarrel with Ulu. He is still our protector, even though we no longer fear Abam warriors at night. But I will not see with these eyes of mine his priest making himself lord over us. My father told me many things, but he did not tell me that Ezeulu was king in Umuaro. Who is he, anyway? Does anybody here enter his compound through the man's gate? If Umuaro decided to have a king we know where he would come from. Since when did Umuachala become head of the six villages? We all know that it was jealousy among the big villages that made them give the priesthood to the weakest. We shall fight for our farmland and for the contempt Okperi has poured on us. Let us not listen to anyone trying to frighten us with the name of Ulu. If a man says yes his *chi* also says yes. And we have all heard how the people of Aninta dealt with their deity when he failed them. Did they not carry him to the boundary between them and their neighbours and set fire on him? I salute you.'

The war was waged from one Afo to the next. On the day it began Umuaro killed two men of Okperi. The next day was Nkwo, and so there was no fighting. On the two following days, Eke and Oye, the fighting grew fierce. Umuaro killed four men and Okperi replied with three, one of the three being Akukalia's brother, Okoye. The next day, Afo, saw the war brought to a sudden close. The white man, Wintabota, brought soldiers to Umuaro and stopped it. The story of what these soldiers did in Abame was still told with fear, and so Umuaro made no effort to resist but laid down their arms. Although they were not yet satisfied they could say without shame that Akukalia's death had been avenged, that they had provided him with three men on whom to rest his head. It was also a good thing perhaps that the war was stopped. The death of Akukalia and his brother in one and the same dispute showed that Ekwensu's hand was in it.

The white man, not satisfied that he had stopped the war, had gathered all the guns in Umuaro and asked the soldiers to break them in the face of all, except three or four which he carried away. Afterwards he sat in judgement over Umuaro and Okperi and gave the disputed land to Okperi.

Chapter Three

Captain T. K. Winterbottom stood at the veranda of his bungalow on Government Hill to watch the riot of the year's first rain. For the past month or two the heat had been building up to an unbearable pitch. The grass had long been burnt out, and the leaves of the more hardy trees had taken on the red and brown earth colour of the country. There was only two hours' respite in the morning before the country turned into a furnace and perspiration came down in little streams from the head and neck. The most exasperating was the little stream that always coursed down behind the ear like a fly, walking. There was another moment of temporary relief at sundown when a cool wind blew. But this treacherous beguiling wind was the great danger of Africa. The unwary European who bared himself to it received the death-kiss.

Captain Winterbottom had not known real sleep since the dry, cool harmattan wind stopped abruptly in December; and it was now mid-February. He had grown pale and thin, and in spite of the heat his feet often felt cold. Every morning after the bath which he would have preferred cold but must have hot to stay alive (since Africa never spared those who did what they liked instead of what they had to do), he looked into the mirror and saw his gums getting whiter and whiter. Perhaps another bout of fever was on the way. At night he had to imprison himself inside a mosquito-net which shut out whatever air movement there was outside. His bedclothes were sodden and his head formed a waterlogged basin on the pillow. After the first stretch of unrestful sleep he would lie awake, tossing about until he was caught in the distant throb of drums. He would wonder what unspeakable rites went on in the forest at night, or was it the heart-beat of the

African darkness? Then one night he was terrified when it suddenly occurred to him that no matter where he lay awake at night in Nigeria the beating of the drums came with the same constancy and from the same elusive distance. Could it be that the throbbing came from his own heat-stricken brain? He attempted to smile it off but the skin on his face felt too tight. This dear old land of waking nightmares!

Fifteen years ago Winterbottom might have been so depressed by the climate and the food as to have doubts about service in Nigeria. But he was now a hardened coaster, and although the climate still made him irritable and limp, he would not now exchange the life for the comfort of Europe. His strong belief in the value of the British mission in Africa was, strangely enough, strengthened during the Cameroon campaign of 1916 when he fought against the Germans. That was how he had got the title of captain but unlike many other colonial administrators who also saw active service in the Cameroon he carried his into peacetime.

Although the first rain was overdue, when it did come it took people by surprise. Throughout the day the sun had breathed fire as usual and the world had lain prostrate with shock. The birds which sang in the morning were silenced. The air stood in one spot, vibrating with the heat; the trees hung limp. Then without any sign a great wind arose and the sky darkened. Dust and flying leaves filled the air. Palm trees and coconut trees swayed from their waists; their tops gave them the look of giants fleeing against the wind, their long hair streaming behind them.

Winterbottom's servant, John, rushed around closing doors and windows and picking up papers and photographs from the floor. Sharp and dry barks of thunder broke into the tumult. The world which had dozed for months was suddenly full of life again, smelling of new leaves to be born. Winterbottom, at the railing of his veranda, was also a changed man. He let the dust blow into his eyes and for once envied the native children running around naked and singing to the coming rain.

'What are they saying?' he asked John, who was now carrying in the deck-chairs.

'Dem talk say make rain come quick quick.'

Four other children ran in from the direction of the Boys' quarters to join the rest on Winterbottom's lawn which was the only space big enough for their play.

'Are all these your pickin, John?' There was something like envy in his voice.

'No, sir,' said John, putting down the chair and pointing. 'My pickin na dat two wey de run yonder and dat yellow gal. Di oder two na Cook im pickin. Di oder one yonder na Gardener him brodder pickin.'

They had to shout to be heard. The sky was now covered with restless, black clouds except at the far horizon where a narrow rim of lightness persisted. Long streaks of lightning cracked the clouds angrily and impatiently only to be wiped off again.

When it began the rain fell like large pebbles. The children intensified their singing as the first frozen drops hit them. Sometimes it was quite painful, but it only made them laugh the more. They scrambled to pick up the frozen drops and throw them into their mouths before they melted.

It rained for almost an hour and stopped clean. The trees were washed green and the leaves fluttered happily. Winterbottom looked at his watch and it was almost six. In the excitement of the year's first rain he had forgotten his tea and biscuits which John had brought in just before five; he picked up a biscuit and began to munch. Then he remembered that Clarke was coming to dinner and went to the kitchen to see what Cook was doing.

Okperi was not a very big station. There were only five Europeans living on Government Hill: Captain Winterbottom, Mr Clarke, Roberts, Wade and Wright. Captain Winterbottom was the District Officer. The Union Jack flying in front of his bungalow declared he was the King's representative in the district. He took the salute on Empire Day at the march past of all the school-children in the area – one of the few occasions when he wore his white uniform and sword. Mr Clarke was his Assistant District Officer. He was only four weeks old in the station, and had come to replace poor John Macmillan, who had died from cerebral malaria.

The other Europeans did not belong to the Administration. Roberts was an Assistant Superintendent of Police in charge of the local detachment. Wade was in charge of the prison; he was also called Assistant Superintendent. The other man, Wright, did not really belong to the station. He was a Public Works Department man supervising the new road to Umuaro. Captain Winterbottom had already had cause to talk to him seriously about his behaviour, especially with native women. It was absolutely imperative, he told him, that every European in Nigeria, particularly those in such a lonely outpost as Okperi, should not lower themselves in the eyes of the natives. In such a place the District Officer was something of a school prefect, and Captain Winterbottom was determined to do his duty. He would go as far as barring Wright from the club unless he showed a marked change.

The club was the old Regimental Mess the army left behind when their work of pacification was done in these parts and then moved on. It was a small wooden bungalow containing the mess-room, ante-room, and a veranda. At present the mess-room was used as bar and lounge, the ante-room as library where members saw the papers of two or three months ago and read Reuter's telegrams – ten words twice a week.

Tony Clarke was dressed for dinner, although he still had more than an hour to go. Dressing for dinner was very irksome in the heat, but he had been told by many experienced coasters that it was quite imperative. They said it was a general tonic which one must take if one was to survive in this demoralizing country. For to neglect it could become the first step on the slippery gradient of ever profounder repudiations. Today was quite pleasant because the rain had brought some coolness. But there had been days when Tony Clarke had foregone a proper dinner to avoid the torment of a starched shirt and tie. He was now reading the final chapter of *The Pacification of the Primitive Tribes of the Lower Niger*, by George Allen, which Captain Winterbottom had lent him. From time to time he glanced at his gold watch, a present from his father when he left home for service in Nigeria or, as George Allen would have said, to answer the call. He had now had the book for over a fortnight and must finish and take it back this evening. One of the ways in which the tropics were affecting him was the speed of his reading, although in its own right the book was also pretty dull; much too smug for his taste. But he was now finding the last few paragraphs quite stirring. The chapter was headed THE CALL.

'For those seeking but a comfortable living and a quiet occupation Nigeria is closed and will be closed until the earth has lost some of its deadly fertility and until the people live under something like sanitary conditions. But for those in search of strenuous life, for those who can deal with men as others deal with material, who can grasp great situations, coax events, shape destinies and ride on the crest of the wave of time Nigeria is holding out her hands. For the men who in India have made the Briton the law-maker, the organizer, the engineer of the world this new, old land has great rewards and honourable work. I know we can find the men. Our mothers do not draw us with nervous grip back to the fireside of boyhood, back into the home circle, back to the purposeless sports of middle life; it is our greatest pride that they do – albeit tearfully – send us fearless and erect, to lead the backward races into line. "Surely we are the people!" Shall it be the Little Englander for whom the Norman fought the Saxon on his field? Was it for him the archers bled at Crecy and Poitiers, or Cromwell drilled his men? Is it only for the desk our youngsters read of Drake and Frobisher, of Nelson, Clive and men like Mungo Park? Is it for the counting-house they learn of Carthage, Greece and Rome? No, no; a thousand times no! The British race will take its place, the British blood will tell. Son after son will leave the Mersey, strong in the will of his parents today, stronger in the deed of his fathers in the past, braving the climate, taking the risks, playing his best in the game of life.'

'That's rather good,' said Mr Clarke, and glanced at his watch again. Captain Winterbottom's bungalow was only two minutes' walk away, so there was plenty of time. Before he came to Okperi Clarke had spent two months at Headquarters being broken in, and he would never forget the day he was invited to dinner by His Honour the Lieutenant-Governor. For some curious reason he had imagined that the time was eight o'clock and arrived at Government House on the dot. The glittering Reception Hall was empty and Clarke would have gone into the front garden to wait had not one of the stewards come forward and offered him a drink. He sat uneasily on the edge of a chair with a glass of sherry in his hand, wondering whether he should not even now withdraw into the shade of one of the trees in the garden until the other guests arrived. Then it was too late. Someone was descending the stairs at a run, whistling uninhibitedly. Clarke sprang to his feet. His Honour glowered at him for a brief moment before he came forward to shake hands. Clarke introduced himself and was about to apologize. But H.H. gave him no chance.

'I was under the impression that dinner was at eight-fifteen.' Just then his aide-de-camp came in and, seeing a guest, looked worried, shook his watch and listened for its ticking.

'Don't worry, John. Come and meet Mr Clarke who came a little early.' He left the two together and went upstairs again. Throughout the dinner he never spoke to Clarke again. Very soon other guests began to arrive. But they were all very senior people and took no interest at all in poor Clarke. Two of them had their wives; the rest including H.H. were either unmarried or had wisely left their wives at home in England.

The worst moment for Clarke came when H.H. led his guests into the Dining-Room and Clarke could not find his name anywhere. The rest took no notice; as soon as H.H. was seated they all took their places. After what looked to Clarke like hours the A.D.C. noticed him and sent one of the stewards to get a chair. Then he must have had second thoughts, for he stood up and offered his own place to Clarke.

Captain Winterbottom was drinking brandy and ginger ale when Tony Clarke arrived.

'It's nice and cool today, thank God.'

'Yes, the first rain was pretty much overdue,' said Captain Winterbottom.

'I had no idea what a tropical storm looked like. It will be cooler now, I suppose.'

'Well, not exactly. It will be fairly cool for a couple of days that's all. You see, the rainy season doesn't really begin until May or even June. Do sit down. Did you enjoy that?'

'Yes, thank you very much. I found it most interesting. Perhaps Mr Allen is a trifle too dogmatic. One could even say a little smug.'

Captain Winterbottom's Small Boy, Boniface, came forward with a silver tray.

'What Massa go drink?'

'I wonder.'

'Why not try some Old Coaster?'

'What's that?'

'Brandy and ginger ale.'

'Right. That's fine.' For the first time he looked at the Small Boy in his starched white uniform and saw that he was remarkably handsome.

Captain Winterbottom seemed to read his thought.

'He's a fine specimen, isn't he? He's been with me four years. He was a little boy of about thirteen – by my own calculation, they've no idea of years – when I took him on. He was absolutely raw.'

'When you say they've no idea of years . . .'

'They understand seasons, I don't mean that. But ask a man how old he is and he doesn't begin to have an idea.'

The Small Boy came back with the drink.

'Thank you very much,' said Mr Clarke as he took it.

'Yessah.'

Thousands of flying ants swarmed around the tilley lamp on a stand at the far corner. They soon lost their wings and crawled on the floor. Clarke watched them with great interest, and then asked if they stung.

'No, they are quite harmless. They are driven out of the ground by the rain.'

The crawling ones were sometimes hooked up in twos at their tails.

'It was rather interesting what you said about Allen. A little smug, I think you said.'

'That was the impression I had – sometimes. He doesn't allow, for instance, for there being anything of value in native institutions. He might really be one of the missionary people.'

'I see you are one of the progressive ones. When you've been here as long as Allen was and understood the native a little more you might begin to see things in a slightly different light. If you saw, as I did, a man buried alive up to his neck with a piece of roast yam on his head to attract vultures you know . . . Well, never mind. We British are a curious bunch, doing everything half-heartedly. Look at the French. They are not ashamed to teach their culture to backward races under their charge. Their attitude to the native ruler is clear. They say to him: "This land has belonged to you because you have been strong enough to hold it. By the same token it now belongs to us. If you are not satisfied come out and fight us." What do we British do? We flounder from one expedient to its opposite. We do not only promise to secure old savage tyrants on their thrones – or more likely filthy animal skins – we not only do that, but we now go out of our way to invent chiefs where there were none before. They make me sick.' He swallowed what was left in his glass and shouted to Boniface for another glass. 'I wouldn't really mind if this dithering was left to old fossils in Lagos, but when young Political Officers get infected I just give up. If someone is positive we call him smug.'

Mr Clarke admitted that whatever judgement he made was made in ignorance and that he was open to correction.

'Boniface!'

'Yessah.'

'Bring another drink for Mr Clarke.'

'No really I think I've had . . .'

'Nonsense. Dinner won't be ready for another hour at least. Try something else if you prefer. Whisky?' Clarke accepted another brandy with great reluctance.

'That's a very interesting collection of firearms.' Mr Clarke had been desperately searching for a new subject. Then luckily he lit on a collection of quaint-looking guns arranged like trophies near the low window of the living-room. 'Are they native guns?' He had stumbled on a redeeming theme.

Captain Winterbottom was transformed.

'Those guns have a long and interesting history. The people of Okperi and their neighbours, Umuaro, are great enemies. Or they were before I came into the story. A big savage war had broken out between them over a piece of land. This feud was made worse by the fact that Okperi welcomed missionaries and government while

Umuaro, on the other hand, has remained backward. It was only in the last four or five years that any kind of impression has been made there. I think I can say with all modesty that this change came about after I had gathered and publicly destroyed all firearms in the place except, of course, this collection here. You will be going there frequently on tour. If you hear anyone talking about Otiji-Egbe, you know they are talking about me. Otiji-Egbe means Breaker of Guns. I am even told that all children born in that year belong to a new age-grade of the Breaking of the Guns.'

'That's most interesting. How far is this other village, Umuaro?' Clarke knew instinctively that the more ignorant he seemed the better.

'Oh, about six miles, not more. But to the native that's a foreign country. Unlike some of the more advanced tribes in Northern Nigeria, and to some extent Western Nigeria, the Ibos never developed any kind of central authority. That's what our headquarters people fail to appreciate.'

'Yes. I see.'

'This war between Umuaro and Okperi began in a rather interesting way. I went into it in considerable detail . . . Boniface! How are you doing, Mr Clarke? Fine? You ought to drink more; it's good for malaria . . . As I was saying, this war started because a man from Umuaro went to visit a friend in Okperi one fine morning and after he'd had one or two gallons of palm wine – it's quite incredible how much of that dreadful stuff they can tuck away – anyhow, this man from Umuaro having drunk his friend's palm wine reached for his *ikenga* and split it in two. I may explain that *ikenga* is the most important fetish in the Ibo man's arsenal, so to speak. It represents his ancestors to whom he must make daily sacrifice. When he dies it is split in two; one half is buried with him and the other half is thrown away. So you can see the implication of what our friend from Umuaro did in splitting his host's fetish. This was, of course, the greatest sacrilege. The outraged host reached for his gun and blew the other fellow's head off. And so a regular war developed between the two villages, until I stepped in. I went into the question of the ownership of the piece of land which was the remote cause of all the unrest and found without any shade of doubt that it belonged to Okperi. I should mention that every witness who testified before me – from both sides without exception – perjured themselves. One thing you must remember in dealing with natives is that like children they are great liars. They don't lie simply to get out of trouble. Sometimes they would spoil a good case by a pointless lie. Only one man – a kind of priest-king in Umuaro – witnessed against his own people. I have not found out what it was, but I think he must have had some pretty fierce tabu working on him. But he was a most impressive figure of a man. He was very light in complexion, almost red. One finds people like that now and again among the Ibos. I have a theory that the Ibos in the distant past assimilated a small non-negroid tribe of the same complexion as the Red Indians.'

Winterbottom stood up. 'Now what about some dinner,' he said.

Chapter Four

In the five years since the white man broke the guns of Umuaro the enmity between Ezeulu and Nwaka of Umunneora grew and grew until they were at the point which Umuaro people called *kill and take the head*. As was to be expected this enmity spread through their two villages and before long there were several stories of poisoning. From then on few people from the one village would touch palm wine or kolanut which had passed through the hands of a man from the other.

Nwaka was known for speaking his mind; he never paused to bite his words. But many people trembled for him that night in his compound when he had all but threatened Ulu by reminding him of the fate of another deity that failed his people. It was true that the people of Aninta burnt one of their deities and drove away his priest. But it did not follow that Ulu would also allow himself to be bullied and disgraced. Perhaps Nwaka counted on the protection of the personal god of his village. But the elders were not foolish when they said that a man might have Ngwu and still be killed by Ojukwu.

But Nwaka survived his rashness. His head did not ache, nor his belly; and he did not groan in the middle of the night. Perhaps this was the meaning of the recitative he sang at the Idemili festival that year. He had a great Mask which he assumed on this and other important occasions. The Mask was called Ogalanya or Man of Riches, and at every Idemili festival crowds of people from all the villages and their neighbours came to the *ilo* of Umunneora to see this great Mask bedecked with mirrors and rich cloths of many colours.

That year the Mask spoke a monologue full of boast. Some of those who knew the language of ancestral spirits said that Nwaka spoke of his challenge to Ulu.

Folk assembled, listen and hear my words. There is a place, Beyond Knowing, where no man or spirit ventures unless he holds in his right hand his kith and in his left hand his kin. But I, Ogalanya, Evil Dog that Warms His Body through the Head, I took neither kith nor kin and yet went to this place.

The flute called him Ogalanya Ajo Mmo, and the big drum replied.

When I got there the first friend I made turned out to be a wizard. I made another friend and found he was a poisoner. I made my third friend and he was a leper. I, Ogalanya, who cuts kpom and pulls waa, I made friends with a leper from whom even a poisoner flees.

The flute and the drum spoke again. Ogalanya danced a few steps to the right and then to the left, turned round sharply and saluted empty air with his matchet.

I returned from my sojourn. Afo passed, Nkwo passed, Eke passed, Oye passed. Afo came round again. I listened, but my head did not ache, my belly did not ache; I did not feel dizzy.

Tell me, folk assembled, a man who did this, is his arm strong or not?

The crowd replied: 'His arm is indeed very strong.' The flute and all the drums joined in the reply.

In the five years since these things happened people sometimes ask themselves how a man could defy Ulu and live to boast. It was better to say that it was not Ulu the man taunted; he had not called the god's name. But if it was, where did Nwaka get this power? For when we see a little bird dancing in the middle of the pathway we must know that its drummer is in the near-by bush.

Nwaka's drummer and praise-singer was none other than the priest of Idemili, the personal deity of Umunneora. This man, Ezidemili, was Nwaka's great friend and mentor. It was he who fortified Nwaka and sent him forward. For a long time no one knew this. There were few things happening in Umuaro which Ezeulu did not know. He knew that the priest of Idemili and Ogwugwu and Eru and Udo had never been happy with their secondary role since the villages got together and made Ulu and put him over the older deities. But he would not have thought that one of them would go so far as to set someone to challenge Ulu. It was only the incident of the sacred python that opened Ezeulu's eyes. But that was later.

The friendship between Nwaka and Ezidemili began in their youth. They were often seen together. Their mothers had told them that they were born within three days of each other, Nwaka being the younger. They were good wrestlers. But in other ways they were very different. Nwaka was tall and of a light skin; Ezidemili was very small and black as charcoal; and yet it was he who had the other like a goat on a lead. Later their lives took different paths, but Nwaka still sought the other's advice before he did any important thing. This was strange because Nwaka was a great man and a great orator who was called Owner of Words by his friends.

It was his friendship with Ezidemili which gradually turned him into Ezeulu's mortal enemy. One of the ways Ezidemili accomplished this was to constantly assert that in the days before Ulu the true leaders of each village had been men of high title like Nwaka.

One day as Nwaka sat with Ezidemili in his *obi* drinking palm wine and talking about the affairs of Umuaro their conversation turned, as it often did, on Ezeulu.

'Has anybody ever asked why the head of the priest of Ulu is removed from the body at death and hung up in the shrine?' asked Ezidemili rather abruptly. It was as though the question having waited for generations to be asked had now broken through by itself. Nwaka had no answer to it. He knew that when an Ezeulu or an Ezidemili died their heads were separated from their body and placed in their shrine. But no one had ever told him why this happened.

'In truth I do not know,' he said.

'I can tell you that even Ezeulu does not know.'

Nwaka emptied the wine in his horn and hit it twice on the floor. He knew that a great story was coming, but did not want to appear too expectant. He poured himself another hornful.

'It is a good story, but I do not think that I have ever told it to anyone before. I heard it from the mouth of the last Ezidemili just before he died.' He paused and drank a little from his horn. 'This palm wine has water in it. Every boy in Umuaro knows that Ulu was made by our fathers long ago. But Idemili was there at the beginning of things. Nobody made it. Do you know the meaning of Idemili?'

Nwaka shook his head slightly because of the horn at his lips.

'Idemili means Pillar of Water. As the pillar of this house holds the roof so does Idemili hold up the Raincloud in the sky so that it does not fall down. Idemili belongs to the sky and that is why I, his priest, cannot sit on bare earth.'

Nwaka nodded his head . . . Every boy in Umuaro knew that Ezidemili did not sit on bare earth.

'And that is why when I die I am not buried in the earth, because the earth and the sky are two different things. But why is the priest of Ulu buried in the same way? Ulu has no quarrel with earth; when our fathers made it they did not say that his priest should not touch the earth. But the first Ezeulu was an envious man like the present one; it was he himself who asked his people to bury him with the ancient and awesome ritual accorded to the priest of Idemili. Another day when the present priest begins to talk about things he does not know, ask him about this.'

Nwaka nodded again in admiration and fillipped his fingers.

The place where the Christians built their place of worship was not far from Ezeulu's compound. As he sat in his *obi* thinking of the Festival of the Pumpkin Leaves, he heard their bell: GOME, GOME, GOME, GOME, GOME. His mind turned from the festival to the new religion. He was not sure what to make of it. At first he had thought that since the white man had come with great power and conquest it was necessary that some people should learn the ways of his deity. That was why he had agreed to send his son, Oduche, to learn the new ritual. He also wanted him to learn the white man's wisdom, for Ezeulu knew from what he saw of Wintabota and the stories he heard about his people that the white man was very wise.

But now Ezeulu was becoming afraid that the new religion was like a leper. Allow him a handshake and he wants to embrace. Ezeulu had already spoken strongly to his son who was becoming more strange every day. Perhaps the time had come to bring him out again.

But what would happen if, as many oracles prophesied, the white man had come to take over the land and rule? In such a case it would be wise to have a man of your family in his band. As he thought about these things Oduche came out from the inner compound wearing a white singlet and a towel which they had given him in the school. Nwafo came out with him, admiring his singlet. Oduche saluted his father and set out for the mission because it was Sunday morning. The bell continued ringing in its sad monotone.

Nwafo came back to the *obi* and asked his father whether he knew what the bell was saying. Ezeulu shook his head.

'It is saying: Leave your yam, leave your cocoyam and come to church. That is what Oduche says.'

'Yes,' said Ezeulu thoughtfully. 'It tells them to leave their yam and their cocoyam, does it? Then it is singing the song of extermination.'

They were interrupted by loud and confused talking inside the compound, and Nwafo ran out to see what it was. The voices were getting louder and Ezeulu who normally took no interest in women's shouting began to strain his ear. But Nwafo soon rushed back.

'Oduche's box is moving,' he said, out of breath with excitement. The tumult in the compound grew louder. As usual the voice of Ezeulu's daughter, Akueke, stood out above all others.

'What is called "Oduche's box is moving"?' he asked, rising with deliberate slowness to belie his curiosity.

'It is moving about the floor.'

'There is nothing that a man will not hear nowadays.' He went into his inner compound through the door at the back of his *obi*. Nwafo ran past him to the group of excited women outside his mother's hut. Akueke and Matefi did most of the talking. Nwafo's mother, Ugoye, was speechless. Now and again she rubbed her palms together and showed them to the sky.

Akueke turned to Ezeulu as soon as she saw him. 'Father, come and see what we are seeing. This new religion . . .'

'Shut your mouth,' said Ezeulu, who did not want anybody, least of all his own daughter, to continue questioning his wisdom in sending one of his sons to join the new religion.

The wooden box had been brought from the room where Oduche

and Nwafo slept and placed in the central room of their mother's hut where people sat during the day.

The box, which was the only one of its kind in Ezeulu's compound, had a lock. Only people of the church had such boxes made for them by the mission carpenter and they were highly valued in Umuaro. Oduche's box was not actually moving; but it seemed to have something inside it struggling to be free. Ezeulu stood before it wondering what to do. Whatever was inside the box became more violent and actually moved the box around. Ezeulu waited for it to calm down a little, bent down and carried the box outside. The women and children scattered in all directions.

'Whether it be bad medicine or good one, I shall see it today,' he said as he carried the box at arm's length like a potent sacrifice. He did not pass through his *obi*, but took the door in the red-earth wall of his compound. His second son, Obika, who had just come in followed him. Nwafo came closely behind Obika, and the women and children followed fearfully at a good distance. Ezeulu looked back and asked Obika to bring him a matchet. He took the box right outside his compound and finally put it down by the side of the common footpath. He looked back and saw Nwafo and the women and children.

'Every one of you go back to the house. The inquisitive monkey gets a bullet in the face.'

They moved back not into the compound but in front of the *obi*. Obika took a matchet to his father who thought for a little while and put the matchet aside and sent him for the spear used in digging up yams. The struggling inside the box was as fierce as ever. For a brief moment Ezeulu wondered whether the wisest thing was not to leave the box there until its owner returned. But what would it mean? That he, Ezeulu, was afraid of whatever power his son had imprisoned in a box. Such a story must never be told of the priest of Ulu.

He took the spear from Obika and wedged its thin end between the box and its lid. Obika tried to take the spear from him, but he would not hear it.

'Stand aside,' he told him. 'What do you think is fighting inside? Two cocks?' He clenched his teeth in an effort to lever the top open. It was not easy and the old priest was covered with sweat by the time he succeeded in forcing the box. What they saw was enough to blind a man. Ezeulu stood speechless. The women and the children who had watched from afar came running down. Ezeulu's neighbour, Anosi, who was passing by branched in, and soon a big crowd had gathered. In the broken box lay an exhausted royal python.

'May the Great Deity forbid,' said Anosi.

'An abomination has happened,' said Akueke.

Matefi said: 'If this is medicine, may it lose its potency.'

Ezeulu let the spear fall from his hand. 'Where is Oduche?' he asked. No one answered. 'I said where is Oduche?' His voice was terrible.

Nwafo said he had gone to church. The sacred python now raised its head above the edge of the box and began to move in its dignified and unhurried way.

'Today I shall kill the boy with my own hands,' said Ezeulu as he picked up the matchet which Obika had brought at first.

'May the Great Deity forbid such a thing,' said Anosi.

'I have said it.'

Oduche's mother began to cry, and the other women joined her. Ezeulu walked slowly back to his *obi* with the matchet. The royal python slid away into the bush.

'What is the profit of crying?' Anosi asked Ugoye. 'Won't you find where your son is and tell him not to return home today?'

'He has spoken the truth, Ugoye,' said Matefi. 'Send him away to your kinsmen. We are fortunate the python is not dead.'

'You are indeed fortunate,' said Anosi to himself as he continued on his way to Umunneora to buy seed-yams from his friend. 'I have already said that what this new religion will bring to Umuaro wears a hat on its head.' As he went he stopped and told anyone he met what Ezeulu's son had done. Before midday the story had reached the ears of Ezidemili whose deity, Idemili, owned the royal python.

It was five years since Ezeulu promised the white man that he would send one of his sons to church. But it was only two years ago that he fulfilled the promise. He wanted to satisfy himself that the white man had not come for a short visit but to build a house and live.

At first Oduche did not want to go to church. But Ezeulu called him to his *obi* and spoke to him as a man would speak to his best friend and the boy went forth with pride in his heart. He had never heard his father speak to anyone as an equal.

'The world is changing,' he had told him. 'I do not like it. But I am like the bird Eneke-nti-oba. When his friends asked him why he was always on the wing he replied: "Men of today have learnt to shoot without missing and so I have learnt to fly without perching." I want one of my sons to join these people and be my eye there. If there is nothing in it you will come back. But if there is something there you will bring home my share. The world is like a Mask dancing. If you want to see it well you do not stand in one place. My spirit tells me that those who do not befriend the white man today will be saying *had we known* tomorrow.'

Oduche's mother, Ugoye, was not happy that her son should be chosen for sacrifice to the white man. She tried to reason with her husband, but he was impatient with her.

'How does it concern you what I do with my sons? You say you do not want Oduche to follow strange ways. Do you not know that in a great man's household there must be people who follow all kinds of strange ways? There must be good people and bad people, honest workers and thieves, peace-makers and destroyers; that is the mark of a great *obi*. In such a place, whatever music you beat on your drum there is somebody who can dance to it.'

If Oduche had any reluctance left after his father had talked to him it was removed as soon as he began to go to church. He found that he could learn very quickly and he began to think of the day when he could speak the language of the white man, just as their teacher, Mr Molokwu, had spoken with Mr Holt when he had visited their church. But there was somebody else who had impressed Oduche even more. His name was Blackett, a West Indian missionary. It was said that this man although black had more knowledge than white men. Oduche thought that if he could get one-tenth of Blackett's knowledge he would be a great man in Umuaro.

He made very good progress and was popular with his teacher and members of the church. He was younger than most other converts, being only fifteen or sixteen. The teacher, Mr Molokwu, expected great things of him and was preparing him for baptism when he was transferred to Okperi. The new teacher was a man from the Niger Delta. He spoke the white man's language as if it was his own. His name was John Goodcountry.

Mr Goodcountry told the converts of Umuaro about the early Christians of the Niger Delta who fought the bad customs of their people, destroyed shrines and killed the sacred iguana. He told them of Joshua Hart, his kinsman, who suffered martyrdom in Bonny.

'If we are Christians, we must be ready to die for the faith,' he said. 'You must be ready to kill the python as the people of the rivers killed the iguana. You address the python as Father. It is nothing but a snake, the snake that deceived our first mother, Eve. If you are afraid to kill it do not count yourself a Christian.'

The first Umuaro man to kill and eat a python was Josiah Madu of Umuagu. But the story did not spread outside the little group of Christians, most of whom refused, however, to follow Josiah's example. They were led by Moses Unachukwu, the first and the most famous convert in Umuaro.

Unachukwu was a carpenter, the only one in all those parts. He had learnt the trade under the white missionaries who built the Onitsha Industrial Mission. In his youth he had been conscripted to carry the loads of the soldiers who were sent to destroy Abame as a reprisal for the killing of a white man. What Unachukwu saw during that punitive expedition taught him that the white man was not a thing of fun. And so after his release he did not return to Umuaro but made his way to Onitsha, where he became house-boy to the carpenter-missionary, J. P. Hargreaves. After over ten years' sojourn in a strange land, Unachukwu returned to Umuaro with the group of missionaries who succeeded after two previous failures in planting the new faith among his people. Unachukwu regarded the success of this third missionary effort as due largely to himself. He saw his sojourn in Onitsha as a parallel to that of the Moses of the Old Testament in Egypt.

As the only carpenter in the neighbourhood Moses Unachukwu built almost single-handed the new church in Umuaro. Now he was not only a lay reader but a pastor's warden although Umuaro did not have a pastor as yet, only a catechist. But it showed the great esteem in which Moses Unachukwu was held in the young church. The last catechist, Mr Molokwu, consulted him in whatever he did. Mr Goodcountry, on the other hand, attempted from the very first to ignore him. But Moses was not a man to be ignored lightly.

Mr Goodcountry's teaching about the sacred python gave Moses the first opportunity to challenge him openly. To do this he used not only the Bible but, strangely enough for a convert, the myths of Umuaro. He spoke with great power for, coming as he did from the village which carried the priesthood of Idemili, he knew perhaps more than others what the python was. On the other side, his great knowledge of the Bible and his sojourn in Onitsha which was the source of the new religion gave him confidence. He told the new teacher quite bluntly that neither the Bible nor the catechism asked converts to kill the python, a beast full of ill omen.

'Was it for nothing that God put a curse on its head?' he asked, and then turned abruptly into the traditions of Umuaro. 'Today there are six villages in Umuaro; but this has not always been the case. Our fathers tell us that there were seven before, and the seventh was called Umuama.' Some of the converts nodded their support. Mr Goodcountry listened patiently and contemptuously.

'One day six brothers of Umuama killed the python and asked one of their number, Iweka, to cook yam pottage with it. Each of them brought a piece of yam and a bowl of water to Iweka. When he finished cooking the yam pottage the men came one by one and took their pieces of yam. Then they began to fill their bowls to the mark with the yam stew. But this time only four of them took their measure before the stew got finished.'

Moses Unachukwu's listeners smiled, except Mr Goodcountry who sat like a rock. Oduche smiled because he had heard the story as a little boy and forgotten it until now.

'The brothers began to quarrel violently, and then to fight. Very soon the fighting spread throughout Umuama, and so fierce was it that the village was almost wiped out. The few survivors fled their village, across the great river to the land of Olu where they are scattered today. The remaining six villages seeing what had happened to Umuama went to a seer to know the reason, and he told them that the royal python was sacred to Idemili; it was this deity which had punished Umuama. From that day the six villages decreed that henceforth anyone who killed the python would be regarded as having killed his kinsman.' Moses ended by counting on his fingers the villages and clans which also forbade the killing of the snake. Then Mr Goodcountry spoke.

'A story such as you have just told us is not fit to be heard in the house of God. But I allowed you to go on so that all may see the foolishness of it.' There was murmuring from the congregation which might have stood either for agreement or disagreement.

'I shall leave it to your own people to answer you.' Mr Goodcountry looked round the small congregation, but no one spoke. 'Is there no one here who can speak up for the Lord?'

Oduche who had thus far inclined towards Unachukwu's position had a sudden stab of insight. He raised his hand and was about to put it down again. But Mr Goodcountry had seen him.

'Yes?'

'It is not true that the Bible does not ask us to kill the serpent. Did not God tell Adam to crush its head after it had deceived his wife?' Many people clapped for him.

'Do you hear that, Moses?'

Moses made to answer, but Mr Goodcountry was not going to give him another opportunity.

'You say you are the first Christian in Umuaro, you partake of the Holy Meal; and yet whenever you open your mouth nothing but heathen filth pours out. Today a child who sucks his mother's breast has taught you the Scriptures. Is it not as Our Lord himself said that the first shall become last and the last become first. The world will pass away but not one single word of Our Lord will be set aside.' He turned to Oduche. 'When the time comes for your baptism you will be called Peter; on this rock will I build my Church.'

This caused more clapping from a part of the congregation. Moses was now fully aroused.

'Do I look to you like someone you can put in your bag and walk away?' he asked. 'I have been to the fountainhead of this new religion and seen with my own eyes the white people who brought it. So I want to tell you now that I will not be led astray by outsiders who choose to weep louder than the owners of the corpse. You are not the first teacher I have seen; you are not the second; you are not the third. If you are wise you will face the work they sent you to do here and take your hand off the python. You can say that I told you so. Nobody here has complained to you that the python has ever blocked his way as he came to church. If you want to do your work in peace you will heed what I have said, but if you want to be the lizard that ruined his own mother's funeral you may carry on as you are doing.' He turned to Oduche. 'As for you they may call you Peter or they may call you Paul or Barnabas; it does not pull a hair from me. I have nothing to say to a mere boy who should be picking palm nuts for his mother. But since you have also become our teacher I shall be waiting for the day when you will have the courage to kill a python in this Umuaro. A coward may cover the ground with his words but when the time comes to fight he runs away.'

At that moment Oduche took his decision. There were two pythons – a big one and a small one – which lived almost entirely in his mother's hut, on top of the wall which carried the roof. They did no harm and kept the rats away; only once were they suspected of frightening away a hen and swallowing her eggs. Oduche decided that he would hit one of them on the head with a big stick. He would do it so carefully and secretly that when it finally died people would think it had died of its own accord.

Six days passed before Oduche found a favourable moment, and during this time his heart lost some of its strength. He decided to take the smaller python. He pushed it down from the wall with his stick but could not bring himself to smash its head. Then he thought he heard people coming and had to act quickly. With lightning speed he picked it up as he had seen their neighbour, Anosi, do many times, and carried it into his sleeping-room. A new and exciting thought came to him then. He opened the box which Moses had built for him, took out his singlet and towel and locked the python inside. He felt a great relief within. The python would die for lack of air, and he would be responsible for its death without being guilty of killing it, which seemed to him a very happy compromise.

Ezeulu's first son, Edogo, had left home early that day to finish the mask he was carving for a new ancestral spirit. It was now only five days to the Festival of the Pumpkin Leaves when this spirit was expected to return from the depths of the earth and appear to men as a Mask. Those who would act as his attendants were making great plans for his coming; they had learnt their dance and were now anxious about the mask Edogo was carving for them. There were other carvers in Umuaro besides him; some of them were even better. But Edogo had a reputation for finishing his work on time unlike Obiako, the master carver, who only took up his tools when he saw his customers coming. If it had been any other kind of carving Edogo would have finished it long ago, working at it any moment his hands were free. But a mask was different; he could not do it in the home under the profane gaze of women and children but had to retire to the spirit-house built for such work at a secluded corner of the Nkwo market place where no one who had not been initiated into the secret of Masks would dare to approach.

The hut was dark inside although the eye got used to it after a short while. Edogo put down the white *okwe* wood on which he was going to work and then unslung his goatskin bag in which he carried his tools. Apart from the need for secrecy, Edogo had always found the atmosphere of this hut right for carving masks. All around him were older masks and other regalia of ancestral spirits, some of them older than even his father. They produced a certain ambience which gave power and cunning to his fingers. Most of the masks were for fierce, aggressive spirits with horns and teeth the size of fingers. But four of them belonged to maiden-spirits and were delicately beautiful. Edogo remembered with a smile what Nwanyinma told him when he first married his wife. Nwanyinma was a widow with whom he had made friends in his bachelor days. In her jealousy against the younger rival she had told Edogo that the only woman whose breasts stayed erect year after year was the maiden-spirit.

Edogo sat down on the floor near the entrance where there was the most light and began to work. Now and again he heard people talking as they passed through the market place from one village of Umuaro to another. But when his carving finally got hold of him he heard no more voices.

The mask was beginning to come out of the wood when Edogo suddenly stopped and turned his ear in the direction of the voices which had broken into his work. One of the voices was very familiar; yes, it was their neighbour, Anosi. Edogo listened very hard and then stood up and went to the wall nearest the market centre. He could now hear quite clearly. Anosi seemed to be talking to two or three other men he had just met.

'Yes. I was there and saw it with my own eyes,' he was saying. 'I would not have believed it had somebody else told me. I saw the box opened and a python inside it.'

'Do not repeat it,' said one of the others. 'It cannot be true.'

'That is what everybody says: it cannot be true. But I saw it with my own eyes. Go to Umuachala now and see the whole village in turmoil.'

'What that man Ezeulu will bring to Umuaro is pregnant and nursing a baby at the same time.'

'I have heard many things, but never till today have I heard of an abomination of this kind.'

By the time Edogo reached home his father was still in a very bad temper, only that now his anger was not so much against Oduche as against all the double-faced neighbours and passers-by whose words of sympathy barely concealed the spitefulness in their hearts. And even if they had been sincere Ezeulu would still have resented anybody making him an object of pity. At first his anger smouldered inwardly. But the last group of women who went in to see his wives, looking like visitors to a place of death, inflamed his wrath. He heard them in the inner compound shouting: 'E-u-u! What shall we do to the children of today?' Ezeulu strode into the compound and ordered them to leave.

'If I see any one of you still here when I go and come back she will know that I am an evil man.'

'What harm have we done in coming to console another woman?'

'I say leave this place at once!'

The women hurried out saying: 'Forgive us; we have erred.'

It was therefore a very irate Ezeulu to whom Edogo told his story of what he had heard at the Nkwo market place. When he finished his father asked him curtly:

'And what did you do when you heard that?'

'What should I have done?' Edogo was surprised and a little angry at his father's tone.

'Don't you hear him?' asked Ezeulu of no one. 'My first son, somebody says to your hearing that your father has committed an abomination, and you ask me what you should have done. When I was your age I would have known what to do. I would have come out and broken the man's head instead of hiding in the spirit-house.'

Edogo was now really angry but he controlled his tongue. 'When you were my age your father did not send one of his sons to worship the white man's god.' He walked away to his own hut full of bitterness for having broken off his carving to come and see what was happening at home, only to be insulted.

'I blame Obika for his fiery temper,' thought Ezeulu, 'but how much better is a fiery temper than this cold ash!' He inclined backwards and rested his head on the wall behind him and began to gnash his teeth.

It was a day of annoyance for the Chief Priest – one of those days when it seemed he had woken up on the left side. As if he had not borne enough vexation already he was now visited, at sunset, by a young man from Umunneora. Because of the hostility between Ezeulu's village and Umunneora he did not offer the man kolanut lest he should have a belly-ache later and attribute it to Ezeulu's hospitality. The man did not waste much time before he gave his message.

'I am sent by Ezidemili.'

'True? I trust he is well.'

'He is well,' replied the messenger. 'But at the same time he is not.'

'I do not understand you.' Ezeulu was now very alert. 'If you have a message, deliver it because I have no time to listen to a boy learning to speak in riddles.'

The young man ignored the insult. 'Ezidemili wants to know what you are going to do about the abomination which has been committed in your house.'

'That what happened?' asked the Chief Priest, holding his rage firmly with two hands.

'Should I repeat what I have just said?'

'Yes.'

'All right. Ezidemili wants to know how you intend to purify your house of the abomination that your son committed.'

'Go back and tell Ezidemili to eat shit. Do you hear me? Tell Ezidemili that Ezeulu says he should go and fill his mouth with shit. As for you, young man, you may go in peace because the world is no longer what it was. If the world had been what it was I would have given you something to remind you always of the day you put your head into the mouth of a leopard.' The young man wanted to say something but Ezeulu did not allow him.

'If you want to do something with your life, take my advice and say not another word here.' Ezeulu rose threateningly to his full height; the young man decided to heed his advice and rose to go.

Chapter Five

Captain T. K. Winterbottom stared at the memorandum before him with irritation and a certain amount of contempt. It came from the Lieutenant-Governor through the Resident through the Senior District Officer to him, the last two adding each his own comment before passing the buck down the line. Captain Winterbottom was particularly angry at the tone of the Senior District Officer's minute. It was virtually a reprimand for what he was pleased to describe as Winterbottom's stonewalling on the issue of the appointment of Paramount Chiefs. Perhaps if this minute had been written by any other person Captain Winterbottom would not have minded so much; but Watkinson had been his junior by three years and had been promoted over him.

'Any fool can be promoted,' Winterbottom always told himself and his assistants, 'provided he does nothing but try. Those of us who have a job to do have no time to try.'

He lit his pipe and began to pace his spacious office. He had designed it himself and had made it open and airy. As he walked up and down he noticed for the first time, although it had always been there, the singing of prisoners, as they cut the grass outside. It was amazing how tall it had grown with the two rainfalls which had come so close together. He went to the window and watched the prisoners for a while. One of them supplied the beat with something that looked like a piece of stone on an empty bottle and sang a short solo; the others sang the chorus and swung their blades to the beat. Captain Winterbottom removed his pipe, placed it on the window-sill, cupped his hands over his mouth and shouted: 'Shut up there!' They all looked up and saw who it was and stopped their music. Their blades went up and down haphazardly thereafter. Then their warder who had been standing under the shade of a mango tree a little distance away thought it was safest to take his men to another spot where they would not disturb the D.O. So he marched them off in a ragged double file to another part of Government Hill. They all wore dirty-white jumpers made from baft and a skull cap to match. Two of them carried headpans and the soloist clutched his bottle and stone. As soon as they settled down in their new place he raised a song and blades swung up and down to the beat:

> When I cut grass and you cut
> What's your right to call me names?

Back at his desk Captain Winterbottom read the Lieutenant-Governor's memorandum again:

'My purpose in these paragraphs is limited to impressing on all Political Officers working among the tribes who lack Natural Rulers the vital necessity of developing without any further delay an effective system of "indirect rule" based on native institutions.

'To many colonial nations native administration means government by white men. You are all aware that H.M.G. considers this policy as mistaken. In place of the alternative of governing directly through Administrative Officers there is the other method of trying while we endeavour to purge the native system of its abuses to build a higher civilization upon the soundly rooted native stock that had its foundation in the hearts and minds and thoughts of the people and therefore on which we can more easily build, moulding it and establishing it into lines consonant with modern ideas and higher standards, and yet all the time enlisting the real force of the spirit of the people, instead of killing all that out and trying to start afresh. We must not destroy the African atmosphere, the African mind, the whole foundation of his race . . .'

Words, words, words. Civilization, African mind, African atmosphere. Has His Honour ever rescued a man buried alive up to his neck, with a piece of roast yam on his head to attract vultures? He began to pace up and down again. But why couldn't someone tell the bloody man that the whole damn thing was stupid and futile. He knew why. They were all afraid of losing their promotion or the O.B.E.

Mr Clarke walked in to say he was off on his first tour of the district. Captain Winterbottom waved him away with 'Have a good trip' which he said almost without looking at him. But as he turned to go he called him back.

'When you are in Umuaro find out as much as you can – very discreetly of course – about Wright and his new road. I've heard all kinds of ugly stories of whippings and that kind of business. Without prejudging the issue I may say that I wouldn't put anything past Wright, from sleeping with native women to birching their men . . . All right I'll see you in a week's time. Take care of yourself. Remember, no chances with the water. Have a good trip.'

This short interruption made it possible for Captain Winterbottom to return to the Lieutenant-Governor's memorandum with diminished anger. Instead he now felt tired and resigned. The great tragedy of British colonial administration was that the man on the spot who knew his African and knew what he was talking about found himself being constantly overruled by starry-eyed fellows at Headquarters.

Three years ago they had put pressure on Captain Winterbottom to appoint a Warrant Chief for Okperi against his better judgement. After a long palaver he had chosen one James Ikedi, an intelligent fellow who had been among the very first people to receive missionary education in these parts. But what had happened? Within three months of this man receiving his warrant Captain Winterbottom began to hear rumours of his high-handedness. He had set up an illegal court and a private prison. He took any woman who caught his fancy without paying the customary bride-price. Captain Winterbottom went into the whole business thoroughly and uncovered many more serious scandals. He decided to suspend the fellow for six months, and accordingly withdrew his warrant. But after three months the Senior Resident who had just come back from leave and had no first-hand knowledge of the matter ruled that the rascal be reinstated. And no sooner was he back in power than he organized a vast system of mass extortion.

There was at that time a big programme of road and drainage

construction following a smallpox epidemic. Chief James Ikedi teamed up with a notorious and drunken road overseer who had earned the title of Destroyer of Compounds from the natives. The plans for the roads and drains had long been completed and approved by Captain Winterbottom himself and as far as possible did not interfere with people's homesteads. But this overseer went around intimidating the villagers and telling them that unless they gave him money the new road would pass through the middle of their compound. When some of them reported the matter to their chief he told them there was nothing he could do; that the overseer was carrying out the orders of the white man and anyone who had no money to give should borrow from his neighbour or sell his goats or yams. The overseer took his toll and moved on to another compound, choosing only the wealthy villagers. And to convince them that he meant business he actually demolished the compounds of three people who were slow in paying, although no road or drain was planned within half a mile of their homes. Needless to say, Chief Ikedi took a big slice of this illegal tax.

Thinking of this incident Captain Winterbottom could find some excuse for the overseer. He was a man from another clan; in the eyes of the native, a foreigner. But what excuse could one offer for a man who was their blood brother and chief? Captain Winterbottom could only put it down to cruelty of a kind which Africa alone produced. It was this elemental cruelty in the psychological make-up of the native that the starry-eyed European found so difficult to understand.

Chief Ikedi was of course a very clever man and when Captain Winterbottom began to investigate this second scandal it was quite impossible to incriminate him; he had covered up his tracks so well. So Captain Winterbottom lost his main quarry, at any rate for the present; he had no doubt however that he would catch him one of these days. As for the overseer he sentenced him to eighteen months' penal servitude.

There was no doubt whatever in the mind of Captain Winterbottom that Chief Ikedi was still corrupt and high-handed, only cleverer than ever before. The latest thing he did was to get his people to make him an *obi* or king, so that he was now called His Highness Ikedi the First, Obi of Okperi. This among a people who abominated kings!

This was what British administration was doing among the Ibos, making a dozen mushroom kings grow where there was none before.

Captain Winterbottom slept on the Lieutenant-Governor's memorandum and decided that there was little he could do to stop the stupid trend. He had already sacrificed his chances of promotion by too frequently speaking his mind; practically all the officers who joined the Nigerian Service when he did were now Residents and he was not even a Senior District Officer. Not that he cared particularly, but in this matter of Indirect Rule there did not seem to be any point in continuing his objection when fellows who until now had been one with him in opposition had suddenly swung round to blame him for not implementing it. He was now under orders to find a chief and his duty was clear. But he must not repeat the mistake of looking for some mission-educated smart alec. As far as Umuaro was concerned his mind was practically made up. He would go for that impressive-looking fetish priest who alone of all the witnesses who came before him in the Okperi versus Umuaro land case spoke the truth. Provided of course he was still alive. Captain Winterbottom remembered seeing him again once or twice during his routine visits to Umuaro. But that was at least two years ago.

Chapter Six

The outrage which Ezeulu's son committed against the sacred python was a very serious matter; Ezeulu was the first to admit it. But the ill will of neighbours and especially the impudent message sent him by the priest of Idemili left him no alternative but to hurl defiance at them all. He was full of amazement at the calumny which even people he called his friends were said to be spreading against him.

'It is good for a misfortune like this to happen once in a while,' he said, 'so that we can know the thoughts of our friends and neighbours. Unless the wind blows we do not see the fowl's rump.'

He sent for his wife and asked her where her son was. She stood with her arms folded across her breasts and said nothing. For the past two days she had been full of resentment against her husband because it was he who sent Oduche to the church people in spite of her opposition. Why should he now sharpen his matchet to kill him for doing what they taught him in the church?

'Am I talking to a person or a carved *nkwu*?'

'I don't know where he is.'

'You do not know? *He he he he he he,*' he laughed mechanically and then became very serious again. 'You must be telling me in your mind that a man who brings home ant-infested faggots should not complain if he is visited by lizards. You are right. But do not tell me you don't know where your son is . . .'

'Is he my son now?'

He ignored her question.

'Do not tell me you don't know where he is because it is a lie. You may call him out from where you are hiding him. I have not killed anybody before and I will not start with my son.'

'But he will not go to that church again.'

'That is a lie also. I have said that he will go there and he will go. If anybody does not like it he can come and jump on my back.'

That afternoon Oduche returned, looking like a fowl soaked in the rain. He greeted his father fearfully but he ignored him completely. In the inner compound the women welcomed him without enthusiasm. The little children, especially Obiageli, searched him closely as if to see whether he had altered in any way.

Although Ezeulu did not want anybody to think that he was troubled or to make him appear like an object of pity, he did not ignore the religious implications of Oduche's act. He thought about it seriously on the night of the incident. The custom of Umuaro was well known and he did not require the priest of Idemili to instruct him. Every Umuaro child knows that if a man kills the python inadvertently he must placate Idemili by arranging a funeral for the snake almost as elaborate as a man's funeral. But there was nothing in the custom of Umuaro for the man who puts the snake into a box. Ezeulu was not saying that it was not an offence, but it was not serious enough for the priest of Idemili to send him an insulting message. It was the kind of offence which a man put right between himself and his personal god. And what was more the Festival of the New Pumpkin Leaves would take place in a few days. It was he, Ezeulu, who would then cleanse the six villages of this and countless other sins, before the planting season.

Not very long after Oduche's return Ezeulu was visited by one of his in-laws from Umuogwugwu. This man, Onwuzuligbo, was one of those who came to Ezeulu one year this planting season to find out why their kinsman and husband of Ezeulu's daughter had been beaten and carried away from their village.

'It looks as if my death is near,' said Ezeulu.

'Why is that, in-law? Do I look like death?'

'When a man sees an unfamiliar sight, then perhaps his death is coming.'

'You are right, in-law, it is indeed a long time since I came to see you. But we have a saying that the very thing which kills mother rat prevents its little ones from opening their eyes. If all goes well we hope to come and go again as in-laws should.'

Ezeulu sent his son, Nwafo, to bring a kolanut from his mother. Meanwhile he reached for the little wooden bowl which had a lump of white clay in it.

'Here is a piece of *nzu*,' he said as he rolled the chalk towards his guest, who picked it up and drew on the floor between his legs three erect lines and a fourth lying down under them. Then he painted one of his big toes and rolled the chalk back to Ezeulu who put it away again.

After they had eaten a kolanut Onwuzuligbo cleared his throat and thanked Ezeulu, and then asked:

'Is our wife well?'

'Your wife? She is well. Nothing troubles her except hunger. Nwafo, go and call Akueke to salute her husband's kinsman.'

Nwafo soon returned and said she was coming. Akueke came in almost at once. She saluted her father and shook hands with Onwuzuligbo.

'Is your wife, Ezinma, well?' she asked.

'She is well today. Tomorrow is what we do not know.'

'And her children?'

'We have no trouble except hunger.'

'Aaah!' said Akueke, 'that cannot be true. Look how well fed you are.'

When Akueke went back to the inner compound Onwuzuligbo told Ezeulu that his people had sent him to say that they would like to pay a visit to their in-law on the following morning.

'I shall not run away from my house,' said Ezeulu.

'We shall not bring war to you. We are coming to whisper together like in-law and in-law.'

Ezeulu was grateful for the one happy event in a week of trouble and vexation. He sent for his head wife, Matefi and told her to get ready to cook for his in-laws tomorrow.

'Which in-laws?' she asked.

'Akueke's husband and his people.'

'There is no cassava in my hut, and today is not a market.'

'So what do you want me to do?' asked Ezeulu.

'I don't want you to do anything. But Akueke may have some cassava if you ask her.'

'This madness which they say you have must now begin to know its bounds. You are telling me to go and find cassava for you. What has Akueke to do with it; is she my wife? I have told you many times that you are a wicked woman. I have noticed that you will not do anything happily unless it is for yourself or your children. Don't let me speak my mind to you today.' He paused. 'If you want this compound to contain the two of us, go and do what I told you. If Akueke's mother were alive she would not draw a line between her children and yours and you know it. Go away from here before I rise to my feet.'

Although Ezeulu was very anxious for his daughter, Akueke, to return to her husband nobody expected him to say so openly. A man who admitted that his daughter was not always welcome in his home or that he found her presence irksome was in effect telling her husband to treat her as roughly as he liked. So when Akueke's husband finally came round to announcing his intention to take his wife home, Ezeulu made a show of objecting.

'It is right for a man to take his wife home,' he said. 'But I want to remind you that when we begin to plant crops it will be one year since she began to live in my compound. Did you bring yams or cocoyams or cassava to feed her and her child? Or do you think that they are still carrying the breakfast they ate in your house last year?'

Ibe and his people made some vague, apologetic noises.

'What I want to know,' said Ezeulu, 'is how you will pay me for taking care of your wife for one year.'

'In-law, I understand you very well,' said Onwuzuligbo. 'Leave everything to us. You know that a man's debt to his father-in-law can never be fully discharged. When we buy a goat or a cow we pay for it and it becomes our own. But when we marry a wife we must go on paying until we die. We do not dispute that we owe you. Our debt is even greater than you say. What about all the years from her birth to the day we took her from you? Indeed we owe you a great debt, but we ask you to give us time.'

'Let me agree with you,' said Ezeulu, 'but I am agreeing in cowardice.'

Besides Ezeulu's two grown-up sons, Edogo and Obika, his younger brother was also present. His name was Okeke Onenyi. He had said very little so far; but now it appeared to him that his brother was yielding too readily and he decided to speak.

'My in-laws, I salute you. I have not said anything because the man who has no gift for speaking says his kinsmen have said all there is to say. Since you began to speak I have been listening very hard to hear one thing from your mouth, but I have not heard it. Different people have different reasons for marrying. Apart from children which we all want, some men want a woman to cook their meals, some want a woman to help on the farm, others want someone they can beat. What I want to learn from your mouth is whether our in-law has come because he has no one to beat when he wakes up in the morning nowadays.'

Onwuzuligbo promised on behalf of his kinsman that Akueke would not be beaten in future. Then Ezeulu sent for her to find out whether she wanted to return to her husband. She hesitated and then said she would go if her father was satisfied.

'My in-laws, I salute you,' said Ezeulu. 'Akueke will return, but not today. She will need a little time to get ready. Today is Oye; she will come back to you on the Oye after next. When she comes, treat her well. It is not bravery for a man to beat his wife. I know a man and his wife must quarrel; there is no abomination in that. Even brothers and sisters from the same womb do disagree; how much more two strangers. No, you may quarrel, but let it not end in fighting. I shall say no more at present.'

Ezeulu was grateful to Ulu for bringing about so unexpectedly the mending of the quarrel between Akueke and her husband. He was sure that Ulu did it to put him in the right mind for purifying the six villages before they put their crops into the ground. That very evening his six assistants came to him for their orders and he sent them to announce each man in his own village that the Feast of the Pumpkin Leaves would take place on the following Nkwo.

Ugoye was still cooking supper when the crier's *ogene* sounded. Ugoye was notorious for her late cooking. Although Ezeulu often rebuked Matefi for cooking late Ugoye deserved the rebuke even more. But she was wiser than the senior wife; she never cooked late on the days she sent food to her husband. But on all other days her pestle would be heard far into the night. She was particularly slack when, as now, she was forbidden to cook for any grown man on account of her uncleanness.

Her daughter, Obiageli, and Akueke's daughter, Nkechi, were telling each other stories. Nwafo sat on the small mud-seat at the foot of the hut's central pillar watching them with a superior air and pointing out now and again their mistakes.

Ugoye stirred the soup on the fire and tasted it by running her tongue on the back of the ladle. The sound of the *ogene* caught her in the action.

'Keep quiet, you children, and let me hear what they are saying.'

GOME GOME GOME GOME. 'Ora Obodo, listen! Ezeulu has asked me to announce that the Festival of the Pumpkin Leaves will take place on the coming Nkwo.' GOME GOME GOME GOME. 'Ora Obodo! Ezeulu has asked me . . .'

Obiageli had broken off her story so that her mother could hear the crier's message. While she waited impatiently her eyes fell on the soup ladle and, to occupy herself, she picked it up from the wooden bowl where it lay and proceeded to lick it dry.

'Glutton,' said Nwafo. 'It is this lick lick lick which prevents woman from growing a beard.'

'And where, big man, is your beard?' asked Obiageli.

GOME GOME GOME GOME. 'Folks of the village. The Chief Priest of Ulu has asked me to tell every man and every woman that the Festival of the First Pumpkin Leaves will be held on the coming Nkwo market day.' GOME GOME GOME GOME.

The crier's voice was already becoming faint as he took his message down the main pathway of Umuachala.

'Shall we go back to the beginning?' asked Nkechi.

'Yes,' said Obiageli. 'The big ukwa fruit has fallen on Nwaka Dimkpolo and killed him. I shall sing the story and you reply.'

'But I was replying before,' protested Nkechi, 'it is now my turn to sing.'

'You are going to spoil everything now. You know we did not complete the story before the crier came.'

'Do not agree, Nkechi,' said Nwafo. 'She wants to cheat you because she is bigger than you are.'

'Nobody has called your name in this, ant-hill nose.'

'You are asking for a cry.'

'Don't listen to him, Nkechi. After this it will be your turn to sing and I shall reply.' Nkechi agreed and Obiageli began to sing again:

> And who will punish this Water for me?
>> *E-e Nwaka Dimkpolo*
> Earth will dry up this water for me
>> *E-e Nwaka Dimkpolo*
> Who will punish this Earth for me? . . .

'No, no, no,' Nkechi broke in.

'What can happen to Earth, silly girl?' asked Nwafo.

'I said it on purpose to test Nkechi,' said Obiageli.

'It is a lie, as old as you are you can't even tell a simple story.'

'If it pains you, come and jump on my back, ant-hill nose.'

'Mother, if Obiageli abuses me again I shall beat her.'

'Touch her if you dare and I shall cure you of your madness this night.'

'Let us change to another story,' said Obiageli. 'This one has no end.' At the same time she reached for the ladle which had just returned from another visit to the soup pot on the fire. But her mother snatched it from her.

Chapter Seven

The market place was filling up steadily with men and women from every quarter. Because it was specially their day, the women wore their finest cloths and ornaments of ivory and beads according to the wealth of their husbands or, in a few exceptional cases, the strength of their own arms. Most of the men brought palm wine in pots carried on the head or gourds dangling by the side from a loop of rope. The first people to arrive took up positions under the shade of trees and began to drink with their friends, their relations and their in-laws. Those who came after sat in the open which was not hot yet.

A stranger to this year's festival might go away thinking that Umuaro had never been more united in all its history. In the atmosphere of the present gathering the great hostility between Umunneora and Umuachala seemed, momentarily, to lack significance. Yesterday if two men from the two villages had met they would have watched each other's movement with caution and suspicion; tomorrow they would do so again. But today they drank palm wine freely together because no man in his right mind would carry poison to a ceremony of purification; he might as well go out into the rain carrying potent, destructive medicines on his person.

Ezeulu's younger wife examined her hair in a mirror held between her thighs. She could not help feeling that she did a better job on Akueke's hair than Akueke did on hers. But she was very pleased with the black patterns of *uli* and faint yellow lines of *ogalu* on her body. In previous years she would have been among the first to arrive at the market place; she would have been carefree and joyful. But this year her feet seemed to drag because of the load on her mind. She was going to pray for the cleansing of her hut which Oduche had defiled.

She was no longer one of many, many Umuaro women taking part in a general and all-embracing rite. Today she stood in special need. The weight of this feeling all but crushed the long-awaited pleasure of wearing her new ivory bracelets which had earned her so much envy and hostility from her husband's other wife, Matefi.

She was still polishing the ivory when Matefi set out for the Nkwo market place. Before she went she called out from the middle of the compound:

'Is Obiageli's mother ready?'

'No. We shall be following. You need not wait.'

When she was fully prepared Ugoye went behind her hut to the pumpkin which she specially planted after the first rain and cut four leaves, tied them together with banana string and returned to her hut. She put the leaves down on a stool and went to the bamboo shelf to examine the soup pot and the foofoo which Obiageli and Nwafo would eat at midday.

Akueke stooped at the threshold and peeped into Ugoye's hut.

'So you are not ready to go yet? What are you fussing about like a hen in search of a nest?' she asked. 'At this rate we shall find nowhere to stand at the market place.' Then she came into the hut carrying her own bunch of pumpkin leaves. They admired each other's cloths and Akueke praised Ugoye's ivory once again.

As soon as they set out Akueke asked:

'What do you think was Matefi's annoyance this morning?'

'I should ask you; is she not your father's wife?'

'Her face was as big as a mortar. Did she ask if you were ready to go?'

'She did; but it went no deeper than the lips.'

'In all the time I have come across bad people,' said Akueke, 'I have not yet met anyone like her. Her own badness whistles. Since my father asked her to cook for my husband and his people the day before yesterday her belly has been full of bile.'

On ordinary Nkwo days the voice of the market carried far in all directions like the approach of a great wind. Today it was as though all the bees in the world were passing overhead. And people were still flowing in from all the pathways of Umuaro. As soon as they emerged from their compound Ugoye and Akueke joined one such stream.

Every woman of Umuaro had a bunch of pumpkin leaves in her right hand; any woman who had none was a stranger from the neighbouring villages coming to see the spectacle. As they approached Nkwo its voice grew bigger and bigger until it drowned their conversation.

They were just in time to see the arrival of the five wives of Nwaka and the big stir they caused. Each of them wore not anklets but two enormous rollers of ivory reaching from the ankle almost to the knee. Their walk was perforce slow and deliberate, like the walk of an Ijele Mask lifting and lowering each foot with weighty ceremony. On top of all this the women were clad in many coloured velvets. Ivory and velvets were not new in Umuaro but never before had they been seen in such profusion from the house of one man.

Obika and his good friend, Ofoedu, sat with three other young men from Umuagu on the crude mat woven on the ground by exposed roots of an *ogbu* tree. In their midst stood two black pots of palm wine. Just outside their circle one empty pot lay on its side. One of the men was already drunk, but neither Obika nor Ofoedu appeared to have drunk a drop yet.

'Is it true, Obika,' asked one of the men, 'that your new bride has not returned after her first visit?'

'Yes, my friend,' Obika replied light-heartedly. 'My things always turn out differently from other people's. If I drink water it sticks between my teeth.'

'Do not heed him,' said Ofoedu. 'Her mother is ill and her father asked if she could stay back and look after her for a while.'

'Aha, I knew the story I heard could not be true. How could a young bride hesitate over a handsome *ugonachomma* like Obika?'

'Ah, my friend, come out from that,' said the half-drunk man. 'She may not like the size of his penis.'

'But she has never seen it,' said Obika.

'You are talking to small boys of yesterday: She has not seen it!'

Soon after, the great Ikolo sounded. It called the six villages of Umuaro one by one in their ancient order: Umunneora, Umuagu, Umuezeani, Umuogwugwu, Umuisiuzo and Umuachala. As it called each village an enormous shout went up in the market place. It went through the number again but this time starting from the youngest. People began to hurry through their drinking before the arrival of the Chief Priest.

The Ikolo now beat unceasingly; sometimes it called names of important people of Umuaro, like Nwaka, Nwosisi, Igboneme and Uduezue. But most of the time it called the villages and their deities. Finally it settled down to saluting Ulu, the deity of all Umuaro.

Obiozo Ezikolo was now an old man, but his mastery of the king of all drums was still unrivalled. Many years ago when he was still a young man the six villages had decided to confer the *ozo* title on him for his great art which stirred the hearts of his kinsmen so powerfully in times of war. Now in his old age it was a marvel where he got the strength to work as he did. Even climbing on to the Ikolo was a great feat for a man half his age. Now those who were near enough surrounded the drum and looked upwards to admire the ancient drummer. A man well known to him raised his voice and saluted him. He shouted back: 'An old woman is never old when it comes to the dance she knows.' The crowd laughed.

The Ikolo was fashioned in the olden days from a giant iroko tree at the very spot where it was felled. The Ikolo was as old as Ulu himself at whose order the tree was cut down and its trunk hollowed out into a drum. Since those days it had lain on the same spot in the sun and in the rain. Its body was carved with men and pythons and little steps were cut on one side; without these the drummer could not climb to the top to beat it. When the Ikolo was beaten for war it was decorated with skulls won in past wars. But now it sang of peace.

A big *ogene* sounded three times from Ulu's shrine. The Ikolo took it up and sustained an endless flow of praises to the deity. At the same time Ezeulu's messengers began to clear the centre of the market place. Although they were each armed with a whip of palm frond they had a difficult time. The crowd was excited and it was only after a struggle that the messengers succeeded in clearing a small space in the heart of the market place, from which they worked furiously with their whips until they had forced all the people back to form a thick ring at the edges. The women with their pumpkin leaves caused the greatest difficulty because they all struggled to secure positions in front. The men had no need to be so near and so they formed the outside of the ring.

The *ogene* sounded again. The Ikolo began to salute the Chief Priest. The women waved their leaves from side to side across their faces, muttering prayers to Ulu, the god that kills and saves.

Ezeulu's appearance was greeted with a loud shout that must have been heard in all the neighbouring villages. He ran forward, halted abruptly and faced the Ikolo. 'Speak on,' he said to it, 'Ezeulu hears what you say.' Then he stooped and danced three or four steps and rose again.

He wore smoked raffia which descended from his waist to the knee. The left half of his body – from forehead to toes – was painted with white chalk. Around his head was a leather band from which an eagle's feather pointed backwards. On his right hand he carried *Nne Ofo*, the mother of all staffs of authority in Umuaro, and in his left he held a long iron staff which kept up a quivering rattle whenever he stuck its pointed end into the earth. He took a few long strides, pausing on each foot. Then he ran forward again as though he had seen a comrade in the vacant air; he stretched his arm and waved his staff to the right and to the left. And those who were near enough heard the knocking together of Ezeulu's staff and another which no one saw. At this, many fled in terror before the priest and the unseen presences around him.

As he approached the centre of the market place Ezeulu re-enacted the First Coming of Ulu and how each of the four Days put obstacles in his way.

'At that time, when lizards were still in ones and twos, the whole people assembled and chose me to carry their new deity. I said to them:

'"Who am I to carry this fire on my bare head? A man who knows that his anus is small does not swallow an udala seed."

'They said to me:

'"Fear not. The man who sends a child to catch a shrew will also give him water to wash his hand."

'I said: "So be it."

'And we set to work. That day was Eke: we worked into Oye and then into Afo. As day broke on Nkwo and the sun carried its sacrifice I carried my Alusi and, with all the people behind me, set out on that journey. A man sang

with the flute on my right and another replied on my left. From behind the heavy tread of all the people gave me strength. And then all of a sudden something spread itself across my face. On one side it was raining, on the other side it was dry. I looked again and saw that it was Eke.

'I said to him: "Is it you Eke?"'

'He replied: "It is I, Eke, the One that makes a strong man bite the earth with his teeth."'

'I took a hen's egg and gave him. He took it and ate and gave way to me. We went on, past streams and forests. Then a smoking thicket crossed my path, and two men were wrestling on their heads. My followers looked once and took to their heels. I looked again and saw that it was Oye.

'I said to him: "Is it you Oye across my path?"'

'He said: "It is I, Oye, the One that began cooking before Another and so has more broken pots."'

'I took a white cock and gave him. He took it and made way for me. I went on past farmlands and wilds and then I saw that my head was too heavy for me. I looked steadily and saw that it was Afo.

'I said: "Is it you Afo?"'

'He said: "It is I, Afo, the great river that cannot be salted."'

'I replied: "I am Ezeulu, the hunchback more terrible than a leper."'

'Afo shrugged and said: "Pass, your own is worse than mine."'

'I passed and the sun came down and beat me and the rain came down and drenched me. Then I met Nkwo. I looked on his left and saw an old woman, tired, dancing strange steps on the hill. I looked to the right and saw a horse and saw a ram. I slew the horse and with the ram I cleaned my matchet, and so removed that evil.'

By now Ezeulu was in the centre of the market place. He struck the metal staff into the earth and left it quivering while he danced a few more steps to the Ikolo which had not paused for breath since the priest emerged. All the women waved their pumpkin leaves in front of them.

Ezeulu looked round again at all the men and women of Umuaro, but saw no one in particular. Then he pulled the staff out of the ground, and with it in his left hand and the *Mother of Ofo* in his right he jumped forward and began to run round the market place.

All the women set up a long, excited ululation and there was renewed jostling for the front line. As the fleeing Chief Priest reached any section of the crowd the women there waved their leaves round their heads and flung them at him. It was as though thousands and thousands of giant, flying insects swarmed upon him.

Ugoye who had pushed and shoved until she got to the front murmured her prayer over and over again as the Chief Priest approached the part of the circle where she stood:

'Great Ulu who kills and saves, I implore you to cleanse my household of all defilement. If I have spoken it with my mouth or seen it with my eyes, or if I have heard it with my ears or stepped on it with my foot or if it has come through my children or my friends or kinsfolk let it follow these leaves.'

She waved the small bunch in a circle round her head and flung it with all her power at the Chief Priest as he ran past her position.

The six messengers followed closely behind the priest and, at intervals, one of them bent down quickly and picked up at random one bunch of leaves and continued running. The Ikolo drum worked itself into a frenzy during the Chief Priest's flight especially its final stages when he, having completed the full circle of the market place, ran on with increasing speed into the sanctuary of his shrine, his messengers at his heels. As soon as they disappeared the Ikolo broke off its beating abruptly with one last KOME. The mounting tension which had gripped the entire market place and seemed to send its breath going up, up and up exploded with this last beat of the drum and released a vast and deep breathing down. But the moment of relief was very short-lived. The crowd seemed to rouse itself quickly to the knowledge that their Chief Priest was safe in his shrine, triumphant over the sins of Umuaro which he was now burying deep into the earth with the six bunches of leaves.

As if someone had given them a sign, all the women of Umunneora broke out from the circle and began to run round the market place, stamping their feet heavily. At the beginning it was haphazard but soon everyone was stamping together in unison and a vast cloud of dust rose from their feet. Only those whose feet were weighed down by age or by ivory were out of step. When they had gone round they rejoined the standing crowd. Then the women of Umuagu burst through from every part of the huge circle to begin their own run. The others waited and clapped for them; no one ran out of turn. By the time the women of the sixth village ran their race the pumpkin leaves that had lain so thickly all around were smashed and trodden into the dust.

As soon as the running was over the crowd began to break up once more into little groups of friends and relations. Akueke sought out her elder sister, Adeze, whom she had last seen running with the other women of Umuezeani. She did not search very far because Adeze stood out in any crowd. She was tall and bronze-skinned; if she had been a man she would have resembled her father even more than Obika.

'I thought perhaps you had gone home,' said Adeze. 'I saw Matefi just now but she had not seen you at all.'

'How could she see me? I'm not big enough for her to see.'

'Are you two quarrelling again? I thought I saw it on her face. What have you done to her this time?'

'My sister, leave Matefi and her trouble aside and let us talk about better things.'

At that point Ugoye joined them.

'I have been looking for you two all over the market place,' she said. She embraced Adeze whom she called *Mother of my Husband*.

'How are the children?' asked Adeze. 'Is it true you have been teaching them to eat python?'

'You think it is something for making people laugh?' Ugoye sounded very hurt. 'No wonder you are the only person in Umuaro who did not care to come and ask what was happening.'

'Was anything happening? Nobody told me. Was it a fire or did someone die?'

'Do not mind Adeze, Ugoye,' said her sister, 'she is worse than her father.'

'Did you expect what the leopard sired to be different from the leopard?'

No one replied.

'Do not be angry with me, Ugoye. I heard everything. But our enemies and those jealous of us were waiting to see us running up and down in confusion. It is not Adeze will give them that satisfaction. That mad woman, Akueni Nwosisi, whose family has committed every abomination in Umuaro, came running to me to show her pity. I asked her whether someone who put a python in a box was not to be preferred to her kinsman caught behind the house copulating with a she-goat.'

Ugoye and Akueke laughed. They could clearly visualize their aggressive sister putting this question.

'You are coming with us?' asked Akueke.

'Yes, I must see the children. And perhaps I shall exact a fine or two from Ugoye and Matefi; I fear they look after my father half-heartedly.'

'Please, husband, I implore you,' cried Ugoye in mock fear. 'I do my best. It is your father who ill-treats me. And when you talk to him,' she added seriously, 'ask him why at his age he must run like an antelope. Last year he could not get up for days after the ceremony.'

'Don't you know,' asked Akueke looking furtively back to see if a man was near; there was no one; even so she lowered her voice, 'don't you know that in his younger days he used to run as Ogbazulobodo? As Obika does now.'

'It is you people, especially the two of you, who lead him astray. He likes to think that he is stronger than any young man of today and you people encourage him. If he were my father I would let him know the truth.'

'Is he not your husband?' asked Adeze. 'If he dies tomorrow are you not the one to sit in ashes in the cooking-place for seven markets? Is it you or me will wear sackcloth for one year?'

'What am I telling you?' asked Akueke, changing the subject. 'My husband and his people came the other day.'

'What did they come for?'

'What else would they come for?'

'So they are tired of waiting, small beasts of the bush. I thought they were waiting for you to take palm wine to beg them.'

'Don't abuse my husband's people, or we shall fight,' said Akueke pretending anger.

'Please forgive me. I did not know that you and he had suddenly become palm oil and salt again. When are you going back to him?'

'One market come next Oye.'

Chapter Eight

The new road which Mr Wright was building to connect Okperi with its enemy, Umuaro, had now reached its final stages. Even so it would not be finished before the onset of the rainy season if it was left to the paid gang he was using. He had thought of increasing the size of this gang but Captain Winterbottom had told him that far from authorizing any increase he was at that very moment considering a retrenchment as the Vote for Capital Works for the financial year was already largely overspent. Mr Wright had then toyed with the idea of reducing the labourers' pay from threepence a day to something like twopence. But this would not have increased the labour force substantially; not even halving their pay would have achieved the desired result, even if Mr Wright could have found it in his heart to treat the men so meanly. In fact he had got very much attached to this gang and knew their leaders by name now. Many of them were, of course, bone lazy and could only respond to severe handling. But once you got used to them they could be quite amusing. They were as loyal as pet dogs and their ability to improvise songs was incredible. As soon as they were signed on the first day and told how much they would be paid they devised a work song. Their leader sang: *'Lebula toro toro'* and all the others replied: *'A day'*, at the same time swinging their matchets or wielding their hoes. It was a most effective work song and they sang it for many days:

> *Lebula toro toro*
> > *A day*
> *Lebula toro toro*
> > *A day*

And they sang it in English too!

Anyhow there was only one alternative left to Mr Wright if he was to complete the road before June and get away from this hole of a place. He had to use unpaid labour. He asked for permission to do this, and after due consideration Captain Winterbottom gave his approval. In the letter conveying it he pointed out that it was the policy of the Administration to resort to this method only in the most exceptional circumstances . . . 'The natives cannot be an exception to the aphorism that the labourer is worthy of his hire.'

Mr Wright who had come to Government Hill from his P.W.D. Road Camp about five miles away to get this reply, glanced through it, crumpled it and put it in the pocket of his khaki shorts. Like all practical types he had little respect for administrative red tape.

When the leaders of Umuaro were told to provide the necessary labour for the white man's new, wide road they held a meeting and decided to offer the services of the two latest age groups to be admitted into full manhood: the age group that called itself Otakagu, and the one below it which was nicknamed Omumawa.

These two groups never got on well together. They were, like two successive brothers, always quarrelling. In fact it was said that the elder group who when they came of age took the name Devourer Like Leopard were so contemptuous of their younger brothers when they came of age two years later that they nicknamed them Omumawa, meaning that the man's cloth they tied between the legs was a feint to cover small boys' penes. It was a good joke, and so overpowered the attempt of the new group to take a more befitting name. For this reason they nursed a grudge against Otakagu, and a meeting of the two was often like the meeting of fire and gunpowder. Whenever they could, therefore, they went by separate ways; as in the case of the white man's new road. All that Mr Wright asked for was two days in the week, and so the two age groups arranged to work separately on alternate Eke days. On these occasions the white man came over from the paid gang which he had turned into an orderly and fairly skilled force to supervise the free but undisciplined crowd from Umuaro.

Because of his familiarity with the white man's language the carpenter, Moses Unachukwu, although very much older than the two age groups, had come forward to organize them and to take words out of the white man's mouth for them. At first Mr Wright was inclined to distrust him, as he distrusted all uppity natives but he soon found him very useful and was now even considering giving him some little reward when the road was finished. Meanwhile Unachukwu's reputation in Umuaro rose to unprecedented heights. It was one thing to claim to speak the white man's tongue and quite another to be seen actually doing it. The story spread throughout the six villages. Ezeulu's one regret was that a man of Umunneora should have this prestige. But soon, he thought, his son would earn the same or greater honour.

It was the turn of the Otakagu age group to work on the new road on the day following the Festival of the Pumpkin Leaves. Ezeulu's second son, Obika, and his friend, Ofoedu, belonged to this group. But they had drunk so much palm wine on the day before that when all the other people went to work they were still asleep. Obika who had staggered home almost at cock-crow defied the combined effort of his mother and sister to rouse him.

It had happened on the festival day that as Obika and Ofoedu drank with the three men at the market place, one of the men had thrown a challenge to them. The conversation had turned on the amount of palm wine a good drinker could take without losing knowledge of himself.

'It all depends on the palm tree and the tapper,' said one of the men.

'Yes,' agreed his friend, Maduka. 'It depends on the tree and the man who taps it.'

'That is not so. It depends on the man who drinks. You may bring any tree in Umuaro and any tapper,' said Ofoedu, 'and I shall still drink my bellyful and go home with clear eyes.'

Obika agreed with his friend. 'It is true that some trees are stronger than others and some tappers are better than others, but a good drinker will defeat them both.'

'Have you heard of the palm tree in my village which they call Okposalebo?'

Obika and Ofoedu said no.

'Anyone who has not heard of Okposalebo and yet claims to be a good drinker deceives himself.'

'What Maduka says is very true,' said one of the others. 'The wine from this tree is never sold in the market, and no one can drink three hornfuls and still know his way home.'

'This Okposalebo is a very old tree. It is called *Disperser of a Kindred* because two brothers would fight like strangers after drinking two hornfuls of its wine.'

'Tell us another story,' Obika said, filling his horn. 'If the tapper adds medicine to his wine that is another matter, but if you are telling us of the fluid as the tree yields it, then I say tell us another story.'

Then Maduka threw the challenge. 'It is not profitable to speak too many words. The palm tree is not in the distant riverain country, but here in Umuaro. Let us go from here to Nwokafo's compound and ask him to give us a gourd from this tree. It is very costly – the gourd may be *ego-nese* – but I shall pay. If you two drink three hornfuls each and still go home let it be my loss. But if not you must give me *ego-neli* whenever you come to your senses again.'

It was as Maduka had said. The two boasters had fallen asleep where they sat, and when night came he left them there and retired to his bed. But he came out twice in the night and found them still snoring. When he woke up finally in the morning, they were gone. He wished he had seen them depart. Perhaps when they heard their betters talking about palm wine in future they would not open their mouths so wide.

Ofoedu did not seem to have fared as badly as Obika. When he woke up and found that the sun was already shining he rushed to Ezeulu's compound to call Obika. But although they shouted his name and shook him he showed no sign of stirring. Eventually Ofoedu poured a gourd of cold water over him and he woke up. The two then set out to join their age group working on the new road. They were like a pair of Night Masks caught abroad by daylight.

Ezeulu who lay in his *obi* prostrate from the exhaustion of the festival was wakened by all the commotion in the inner compound. He asked Nwafo the meaning of all the noise and was told that they were trying to rouse Obika. He said nothing more, only gnashed his teeth. The young man's behaviour was like a heavy load on his father's head. In a few days, Ezeulu said within himself, Obika's new bride would arrive. She would have come already if her mother had not fallen sick. When she arrived what a husband she would find! A man who could not watch his hut at night because he was dead with palm wine. Where did the manhood of such a husband lie? A man who could not protect his wife if night marauders knocked at his door. A man who was roused in the morning by the women. *Tufia!* spat the old priest. He could not contain his disgust.

Although Ezeulu did not ask for details he knew without being told that Ofoedu was behind this latest episode. He had said it over and over again that this fellow Ofoedu did not contain the smallest drop of human presence inside his entire body. It was hardly two years since he sent everybody running to his father's compound in a false fire alarm for which his father, who was not a rich man, paid a fine of one goat. Ezeulu had told Obika again and again that such a person was not a fit friend for anyone who wanted to do something with his life. But he had not heeded and today there was as little to choose between them as between rotten palm nuts and a broken mortar.

When the two friends first set out to join their age group they walked in silence. Obika felt an emptiness on top as if his head had been numbed by a whole night's fall of dew. But the walking was already doing him some good; the feeling was returning that the head belonged to him.

After one more turning on the narrow, ancient footpath they saw, a little distance ahead of them, a vast opening which was the beginning of the new road. It opened like day after a thick night.

'What do you think of that thing Maduka gave us?' asked Ofoedu. This was the first mention either of them made to the incident of the previous day. Obika did not reply. He merely produced a sound which lay half-way between a sigh of relief and a groan.

'It was not naked palm wine,' said Ofoedu. 'They put some potent herbs in it. When I think of it now we were very foolish to have followed such a dangerous man to his own house. Do you remember that he did not drink even one hornful.'

Obika still said nothing.

'I shall not pay the *ego-neli* to him.'

'Were you thinking at any time that you would pay?' Obika looked surprised. 'I regard anything we said yesterday as words spoken in honour of palm wine.'

They were now on the portion of the new road that had been built. It made one feel lost like a grain of maize in an empty goatskin bag. Obika changed his matchet from the left hand to the right and his hoe from right to left. The feeling of openness and exposure made him alert.

As the new road did not point in the direction of a stream or a market Ofoedu and Obika did not encounter many villagers, only a few women now and again carrying heavy loads of firewood.

'What is that I am hearing?' asked Obika. They were now approaching the old, ragged *egbu* tree from which the night spirits called Onyekulum began their journey loaded with song and gossip in the carefree season after the harvest.

'I was just about to ask you. It sounds like a funeral song.'

As they drew nearer to the work site there was no longer any doubt. It was indeed the dirge with which a corpse was taken into the burial forest:

> Look! a python!
> Look! a python!
> Yes, it lies across the way.

The two men recognized it now and also recognized the singers as men of their age group. They burst out laughing together. Someone had given the ancient song a new and irreverent twist and changed it into a half familiar, half strange and hilarious work song. Ofoedu was certain that he saw the hand of Nweke Ukpaka in it, it was the kind of malicious humour he had.

The approach of Obika and his friend brought about a sudden change among the workers. Their singing stopped and with it the sound of scores of matchets cutting together into tree-trunks. Those who bent forward with hoes to level the cleared parts stopped and straightened up, their feet still planted wide apart, covered with red earth.

Nweke Ukpaka raised his voice and shouted: 'Kwo Kwo Kwo Kwo

Kwo!' All the men replied: 'Kwooooh oh!' and everyone burst out laughing at this imitation of women acknowledging a present.

Mr Wright's irritation mounted dangerously. He clutched the whip in his right hand more firmly and planted the other hand menacingly on his hip. His white helmet made him look even more squat than he was. Moses Unachukwu was talking excitedly to him, but he did not seem to be listening. He stared unwaveringly at the two approaching late-comers and his eyes seemed to Moses to get smaller and smaller. The others wondered what was going to happen. Although the white man always carried a whip he had rarely used it; and when he had done he had appeared to be half joking. But this morning he must have got out of bed from the left side. His face smoked with anger.

Noticing the man's posture Obika put more swagger into his walk. This brought more laughter from the men. He made to pass Mr Wright who, unable to control his anger any more, lashed out violently with his whip. It flashed again and this time caught Obika around the ear, and stung him into fury. He dropped his matchet and hoe and charged. But Moses Unachukwu had thrown himself between the two men. At the same time Mr Wright's two assistants jumped in quickly and held Obika while he gave him half a dozen more lashes on his bare back. He did not struggle at all; he only shivered like the sacrificial ram which must take in silence the blows of funeral dancers before its throat is cut. Ofoedu trembled also, but for once in his life he saw a fight pass before him and could do nothing but look on.

'Are you mad to attack a white man?' screamed Moses Unachukwu in sheer amazement. 'I have heard that not one person in your father's house has a right head.'

'What do you have in mind when you say that?' asked a man from Obika's village who had smelt in Unachukwu's statement the hostility between Umuachala and Umunneora.

The crowd which had hitherto watched in silence now broke hurriedly into the quarrel and before long loud threats were uttered on all sides and at least one person wagged his finger in another's face. It seemed so much easier to deal with an old quarrel than with a new, unprecedented incident.

'Shut up you black monkeys and get down to work!' Mr Wright

had a grating voice but one that carried far. Truce was immediately established. He turned to Unachukwu and said: 'Tell them I shall not tolerate any more slackness.'

Unachukwu translated.

'Tell them this bloody work must be finished by June.'

'The white man says that unless you finish this work in time you will know the kind of man he is.'

'No more lateness.'

'Pardin?'

'Pardon what? Can't you understand plain, simple English? I said there will be no more late-coming.'

'Oho. He says everybody must work hard and stop all this shit-eating.'

'I have one question I want the white man to answer.' This was Nweke Ukpaka.

'What's that?'

Unachukwu hesitated and scratched his head. 'Dat man wan axe master queshon.'

'No questions.'

'Yessah.' He turned to Nweke. 'The white man says he did not leave his house this morning to come and answer your questions.'

The crowd grumbled. Wright shouted that if they did not immediately set to work they would be seriously dealt with. There was no need to translate this; it was quite clear.

The matchets began to sound again on tree-trunks and those who worked with hoes bent down once more. But as they worked they arranged a meeting.

Nothing came of it. The first disagreement was over the presence of Moses Unachukwu. Many people – largely from Umuachala village – saw no reason why a man of another age group should sit in on their deliberations. Others pointed out that this was a special meeting to discuss the white man and for that reason it would be foolish to exclude the only kinsman who knew the ways of these white people. At this point Ofoedu stood up and, to everyone's surprise, joined those who wanted Moses to stay.

'But my reason is different,' he added. 'I want him to say before us all what he said before the white man about Obika's family. I want him also to say before us all whether it is true that he incited the white man to whip our comrade. When he has given us these answers he may go away. You ask me why he should go away? I shall tell you. This is a meeting of Otakagu age group. He belongs to Akakanma. And let me remind you all, but especially those who are murmuring and interrupting me, that he also belongs to the white man's religion. But I do not want to talk about that now. All I say is that Unachukwu should answer the questions I have asked, and after that he may go and take with him all his knowledge of the white man's ways. We have all heard stories of how he came by this knowledge. We have heard that when he left Umuaro he went to cook like a woman in the white man's kitchen and lick his plates . . .'

The rest of Ofoedu's speech was drowned in the tumult that broke out. It was just like Ofoedu, many people were saying, to open his mouth and let out his words alive without giving them as much as a bite with his teeth. Others said he had spoken the truth. Anyhow, it took a very long time to establish peace again. Moses Unachukwu was saying something but no one heard, until the tumult had spent itself. By then his voice had gone hoarse.

'If you ask me to go away I shall do so at once.'

'Do not go!'

'We permit you to stay!'

'But if I go away it will not be due to the barking of that mad dog. If there were any shame left in the world how could that beast of the bush who could not give his father a second burial stand up before you and pass shit through his mouth . . .'

'It is enough!'

'We have not come here to abuse ourselves!'

When the discussion began again someone suggested that they should go to the elders of Umuaro and tell them that they could no longer work on the white man's road. But as speaker after speaker revealed the implications of such a step it lost all support. Moses told them that the white man would reply by taking all their leaders to prison at Okperi.

'You all know how friendly we are with Okperi. Do you think that any Umuaro man who goes to prison there will come back alive? But that apart, do you forget that this is the moon of planting? Do you want to grow this year's crops in the prison house in a land where your fathers owe a cow? I speak as your elder brother. I have travelled in Olu and I have travelled in Igbo, and I can tell you that there is no escape from the white man. He has come. When Suffering knocks at your door and you say there is no seat left for him, he tells you not to worry because he has brought his own stool. The white man is like that. Before any of you here was old enough to tie a cloth between the legs I saw with my own eyes what the white man did to Abame. Then I knew there was no escape. As daylight chases away darkness so will the white man drive away all our customs. I know that as I say it now it passes by your ears, but it will happen. The white man has power which comes from the true God and it burns like fire. This is the God about Whom we preach every eighth day . . .'

Unachukwu's opponents were now shouting that this was a meeting of an age group, that they had not assembled to join with him in chewing the seed of foolishness which they called their new religion.

'We are talking about the white man's road,' said a voice above the others.

'Yes, we are talking about the white man's road. But when the roof and walls of a house fall in, the ceiling is not left standing. The white man, the new religion, the soldiers, the new road – they are all part of the same thing. The white man has a gun, a matchet, a bow and carries fire in his mouth. He does not fight with one weapon alone.'

Nweke Ukpaka spoke next. 'What a man does not know is greater than he. Those of us who want Unachukwu to go away forget that none of us can say come in the white man's language. We should listen to his advice. If we go to our elders and tell them that we shall no longer work on the white man's road, what do we expect them to do? Will our fathers take up hoes and matchets and go out to work themselves while we sit at home? I know that many of us want to fight the white man. But only a foolish man can go after a leopard with his bare hands. The white man is like hot soup and we must take him slowly-slowly from the edges of the bowl. Umuaro was here before the white man came from his own land to seek us out. We did not ask him to visit us; he is neither our kinsman nor our in-law. We did not steal his goat or his fowl; we did not take his land or his wife. In no way whatever have we done him wrong. And yet he has come to make trouble for us. All we know is that our *ofo* is held high between us and him. The stranger will not kill his host with his visit; when he goes may he not go with a swollen back. I know that the white man does not wish Umuaro well. That is why we must hold our *ofo* by him and give him no cause to say that we did this or failed to do that. For if we give him cause he will rejoice. Why? Because the very house he has been seeking ways of pulling down will have caught fire of its own will. For this reason we shall go on working on his road; and when we finish we shall ask him if he has more work for us. But in dealing with a man who thinks you a fool it is good sometimes to remind him that you know what he knows but have chosen to appear foolish for the sake of peace. This white man thinks we are foolish; so we shall ask him one question. This was the question I had wanted to ask him this morning but he would not listen. We have a saying that a man may refuse to do what is asked of him but may not refuse to be asked, but it seems the white man does not have that kind of saying where he comes from. Anyhow the question which we shall beg Unachukwu to ask him is why we are not paid for working on his road. I have heard that throughout Olu and Igbo, wherever people do this kind of work the white man pays them. Why should our own be different?'

Ukpaka was a persuasive speaker and after him nobody else rose to speak. And the only decision of the meeting was then taken. The Otakagu age group asked Unachukwu to find out, at a well-chosen moment when it was safe to approach the white man, why he had not given them any money for working on his road.

'I shall carry your message to him,' said Unachukwu.

'That message is not complete,' said Nwoye Udora. 'It is not enough to ask him why we are not paid. He knows why and we know why. He knows that in Okperi those who do this kind of work are paid. Therefore the question you should ask him is this: Others are paid for this work; why are we not paid? Or is our own different? It is important to ask whether our own is different.'

This was agreed and the meeting broke up.

'Your words were very good,' someone said to Nwoye Udora as they left the market place. 'Perhaps the white man will tell us whether we killed his father or his mother.'

Ezeulu was not as broken down as his young wife had feared. True he had pains in his feet and thighs and his spittle had a bitter taste. But he had forestalled the worst effects of his exertion by having his body rubbed with a light ointment of camwood as soon as he returned home and by ensuring that a log fire burned beside his low bamboo bed all night. There was no medicine equal to camwood and fire. Very soon the priest would rise as sound as newly fired clay.

If anyone had told Ezeulu about his younger wife's concern he would have laughed. It showed how little of a man his wives knew especially when, like Ugoye, they were no older than the man's first children. If Ugoye had known her husband in his earliest years as priest she might have realized that the exhaustion he felt after the festival had nothing to do with advancing age. Had it been that Ezeulu would not have yielded to it. His daughters made light of the wife's concern because they were wiser, being his daughters. They knew that this was a necessary conclusion to the festival. It was part of the sacrifice. For who could trample the sins and abominations of all Umuaro into the dust and not bleed in the feet? Not even a priest as powerful as Ezeulu could hope to do that.

The story that the white man had whipped Obika spread through the villages while the age group held its meeting under the shade of ogbu trees in the market place. The story was brought home to Ezeulu's compound by Edogo's wife who was returning from the bush with a bundle of firewood on her head. Ezeulu was wakened from sleep by Obika's mother and sister weeping. He threw off the mat with which he had covered himself and sprang to his feet, his mind having run immediately to death. But then he heard Edogo's wife talking, which would not happen if anyone had died. He sat down on the edge of his bed and, raising his voice, called Edogo's wife. She immediately came into the *obi* followed by her husband who had been carving an iroko door for the compound of a titled man when his wife returned.

'What are you saying?' Ezeulu asked Amoge. She repeated the story she had heard.

'Whip?' he asked, unable to understand. 'But what offence did he commit?'

'Those who told the story did not say.'

Ezeulu screwed his face in thought. 'I think he was late in going. But the white man would not whip a grown man who is also my son for that. He would be asked to pay a fine to his age group for being late; he would not be whipped. Or perhaps he hit the white man first . . .'

Edogo was touched by the distress which his father felt but tried to conceal. It ought to have made him jealous of his younger brother but did not.

'I think I shall go to Nkwo where they are meeting,' said Edogo. 'I cannot yet find meaning in this story.' He returned to his hut, took his matchet and made to go out.

His father who was still trying to understand how it could have happened called after him. When he came back into his *obi* Ezeulu advised him not to be rash.

'From what I know of your brother he is likely to have struck the first blow. Especially as he was drunk when he left home.' There was already a change in his tone, and Edogo nearly smiled.

He set out again, wearing only his work cloth – a long, thin strip passed between the legs and secured around the waist, with one end dangling in front and the other behind.

Obika's mother came out of the compound sniffling and drawing the back of her fist across her eyes.

'Where is that one going?' asked Ezeulu. 'I see that those who will fight the white man are lining up.' He laughed as Matefi turned round to hear what he was saying. 'Go back to your hut, woman!' Edogo had now reached the main footpath and turned left.

Ezeulu now sat down on the iroko panel with his back against the wall so that he could see the approaches to his compound. His mind raced up and down in different directions trying vainly to make sense of the whipping story. Now he was thinking about the white man who did it. Ezeulu had seen him and heard his voice when he spoke to the elders of Umuaro about the new road. When the story had first spread that a white man was coming to talk to the elders Ezeulu had thought it would be his friend, Wintabota, the Destroyer of Guns. He had been greatly disappointed when he saw it was another white man. Wintabota was tall and erect and carried himself like a great man. His voice sounded like thunder. This other man was short and thick, as hairy as a monkey. He spoke in a queer way without opening his mouth. Ezeulu thought he must be some kind of manual labourer in the service of Wintabota.

Some people appeared at the junction of the main footpath and the approaches to Ezeulu's compound. He jerked his head forward, but the men passed.

Ezeulu came finally to the conclusion that unless his son was at fault he would go in person to Okperi and report the white man to his master. His thoughts were stopped by the sudden appearance of Obika and Edogo. Behind them came a third whom he soon recognized as Ofoedu. Ezeulu could never get used to this worthless young man who trailed after his son like a vulture after a corpse. He was filled with anger which was so great that it also engulfed his son.

'What was the cause of the whipping?' he asked Edogo, ignoring the other two. Obika's mother and all the others in the compound had now hastened into Ezeulu's *obi*.

'They were late for work.'

'Why were you late?'

'I have not come home to answer anybody's questions,' Obika shouted.

'You may answer or not as you please. But let me tell you that this is only the beginning of what palm wine will bring to you. The death that will kill a man begins as an appetite.'

Obika and Ofoedu walked out.

Chapter Nine

Edogo's homestead was built against one of the four sides of his father's compound so that they shared one wall between them. It was a very small homestead with two huts, one for Edogo and the other for his wife, Amoge. It was built deliberately small for, like the compounds of many first sons, it was no more than a temporary home where the man waited until he could inherit his father's place.

Of late another small compound had been built on the other side of Ezeulu's for his second son, Obika. But it was not quite as small as Edogo's. It also had two huts, one for Obika and the other for the bride who was soon to come.

As one approached Ezeulu's compound off the main village pathway Edogo's place stood on the left and Obika's on the right.

When Obika walked away with his friend, Edogo returned to the shade of the ogbu tree in front of his compound to resume work on the door he was carving. It was nearly finished and after it he would leave carving for a while and face his farm work. He envied master craftsmen like Agwuegbo whose farms were cultivated for them by their apprentices and customers.

As he carved his mind kept wandering to his wife's hut from where the cry of their only child was reaching him. He was their second child, the first having died after three months. The one that died had brought sickness with him into the world; a ridge ran down the middle of his head. But the second, Amechi, had been different. At his birth he had seemed so full of life. Then at about the sixth month he had changed overnight. He stopped sucking his mother's breast and his skin took the complexion of withering cocoyam leaves. Some people said perhaps Amoge's milk had gone bitter. She was asked to squirt some of it into a bowl to see if it would kill an ant. But the little ant which was dropped into it stayed alive; so the fault was not with the milk.

Edogo's mind was in pain over the child. Some people were already saying that perhaps he was none other than the first one. But Edogo and Amoge never talked about it; the woman especially was afraid. Since utterance had power to change fear into a living truth they dared not speak before they had to.

In her hut Amoge sat on a low stool, her crying child set on the angle of her two feet which she had brought together to touch at the heels. After a while she lifted her feet and child together on to another spot leaving behind on the floor a round patch of watery, green excrement. She looked round the room but did not seem to find what she wanted. Then she called: *Nwanku! Nwanku! Nwanku!* A wiry, black dog rushed in from outside and made straight for the excrement which disappeared with four or five noisy flicks of its tongue. Then it sat down with its tail wagging on the floor. Amoge moved her feet and child once again but this time all that was left behind was a tiny green drop. Nwanku did not consider it big enough to justify getting up; it merely stretched its neck and took it up with the corner of the tongue and sat up again to wait. But the child had finished and the dog was soon trying without success to catch a fly between its jaws.

Edogo's thoughts refused to stay on the door he was carving. Once again he put down the hammer and changed the chisel from his left hand to the right. The child had now stopped crying and Edogo's thoughts wandered to the recent exchange of words between his father and brother. The trouble with Ezeulu was that he could never see something and take his eyes away from it. Everybody agreed that Obika's friendship with Ofoedu would not bring about any good, but Obika was no longer a child and if he refused to listen to advice he should be left alone. That was what their father could never learn. He must go on treating his grown children like little boys, and if they ever said no there was a big quarrel. This was why the older his children grew the more he seemed to dislike them. Edogo remembered how much his father had liked him when he was a boy and how with the passage of years he had transferred his affection first to Obika and then to Oduche and Nwafo. Thinking of it now Edogo could not actually remember that their father had ever shown much affection for Oduche. He seemed to have lingered too long on Obika (who of all his sons resembled him most in appearance) and then by-passed Oduche for Nwafo. What would happen if the old man had another son tomorrow? Would Nwafo then begin to lose favour in his eyes? Perhaps. Or was there more to it than that? Was there something in the boy which told their father that at last a successor to the priesthood had come? Some people said Nwafo was in every way an image of Ezeulu's father. Actually Edogo would feel greatly relieved if on the death of their father the diviner's string of beads fell in favour of Nwafo. 'I do not want to be Chief Priest,' he heard himself saying aloud. He looked round instinctively to see if anyone had been near enough to have heard him. 'As for Obika,' he thought, 'things like the priesthood did not come near his mind.' Which left only Oduche and Nwafo. But as Ezeulu had turned Oduche over to the new religion he could no longer be counted. A strange thought seized Edogo now. Could it be that their father had deliberately sent Oduche to the religion of the white man so as to disqualify him for the priesthood of Ulu? He put down the chisel with which he was absentmindedly straightening the intersecting lines on the iroko door. That would explain it! The priesthood would then fall on his youngest and favourite son. The reason which Ezeulu gave for his strange decision had never convinced anyone. If as he said he merely wanted one of his sons to be his eye and ear at this new assembly why did he not send Nwafo who was close to his thoughts? No, that was not the reason. The priest wanted to have a hand in the choice of his successor. It was what anyone who knew Ezeulu would expect him to do. But was he not presuming too much? The choice of a priest lay with the deity. Was it likely that he would let the old priest force his hand. Although Edogo and Obika did not seem attracted to the office that would not prevent the deity from choosing either of them or even Oduche, out of spite. Edogo's thinking now became confused. If Ulu should choose him to be Chief Priest what would he do? This thought had never worried him before because he had always taken it for granted that Ulu would not want him. But the way he saw things now there was no certainty about that. Would he be happy if the diviner's beads fell in his favour? He could not say.

Perhaps the only sure happiness it would give him was the knowledge that his father's partiality for his younger sons had been frustrated by the deity himself. From Ani-Mmo where dead men went Ezeulu would look up and see the ruin of all his plans.

Edogo was surprised by this depth of ill-will for his father and relented somewhat. He remembered what his mother used to say when she was alive, that Ezeulu's only fault was that he expected everyone – his wives, his kinsmen, his children, his friends and even his enemies – to think and act like himself. Anyone who dared to say no to him was an enemy. He forgot the saying of the elders that if a man sought for a companion who acted entirely like himself he would live in solitude.

Ezeulu was sitting at the same spot long after his quarrel with Obika. His back was set against the wall and his gaze on the approaches to his compound. Now and again he seemed to study the household shrine standing against the low threshold wall in front of him. On his left there was a long mud-seat with goatskins spread on it. The eaves on that part of the hut were cut back so that Ezeulu could watch the sky for the new moon. In the daytime light came into the hut mostly from that part. Nwafo squatted on the mud-seat, facing his father. At the other end of the room, on Ezeulu's right, stood his low bamboo bed; beside it a fire of ukwa logs smouldered.

Without changing his fixed gaze Ezeulu began suddenly to talk to Nwafo.

'A man does not speak a lie to his son,' he said. 'Remember that always. To say *My father told me* is to swear the greatest oath. You are only a little boy, but I was no older when my father began to confide in me. Do you hear what I am saying?'

Nwafo said yes.

'You see what has happened to your brother. In a few days his bride will come and he will no longer be called a child. When strangers see him they will no longer ask *Whose son is he?* but *Who is he?* Of his wife they will no longer say *Whose daughter?* but *Whose wife?* Do you understand me?' Nwafo saw that his face was beginning to shine with sweat. Someone was coming towards the hut and he stopped talking.

'Who is that?' Ezeulu screwed up his eyes in an effort to see. Nwafo jumped down from the mud-seat and came to the centre of the hut to see.

'It is Ogbuefi Akuebue.'

Akuebue was one of the very few men in Umuaro whose words gained entrance into Ezeulu's ear. The two men were in the same age group. As he drew near he raised his voice and asked: 'Is the owner of this house still alive?'

'Who is this man?' asked Ezeulu. 'Did they not say that you died two markets come next Afo?'

'Perhaps you do not know that everyone in your age group has long died. Or are you waiting for mushrooms to sprout from your head before you know that your time is over?' Akuebue was now inside the hut but he still maintained the posture he had assumed to pass under the low eaves – the right hand supported above the knee and the body bent at the waist. Without rising to his full height he shook hands with the Chief Priest. Then he spread his goatskin on the floor near the mud-seat and sat down.

'How are your people?'

'They are quiet.' This was always how Akuebue answered about his family. It amused Nwafo greatly. He had an image in his mind of this man's wives and children sitting quietly with their hands between their laps.

'And yours?' he asked Ezeulu.

'Nobody has died.'

'Do they say that Obika was whipped by the white man?'

Ezeulu opened both palms to the sky and said nothing.

'What did they say was his offence?'

'My friend, let us talk about other things. There was a time when a happening such as this would have given me a fever; but that time has passed. Nothing is anything to me any more. Go and ask your mother to bring me a kolanut, Nwafo.'

'She was saying this morning that her kolanuts were finished.'

'Go and ask Matefi then.'

'Must you worry about kolanuts every time? I am not a stranger.'

'I was not taught that kolanut was the food of strangers,' said Ezeulu. 'And besides do not our people say that he is a fool who treats his brother worse than a stranger? But I know what you are afraid of; they tell me you have lost all your teeth.' As he said this he reached for a lump of white clay in a four-sided wooden bowl shaped like the head of a lizard and rolled it on the floor towards Akuebue who picked it up and drew four upright lines with it on the floor. Then he painted the big toe of his right foot and rolled the chalk back to Ezeulu and he put it away again in the wooden bowl.

Nwafo was soon back with a kolanut in another bowl.

'Show it to Akuebue,' said his father.

'I have seen it,' replied Akuebue.

'Then break it.'

'No. The king's kolanut returns to his hands.'

'If you say so.'

'Indeed I say so.'

Ezeulu took the bowl from Nwafo and set it down between his legs. Then he picked up the kolanut in his right hand and offered a prayer. He jerked the hand forward as he said each sentence, his palm open upwards and the thumb holding down the kolanut on the four fingers.

'Ogbuefi Akuebue, may you live, and all your people. I too will live with all my people. But life alone is not enough. May we have the things with which to live it well. For there is a kind of slow and weary life which is worse than death.'

'You speak the truth.'

'May good confront the man on top and the man below. But let him who is jealous of another's position choke with his envy.'

'So be it.'

'May good come to the land of Igbo and to the country of the riverain folk.'

Then he broke the kolanut by pressing it between his palms and threw all the lobes into the bowl on the floor.

'O o-o o-o o o o-o,' he whistled. 'Look what has happened here. The spirits want to eat.'

Akuebue craned his neck to see. 'One, two, three, four, five, six. Indeed they want to eat.'

Ezeulu picked up one lobe and threw it outside. Then he picked up another one and put it into his mouth. Nwafo came forward, took the bowl from the floor and served Akuebue. For a short while neither man spoke, only the sound of kolanut as it was crushed between the teeth broke the silence.

'It is strange the way kolanuts behave,' said Ezeulu after he had swallowed twice. 'I do not remember when I last saw one with six lobes.'

'It is indeed very rare, and you only see it when you are not looking for it. Even five is not common. Some years ago I had to buy four or five basketfuls of kolanuts before I could find one with five lobes for a sacrifice. Nwafo, go to your mother's hut and bring me a big calabash of cold water . . . This type of heat is not empty-handed.'

'I think there is water in the sky,' said Ezeulu. 'It is the heat before rain.' As he said this he rose three-quarters erect and walked a few steps to his bamboo bed and took from it his goatskin bag. This bag was sewn together with great cunning; it looked as though the goat which lived in it had been pulled out as one might pull out a snail from its shell. It had four short legs and the tail was intact. Ezeulu took the bag to his seat and began to search arm-deep for his bottle of snuff. When he found it he put it down on the floor and began to look for the small ivory spoon. He soon found that also, and he put the bag away beside him. He took up the little white bottle again, held it up to see how much snuff there was left and then tapped it on his kneecap. He opened the bottle and tipped a little of the content into his left palm.

'Give me a little of that thing to clear my head,' said Akuebue who had just drunk his water.

'Come and get it,' replied Ezeulu. 'You do not expect me to provide the snuff and also the walking around, to give you a wife and find you a mat to sleep on.'

Akuebue rose half-erect with his right hand on the knee and the left palm opened towards Ezeulu. 'I will not dispute with you,' he said. 'You have the yam and you have the knife.'

Ezeulu transferred two spoonfuls of the snuff from his own palm into Akuebue's and then brought out some more from the bottle for himself.

'It is good snuff,' said Akuebue. One of his nostrils carried brown traces of the powder. He took another small heap from his cupped left hand on to his right thumbnail and guided it to the other nostril, throwing his head back and sniffing three or four times. Then he had traces on both nostrils. Ezeulu used the ivory spoon instead of his thumbnail.

'I do not buy my snuff in the market,' said Ezeulu; 'that is why.'

Edogo came in dangling a calabash of palm wine from a short rope tied round its neck. He saluted Akuebue and his father and set down the calabash.

'I did not know that you had palm wine,' said Ezeulu.

'It has just been sent by the owner of the door I am carving.'

'And why do you bring it in the presence of this my friend who took over the stomach of all his dead relatives?'

'But I have not heard Edogo say it was meant for you.' He turned to Edogo and asked: 'Or did you say so?' Edogo laughed and said it was meant for two of them.

Akuebue brought out a big cow's horn from his bag and hit it thrice on the floor. Then he rubbed its edges with his palm to remove dirt. Ezeulu brought out his horn from the bag beside him and held it for Edogo to fill. When he had served him he took the calabash to Akuebue and also filled his horn. Before they drank Ezeulu and Akuebue tipped a little on to the floor and muttered a barely audible invitation to their fathers.

'My body is full of aches,' said Ezeulu, 'and I do not think that palm wine is good for me yet.'

'I can tell you it is not,' said Akuebue who had gulped down the first horn and screwed up his face as though waiting for a sound inside his head to tell him whether it was good wine or not.

Edogo took his father's horn from him and filled himself a measure. Oduche came in then, saluted his father and Akuebue and sat down with Nwafo on the mud-seat. Since he joined the white man's religion he always wore a loincloth of towelling material instead of the thin strip of cloth between the legs. Edogo filled the horn again and offered him but he did not drink. 'What about you, Nwafo?' asked Edogo. He also said no.

'When is it you are going to Okperi?' Ezeulu asked.

'The day after tomorrow.'

'For how long?'

'They say for two markets.'

Ezeulu seemed to be turning this over in his mind.

'What are you going for?' asked Akuebue.

'They want to test our knowledge of the holy book.'

Akuebue shrugged his shoulders.

'I am not sure that you will go,' said Ezeulu. 'But let the days pass and I shall decide.' Nobody said anything in reply. Oduche knew enough about his father not to protest. Akuebue drank another horn of wine and began to gnash his teeth. The voice he had been waiting for had spoken and pronounced the wine good. He knocked the horn on the floor a few times and prayed as he did so.

'May the man who tapped this wine have life to continue his good work. May those of us who drank it also have life. The land of Olu and the land of Igbo.' He rubbed the edges of his horn before putting it away in his bag.

'Drink one horn more,' said Edogo.

Akuebue rubbed his mouth with the back of his hand before replying.

'The only medicine against palm wine is the power to say no.' This statement seemed to bring Ezeulu back to the people around him.

'Before you came in,' he said to Akuebue, 'I was telling that little boy over there that the greatest liar among men still speaks the truth to his own son.'

'It is so,' said Akuebue. 'A man can swear before the most dreaded deity on what his father told him.'

'If a man is not sure of the boundary between his land and his neighbour's,' continued Ezeulu, 'he tells his son: *I think it is here but if there is a dispute do not swear before a deity.*'

'It is even so,' said Akuebue.

'But when a man has spoken the truth and his children prefer to take the lie . . .' His voice had risen with every word towards the dangerous pitch of a curse; then he broke off with a violent shake of the head. When he began again he spoke more quietly. 'That is why a stranger can whip a son of mine and go unscathed, because my son has nailed up his ear against my words. Were it not so that stranger would already have learnt what it was to cross Ezeulu; dogs would have licked his eyes. I would have swallowed him whole and brought him up again. I would have shaved his head without wetting the hair.'

'Did Obika strike the first blow then?' asked Akuebue.

'How do I know? All I can say is that he was blind with palm wine when he left here in the morning. And even when he came back a short while ago it had still not cleared from his eyes.'

'But they say he did not strike the first blow,' said Edogo.

'Were you there?' asked his father. 'Or would you swear before a deity on the strength of what a drunken man tells you? If I was sure of my son do you think I would sit here now talking to you while a man who pokes his finger into my eyes goes home to his bed? If I did nothing else I would pronounce a few words on him and he would know the power in my mouth.' The perspiration was forming on his brow.

'What you say is true,' said Akuebue. 'But in my thinking there is still something for us to do once we find out from those who saw it whether Obika struck the first blow or . . .' Ezeulu did not let him finish.

'Why should I go out looking for strangers to tell me what my son did or did not do? I should be telling them.'

'That is true. But let us first chase away the wild cat, afterwards we blame the hen.' Akuebue turned to Edogo. 'Where is Obika himself?'

'It appears that what I said has not entered your ear,' said Ezeulu. 'Where . . .'

Edogo interrupted him. 'He went out with Ofoedu. He went out because our father did not ask him what happened before blaming him.'

This unexpected accusation stung Ezeulu like the black ant. But he held himself together and, to everybody's surprise, leaned back against the wall and shut his eyes. When he opened them again he began to whistle quietly to himself. Akuebue nodded his head four or five times like a man who had uncovered an unexpected truth. Ezeulu moved his head slightly from side to side and up and down to his almost silent whistling.

'This is what I tell my own children,' said Akuebue to Edogo and the two boys. 'I tell them that a man always has more sense than his children.' It was clear he said this to mollify Ezeulu; but at the same time it was clear he spoke truth. 'Those of you who think they are wiser than their father forget that it is from a man's own stock of sense that he gives out to his sons. That is why a boy who tries to wrestle with his father gets blinded by the old man's loincloth. Why do I speak like this? It is because I am not a stranger in your father's hut and I am not afraid to speak my mind. I know how often your father has pleaded with Obika to leave his friendship with Ofoedu. Why has Obika not heeded? It is because you all – not only Obika but you all, including that little one there – you think you are wiser than your father. My own children are like that. But there is one thing which you all forget. You forget that a woman who began cooking before another must have more broken utensils. When we old people speak it is not because of the sweetness of words in our mouth; it is because we see something which you do not see. Our fathers made a proverb about it. They said that when we see an old woman stop in her dance to point again and again in the same direction we can be sure that somewhere there something happened long ago which touched the roots of her life. When Obika returns tell him what I say, Edogo. Do you hear me?' Edogo nodded. He was wondering whether it was true that a man never spoke a lie to his sons.

Akuebue wheeled round on his buttocks and faced Ezeulu. 'It is the pride of Umuaro,' he said, 'that we never see one party as right and the other wrong. I have spoken to the children and I shall not be afraid to speak to you. I think you are too hard on Obika. Apart from your high position as Chief Priest you are also blessed with a great compound. But in all great compounds there must be people of all minds – some good, some bad, some fearless and some cowardly; those who bring in wealth and those who scatter it, those who give good advice and those who only speak the words of palm wine. That is why we say that whatever tune you play in the compound of a great man there is always someone to dance to it. I salute you.'

Chapter Ten

Although Tony Clarke had already spent nearly six weeks in Okperi most of his luggage, including his crockery, had arrived only a fort-night ago – in fact the day before he went on tour to the bush. That was why he had not been able until now to ask Captain Winterbottom to his house for a meal.

As he awaited the arrival of his guest Mr Clarke felt not a little uneasy. One of the problems of living in a place like this with only four other Europeans (three of whom were supposed to be beneath the notice of Political Officers) was that one had to cope with a guest like Winterbottom absolutely alone. Of course this was not their first social encounter; they had in fact had dinner together not very long ago and things did not altogether grind to a stop. But then Clarke had been guest, without any responsibilities. Today he was going to be host and the onus would rest on him to keep the conversation alive, through the long, arduous ritual of alcohol, food, coffee and more alcohol stretching into midnight. If only he could have invited some-one like John Wright with whom he had struck up a kind of friendship during his recent tour! But such a thing would have been disastrous.

Clarke had shared the lonely thatch-roofed Rest House outside Umuaro with Wright for one night during his tour. Wright had been living in one half of the Rest House for over two weeks then. The Rest House consisted of two enormous rooms each with a camp-bed and an old mosquito-net, a rough wooden table and chair and a cupboard. Just behind the main building there was a thatched shed used as a kitchen. About thirty yards away another hut stood over a dug latrine and wooden seat. Farther away still in the same direction a third hut in very bad repair housed the servants and porters who were sometimes called 'hammock boys'. The Rest House proper was surrounded by a ragged hedge of a native plant which Clarke had never seen anywhere else.

The entire appearance of the place showed that it had not had a caretaker since the last one vanished into the bush with two camp-beds. The beds were replaced but the key to the main building and the latrine was thereafter kept at headquarters so that whenever a European was going on tour and needed to lodge there the native Chief Clerk in Captain Winterbottom's office had to remember to give the key to his head porter or steward. Once when the Police Officer, Mr Wade, had been going to Umuaro the Chief Clerk had forgotten to do this and had had to walk the six or seven miles at night to deliver it. Fortunately for him Mr Wade had not suffered any personal inconvenience as he had sent his boys one day ahead of himself to clean the place up.

As he walked round the premises of the Rest House Tony Clarke felt that he was hundreds of miles from Government Hill. It was quite impossible to believe that it was only six or seven miles away. Even the sun seemed to set in a different direction. No wonder the natives were said to regard a six mile walk as travelling to a foreign country.

Later that evening he and Wright sat on the veranda of the Rest House to drink Wright's gin. In this remote corner, far from the stiff atmosphere of Winterbottom's Government Hill, Clarke was able to discover that he liked Wright very much. He also discovered to his somewhat delighted amazement that in certain circumstances he could contain as much gin as any Old Coaster.

They had only met for very brief moments before. But now they talked like old friends. Clarke thought that for all the other man's squat and rough exterior he was a good and honest Englishman. He found it so refreshing to be talking to a man who did not have the besetting sin of smugness, of taking himself too seriously.

'What do you think the Captain would say, Tony, if he were to see his young Political Officer being nice and friendly to a common road-maker?' His big red face looked almost boyish.

'I don't know and don't much care,' said Clarke, and because the fume of gin was already working on his brain, he added: 'I shall be happy if in all my years in Africa I succeed in building something as good as your road . . .'

'It's good of you to say so.'

'Are we having a celebration to open it?'

'The Captain says no. He says we have already overspent the Vote for it.'

'What does it matter?'

'That's what I want to know. And yet we spend hundreds of pounds building Native Courts all over the division that nobody wants, as far as I can see.'

'I must say though that that is not the Captain's fault.' Clarke was already adopting Wright's half-contemptuous manner of referring to Winterbottom. 'It is the policy of Headquarters which I happen to know the Captain is not altogether in agreement with.'

'Damn the Headquarters.'

'The Captain would approve of that sentiment.'

'Actually, you know, the Captain is not a bad fellow at all. I think that deep down he is quite a decent fellow. One must make allowances for the rough time he's had.'

'In the matter of promotions, you mean?'

'He's been badly treated there too, I'm told,' said Wright. 'Actually I wasn't thinking of that at all. I was thinking of his domestic life. Oh yes. You see during the war while the poor man was fighting the Germans in the Cameroons some smart fellow walked away with his wife at home.'

'Really? I hadn't heard about that.'

'Yes. I'm told he was very badly shaken by it. I sometimes think it was this personal loss during the war that's made him cling to this ridiculous Captain business.'

'Quite possibly. He's the kind of person, isn't he, who would take the desertion of his wife very badly,' said Clarke.

'Exactly. A man as inflexible as him can't take a thing like that.'

In the course of the evening Clarke was given every detail of Winterbottom's marital crisis and he felt really sorry for the man. Wright also seemed to have been touched with sympathy by the very act of telling the story. Without any conscious design the two men dropped their contemptuous reference to *the Captain* and called Winterbottom by his name.

'The real trouble with Winterbottom,' said Wright after deep thought, 'is that he is too serious to sleep with native women.' Clarke was startled out of his own thoughts, and for a brief moment he completely forgot about Winterbottom. On more than one occasion during his present tour he had come up in his mind against the question: How widespread was the practice of white men sleeping with native women?

'He doesn't seem to realize that even Governors have been known to keep dusky mistresses.' He licked his lips.

'I don't think it's a question of knowing or not knowing,' said Clarke. 'He is a man of very high principles, something of a missionary. I believe his father was a Church of England clergyman, which is a far cry from my father, for instance, who is a Bank of England clerical.' They both laughed heartily at this. When Clarke recalled this piece of wit in the morning he realized how much alcohol he must have drunk to find such an inferior joke so amusing.

'I think you are right about the missionary business. He should have come out with the C.M.S. or some such people. By the way, he has been going around lately with the woman missionary doctor at Nkisa. Of course we all have our different tastes, but I would not have thought a woman missionary doctor could provide much fun for a man in this God-forsaken place.'

Clarke wanted to ask about native women – whether they were better than whites, and many other details – but not even the effect of the gin could bring out the questions. Rather he found himself changing the subject and losing this great opportunity. The thoughts he had had since first seeing fully grown girls going about naked were again forced to sleep. Later he would bite his lips in regret.

'From what I heard of Winterbottom at headquarters,' he said, 'I expected to see some sort of buffoon.'

'I know. He is a stock joke at Enugu, isn't he?'

'Whenever I said I was going to Okperi they said: *What! With Old Tom?* and looked pityingly at me. I wondered what was wrong with Old Tom, but no one would say any more. Then one day a very senior officer said to another to my hearing: *Old Tom is always reminding you that he came out to Nigeria in 1910 but he never mentions that in all that time he has not put in a day's work*. It's simply amazing how much back-biting goes on at Enugu.'

'Well,' said Wright, yawning, 'I cannot say myself that Old Tom is the most hard-working man I've ever met; but then who is? Certainly not that lot at Enugu.'

All this was working on Clarke's mind as he awaited Winterbottom's coming. He felt guilty like one who had been caught back-biting one of his own group with an outsider. But then, he told himself in defence, they had said nothing that could be called uncharitable about Winterbottom. All that had happened was that he got to know a few details about the man's life, and felt sorry for him. And that feeling justified the knowledge.

He went into the kitchen for the tenth time that evening to see how Cook was roasting the chicken over a wood fire. It would be terrible if it turned out as tough as the last one Clarke had eaten. Of course all native chicken was tough and very small. But perhaps one shouldn't complain. A fully grown cock cost no more than twopence. Even so one wouldn't mind paying a little more now and again for a good, juicy, English chicken. The look on Cook's face seemed to say that Clarke was coming into the kitchen too frequently.

'How is it coming?'

'Ide try small small,' said Cook, rubbing his smoke-inflamed eyes with his forearm. Clarke looked around vaguely and returned to the veranda of his bungalow. He sat down and looked at his watch again; it was quarter to seven – a full half-hour to go. He began to think up a number of subjects for conversation. His recent tour would have provided enough topics for the evening, but he had just written and submitted a full report on it.

'But this is funny,' he told himself. Why should he feel so nervous because Winterbottom was coming to dinner? Was he afraid of the man? Certainly not! Why all the excitement then? Why should he get so worked up about meeting Winterbottom simply because Wright had told him a few background stories which were in any case common knowledge? From this point Clarke speculated briefly on the nature of knowledge. Did knowledge of one's friends and colleagues impose a handicap on one? Perhaps it did. If so it showed how false was the common assumption that the more facts you could get about others the greater your power over them. Perhaps facts put you at a great disadvantage; perhaps they made you feel sorry and even responsible. Clarke rose to his feet and walked up and down, rather self-consciously. Perhaps this was the real difference between British and French colonial administrations. The French made up their minds about what they wanted to do and did it. The British, on the other hand, never did anything without first sending out a Commission of Inquiry to discover all the facts, which then ham-strung them. He sat down again, glowing with satisfaction.

The dinner was almost entirely satisfactory. There were only two or three uneasy moments throughout the evening; for example when Captain Winterbottom said at the beginning: 'I have just been reading your report on your tour. One could see that you are settling down nicely to your duties.'

'It was all so exciting,' said Clarke, attempting to minimize his part in the success story. 'It's such a wonderful division. I can imagine how you must feel seeing such a happy district growing up under your direction.' He had stopped himself just in time from saying *your wise direction*. Even so he wondered whether this rather obvious attempt to return compliment for compliment was altogether happy.

'One thing worries me, though,' said Winterbottom without any indication that he even heard Clarke's last piece. 'You say in the report that after careful inquiry you were satisfied that there was no truth in all the stories of Wright whipping natives.' Clarke's heart fell. This was the one falsehood in the entire report. In fact he completely forgot to make any inquiries, even if he had known how to set about it. It was only on his return to Okperi that he found a brief, late entry *Wright & natives* scribbled in pencil on the second page of his touring notebook. At first he had worried over it; then he had come to the conclusion that if Wright had in fact been employing unorthodox methods he would have heard of it without making inquiries as such. But since he had heard nothing it was safe to say that the stories were untrue. In any case how did one investigate such a thing? Did one go up to the first native one saw and ask if he had been birched by Wright? Or did one ask Wright? From what Clarke had seen of the man he would not have thought he was that sort.

'My steward is a native of Umuaro,' continued Winterbottom, 'and has just come back after spending two days at home; and he tells me that the whole village was in confusion because a rather important man had been whipped by Wright. But perhaps there's nothing in it.'

Clarke hoped he did not betray his confusion. Anyhow he rallied quickly and said: 'I heard nothing of it on the spot.' The words *on the spot* stung Winterbottom like three wasps. The fellow's cheek! He had been there barely a week and already he was talking as though he owned the district and Winterbottom was the new boy, or some desk-ridden idiot at Headquarters. On the spot indeed! But he chose not to press the matter. He was immersed in his plans for appointing two new Paramount Chiefs in the division and throughout dinner he spoke of nothing else. Clarke was surprised that he no longer spoke with strong feeling. As he watched him across the table he seemed too tired and old. But even that soon passed and a hint of enthusiasm returned to his voice.

'I think I told you the story of the fetish priest who impressed me most favourably by speaking the truth in the land case between these people here and Umuaro.'

'Yes, I think you did.' Clarke was nervously watching his guest in difficulty with a piece of chicken. These damned native birds!

'Well, I have now decided to appoint him Paramount Chief for Umuaro. I've gone through the records of the case again and found that the man's title is Eze Ulu. The prefix *eze* in Ibo means king. So the man is a kind of priest-king.'

'That means, I suppose,' said Clarke, 'that the new appointment would not altogether be strange to him.'

'Exactly. Although I must say that I have never found the Ibo man backward in acquiring new airs of authority. Take this libertine we made Chief here. He now calls himself His Highness Obi Ikedi the First of Okperi. The only title I haven't yet heard him use is *Fidei Defensor*.'

Clarke opened his mouth to say that the love of title was a universal human failing but thought better of it.

'The man was a complete nonentity until we crowned him, and now he carries on as though he had been nothing else all his life. It's the same with Court Clerks and even messengers. They all manage to turn themselves into little tyrants over their own people. It seems to be a trait in the character of the negro.'

The steward in shining white moved out of the darkness of the kitchen balancing the rest of the boiled potatoes and cauliflower on one hand and the chicken on the other. His heavily starched uniform crackled as he walked over and stood silently on Captain Winterbottom's right.

'Go over to the other side, Stephen,' said Clarke irritably. Stephen grinned and moved over.

'No. I won't have another,' said Winterbottom, and turning to Clarke he added: 'This is very good; one is not usually so lucky with the first cook he gets.'

'Aloysius is not first rate, but I suppose . . . No, I won't have any more, Stephen.'

As they ate fresh fruit salad made from pawpaw, banana and oranges Winterbottom returned to his Paramount Chiefs.

'So as far as Umuaro is concerned I have found their Chief,' he said with one of his rare smiles, 'and they will live happily ever after. I am not so optimistic about Abame who are a pretty wild set anyhow.'

'They are the people who murdered Macdonald?' asked Clarke, half of whose mind was on the salad that had gone a little sour.

'That's right. Actually they're no longer very troublesome – not to us anyhow; the punitive expedition taught them a pretty unforgettable lesson. But they are still very unco-operative. In the whole division they are the least co-operative with their Native Court. Throughout last year the court handled less than a dozen cases and not one was brought to it by the natives themselves.'

'That's pretty grim,' said Clarke without being sure whether he meant it to be ironical or not. But as Winterbottom began to fill in the details of his plans for the two Native Court Areas Clarke could not help being impressed by a new aspect of the man's character. Having been overruled in his opposition to Paramount Chiefs he was now sparing no effort to ensure the success of the policy. Clarke's tutor in Morals at Cambridge had been fond of the phrase *crystalliza-tion of civilization*. This was it.

Over their after-coffee whisky and soda Captain Winterbottom's opposition reared its head momentarily. But that only confirmed Clarke's new opinion of him.

'What I find so heart-rending,' said Winterbottom, 'is not so much the wrong policies of our Administration as our lack of consistency. Take this question of Paramount Chiefs. When Sir Hugh Macdermot first arrived as Governor he sent his Secretary for Native Affairs to investigate the whole business. The fellow came over here and spent a long time discovering the absurdities of the system which I had pointed out all along. Anyhow, from what he said in private conversa-tion it was clear that he agreed with us that it had been an unqualified disaster. That was in 1919. I remember I had just come back from leave . . .' Some strange emotion entered his voice and Clarke saw a rush of blood to his face. He mastered himself and continued: 'More than two years and we still have heard nothing about the man's report. On the contrary the Lieutenant-Governor now asks us to proceed with the previous policy. Where does anyone stand?'

'It is very frustrating,' said Clarke. 'You know I was thinking the other day about our love of Commissions of Inquiry. That seems to me to be the real difference between us and the French. They know what they want and do it. We set up a commission to discover all the facts, as though facts meant anything. We imagine that the more facts we can obtain about our Africans the easier it will be to rule them. But facts . . .'

'Facts are important,' cut in Winterbottom, 'and Commissions of Inquiry could be useful. The fault of our Administration is that they invariably appoint the wrong people and set aside the advice of those of us who have been here for years.'

Clarke felt impotent anger with the man for not letting him finish, and personal inadequacy for not having made the point as beautifully as he had first made it to himself.

Chapter Eleven

The first time Ezeulu left his compound after the Pumpkin Festival was to visit his friend, Akuebue. He found him sitting on the floor of his *obi* preparing seed-yams which he had hired labourers to plant for him next morning. He sat with a short, wooden-headed knife between two heaps of yams. The bigger heap lay to his right on the bare floor. The smaller pile was in a long basket from which he took out one yam at a time, looked at it closely, trimmed it with his knife and put it in the big heap. The refuse lay directly in front of him, between the heaps – large numbers of brown, circular yam-skins chipped off the tail of each seed-yam, and grey, premature tendrils trimmed off the heads.

The two men shook hands and Ezeulu took his rolled goatskin from under his arm, spread it on the floor and sat down. Akuebue asked him about his family and for a while continued to work on his yams.

'They are well,' replied Ezeulu. 'And the people of your compound?'

'They are quiet.'

'Those are very large and healthy seed-yams. Do they come from your own barn or from the market?'

'Do you not know that my portion of the Anietiti land . . . ? Yes. They were harvested there.'

'It is a great land,' said Ezeulu, nodding his head a few times. 'Such a land makes lazy people look like master farmers.'

Akuebue smiled. 'You want to draw me out, but you won't.' He put down the knife and raised his voice to call his son, Obielue, who answered from the inner compound and soon came in, sweating.

'Ezeulu!' he saluted.

'My son.'

He turned to his father to take his message.

'Tell your mother that Ezeulu is greeting her. If she has kolanut let her bring it.' Obielue returned to the inner compound.

'Although I ate no kolanut the last time I went to the house of my friend.' Akuebue said this as though he talked to himself.

Ezeulu laughed. 'What do we say happens to the man who eats and then makes his mouth as if it has never seen food?'

'How should I know?'

'It makes his anus dry up. Did your mother not tell you that?'

Akuebue rose to his feet very slowly because of the pain in his waist.

'Old age is a disease,' he said, struggling to unbend himself with one hand on the hip. When he was three-quarters erect he gave up. 'Whenever I sit for any length of time I have to practise again to walk, like an infant.' He smiled as he toddled to the low entrance wall of his *obi*, took from it a wooden bowl with a lump of chalk in it and offered it to his guest. Ezeulu picked up the chalk and drew five lines with it on the floor – three uprights, a flat one across the top and another below them. Then he painted one of his big toes and dubbed a thin coat of white around his left eye.

Only one of Akuebue's two wives was at home and she soon came into the *obi* to salute Ezeulu and to say that the senior wife had gone to inspect her palm trees for ripe fruit. Obielue returned with a kolanut. He took the wooden bowl from his father, blew into it to remove dust and offered the kolanut in it to Ezeulu.

'Thank you,' said Ezeulu. 'Take it to your father to break.'

'No,' said Akuebue. 'I ask you to break it.'

'That cannot be. We do not by-pass a man and enter his compound.'

'I know that,' said Akuebue, 'but you see that my hands are full and I am asking you to perform the office for me.'

'A man cannot be too busy to break the first kolanut of the day in his own house. So put the yam down; it will not run away.'

'But this is not the first kolanut of the day. I have broken several already.'

'That may be so, but you did not break them in my presence. The time a man wakes up is his morning.'

'All right,' said Akuebue. 'I shall break it if you say so.'

'Indeed I say so. We do not apply an ear-pick to the eye.'

Akuebue took the kolanut in his hand and said: 'We shall both live,' and broke it.

Two gunshots had sounded in the neighbourhood since Ezeulu came in. Now a third went off.

'What is happening there?' he asked. 'Are men leaving the forest now to hunt in the compounds?'

'Oh. You have not heard? Ogbuefi Amalu is very sick.'

'True? And it has reached the point of shooting guns?'

'Yes.' Akuebue lowered his voice out of respect for the bad story. 'What day was yesterday?'

'Eke,' replied Ezeulu.

'Yes, it was on the other Eke that it happened. He was returning home from the farmland he had gone to clear when it struck him down. Before he reached home he was trembling with cold in the noonday heat. He could no longer hold his matchet because his fingers were set like crooks.'

'What do they say it is?'

'From what I saw this morning and yesterday I think it is *aru-mmo*.'

'Please do not repeat it.'

'But I am not telling you that Nwokonkwo or Nwokafo told me. This is what I saw with my own eyes.'

Ezeulu began to gnash his teeth.

'I went to see him this morning. His breath seemed to be scraping his sides with a blunt razor.'

'Who have they hired to make medicine for him?' asked Ezeulu.

'A man called Nwodika from Umuofia. I told them this morning that had I been there when they took the decision I would have told them to go straight to Aninta. There is a doctor there who nips off sickness between his thumb and finger.'

'But if it is the sickness of the Spirits, as you say, there is no medicine for it – except camwood and fire.'

'That is so,' said Akuebue, 'but we cannot put our hands between our laps and watch a sick man for twelve days. We must grope about until what must happen does happen. That is why I spoke of this medicine-man from Aninta.'

'I think you speak of Aghadike whom they call Anyanafummo.'

'You know him. That is the very man.'

'I know many people throughout Olu and Igbo. Aghadike is a great doctor and diviner. But even he cannot carry a battle to the compound of the great god.'

'No man can do that.'

The gun sounded again.

'This gun-shooting is no more than a foolish groping about,' said Ezeulu. 'How can we frighten Spirits away with the noise of a gun? If it were so easy any man who had enough money to buy a keg of gunpowder would live and live until mushrooms sprouted from his head. If I am sick and they bring me a medicine-man who knows more about hunting than herbs I shall send him away and look for another.'

The two men sat for a little while in silence. Then Akuebue said:

'From what I saw this morning we may hear something before another dawn.'

Ezeulu moved his head up and down many times. 'It is a story of great sorrow, but we cannot set fire to the world.'

Akuebue who had stopped working on his yams went back to them now with the proverbial excuse that greeting in the cold harmattan is taken from the fireside.

'That is what our people say,' replied Ezeulu. 'And they also say that a man who visits a craftsman at work finds a sullen host.'

The gun sounded yet again. It seemed to make Ezeulu irritable.

'I shall go over and tell the man that if he has no medicine to give to the sick man he should at least spare the gunpowder they will use for his funeral.'

'Perhaps he thinks that gunpowder is as cheap as wood ash,' said Akuebue, and then more seriously: 'If you go there on your way home say nothing that might make them think you wish their kinsman evil. They may say: What is gunpowder to a man's life?'

Ezeulu did not need two looks at the sick man to see that he could not pass the twelve days which the Spirits gave a man stricken with this disease. If, as Akuebue had said, nothing was heard by tomorrow it would be a thing to tell.

The man's trunk was encased in a thick coat of camwood ointment which had caked and cracked in countless places. A big log fire burned beside the bamboo bed on which he lay and a strong whiff of burning herbs was in the air. His breathing was like the splitting of hard wood. He did not recognize Ezeulu who on entering had greeted those in the room with his eyes alone and made straight for the bedside where he stood for a long time looking down on the sick man in silence. After that he went and sat down with the small crowd of relations talking in very low voices,

'What has a man done to merit this?' he asked.

'That is what we all have been asking,' replied one of the men. 'We were not told to expect it. We woke up one morning to find our shinbone deformed.'

The herbalist sat a little apart from the group, and took no part in the conversation. Ezeulu looked around the room and saw how the man had fortified it against the entry of the Spirits. From the roof hung down three long gourds corked with wads of dry banana leaf. A fourth gourd was the big-bellied type which was often used for carrying palm wine. It hung directly over the sick man. On its neck was a string of cowries, and a bunch of parrots' feathers danced inside it with only their upper half showing. It looked as if something boiled about their feet forcing them to gyrate around the mouth of the gourd. Two freshly sacrificed chicks dangled head downwards on either side of it.

The sick man who had been silent except for his breathing began quite suddenly to groan. Everyone stopped talking. The medicine-man, a ring of white chalk dubbed round one eye and a large leather-covered amulet on his left wrist, rose up and went outside. His flint-gun lay at the threshold, its base on the ground and the barrel pointing into the hut. He picked it up and began to load. The gunpowder was contained in a four-cornered bottle which had once carried the white man's hot drink called Nje-nje. When he had loaded the gun he went to the back of the house and let it off. All the cocks and hens in the neighbourhood immediately set up an alarm as if they had seen a wild animal.

When he returned to the hut he found the sick man even more restless, saying meaningless things.

'Bring me his *ofo*,' he said.

The sick man's brother took the short wooden staff from the house-shrine held by ropes to a rafter. The medicine-man who was now crouching by the bed took it from him and opening the sick man's right hand put it there.

'Hold it!' he commanded pressing the dry fingers round the staff. 'Grasp it, and say no to them! Do you hear me? Say no!'

The meaning of his command seemed at last to seep through many clogged filters to the sick man's mind and the fingers began to close, like claws, slowly round the staff.

'That's right,' said the medicine-man beginning to remove his own hand and to leave the *ofo* in Amalu's grasp. 'Say no to them!'

But as soon as he took his hand completely away Amalu's fingers jerked open and the *ofo* fell down on the floor. The little crowd in the hut exchanged meaningful glances but no words.

Soon after Ezeulu rose to go. 'Take good care of him,' he said.

'Go well,' replied the others.

When Obika's bride arrived with her people and he looked upon her again it surprised him greatly that he had been able to let her go untouched during her last visit. He knew that few other young men of his age would have shown the same restraint which ancient custom demanded. But what was right was right. Obika began to admire this new image of himself as an upholder of custom – like the lizard who fell down from the high iroko tree he felt entitled to praise himself if nobody else did.

The bride was accompanied by her mother who was just coming out of an illness, many girls of her own age and her mother's women friends. Most of the women carried small head-loads of the bride's dowry to which they had all contributed – cooking-pots, wooden bowls, brooms, mortar, pestle, baskets, mats, ladles, pots of palm oil, baskets of cocoyam, smoked fish, fermented cassava, locust beans, heads of salt and pepper. There were also two lengths of cloth, two plates and an iron pot. These last were products of the white man and had been bought at the new trading post at Okperi.

The three compounds of Ezeulu and his sons were already full of relatives and friends before the bride and her people arrived. The twenty or so young maidens attending her were all fully decorated. But the bride stood out among them. It was not only that she was taller than any of them, she was altogether more striking in her looks and carriage. She wore a different coiffure befitting her imminent transition to full womanhood – a plait rather than regular patterns made with a razor.

The girls sang a song called *Ifeoma*. Goodly Thing had come, they said, so let everyone who had good things bring them before her as offering. They made a circle round her and she danced to their song. As she danced her husband-to-be and other members of Ezeulu's family broke through the circle one or two at a time and stuck money on her forehead. She smiled and let the present fall at her feet from where one of the girls picked it up and put it in a bowl.

The bride's name was Okuata. In tallness she took after her father who came of a race of giants. Her face was finely cut and some people already called her Oyilidie because she resembled her husband in comeliness. Her full breasts had a very slight upward curve which would save them from falling and sagging too soon.

Her hair was done in the new *otimili* fashion. There were eight closely woven ridges of hair running in perfect lines from the nape to the front of the head and ending in short upright tufts like a garland of thick bristles worn on the hair-line from ear to ear. She wore as many as fifteen strings of *jigida* on her waist. Most of them were blood-coloured but two or three were black, and some of the blood-coloured strings had been made up with a few black discs thrown in. Tomorrow she would tie a loincloth like a full-grown woman and henceforth her body would be concealed from the public gaze. The strings of *jigida* clinked as she danced. Behind they covered all her waist and the upper part of her buttocks. In front they lay string upon string from under her navel to her genitals, covering the greater part and providing a dark shade for the rest. The other girls were dressed in the same way except that most of them wore fewer strings of *jigida*.

The feasting which followed lasted till sunset. There were pots of yam pottage, foofoo, bitter-leaf soup and *egusi* soup, two boiled legs of goat, two large bowls of cooked *asa* fish taken out whole from the soup and kegs of sweet wine tapped from the raffia palm.

Whenever a particularly impressive item of food was set before the women their song-leader raised the old chant of thanks:

> *Kwo-kwo-kwo-kwo-kwo!*
> Kwo-o-o-oh!
> We are going to eat again as we are wont to do!
> *Who provides?*
> Who is it?
> *Who provides?*
> Who is it?
> *Obika Ezeulu he provides*
> Ayo-o-o-o-o-oh!

But in the end her mother and all the protecting company from her village set out for home again leaving her behind. Okuata felt like an orphan child and tears came down her face. Her mother-in-law took her away into her hut where she would stay until the Sacrifice at the crossroads was performed.

The medicine-man and diviner who had been hired to perform the rite soon arrived and the party set out. In it were Obika, his elder half-brother, his mother and the bride. Ezeulu did not go with them because he rarely left his *obi* after dark. Oduche refused to go so as not to offend the Catechist who preached against sacrifices.

They made for the highway leading to Umuezeani, the village where the bride came from. It was now quite dark and there was no moon. The palm-oil lamp which Obika's mother carried gave little light especially as she had to cup one hand round the wick to protect the flame from the wind. Even so it was blown out twice and she had to go into nearby compounds to light it again – first into Anosi's compound and then into the hut of Membolu's widow.

The medicine-man whose name was Aniegboka walked silently in front of the group. He was a small man but when he spoke he raised his voice as one might do in talking over the compound wall to a neighbour who was hard of hearing. Aniegboka was not one of the famous medicine-men in the clan; he was chosen because he was friendly with Ezeulu's compound and besides the sacrifice he was going to perform did not call for exceptional skill. Children in all the neighbourhood knew him and fled on his approach because they said he could turn a person into a dog by slapping him on the buttocks. But they made fun of him when he was not there because one of his eyes was like a bad cowry. According to the story the eye was damaged by the sharpened end of a banana shaft which Aniegboka – then a little boy – was throwing up and catching again in mid-air.

As the group walked in the dark they passed a few people but only recognized them from their voice when they spoke a greeting. The weak light of the oil lamp seemed to deepen the darkness around them making it difficult for them to see others as easily as they themselves were seen.

There was a soft but constant clatter coming from the big skin bag slung on Aniegboka's shoulder. The bride had a bowl of fired clay in one hand and a hen in the other. Now and again the hen squawked the way hens do when their pen is disturbed by an intruder at night. As she walked in the middle of the file Okuata suffered the struggle of happiness and fear in her thoughts. Obika and Edogo who led the way held their matchets. They spoke now and again but Obika's mind was not in what they said. His ear strained to catch the gentlest clinking together of his bride's *jigida*. He could even isolate her footsteps from all the others behind him. He too was anxious. When he took his wife to his hut after the sacrifice, would he find her at home – as the saying was – or would he learn with angry humiliation that another had broken in and gone off with his prize? That could not be. Everyone who knew her witnessed to her good behaviour. Obika had already chosen an enormous goat as a present for his mother-in-law should his wife prove to be a virgin. He did not know exactly what he would do if he found that he could not take it to her after all.

On his left hand Obika held a very small pot of water by the neck. His half-brother had a bunch of tender palm frond cut from the pinnacle of the tree.

Before long they reached the junction of their highway and another leading to the bride's village along which she had come that very day. They walked a short distance on this road and stopped. The medicine-man chose a spot in the middle of the way and asked Obika to dig a hole there.

'Put down the lamp here,' he told Obika's mother. She did so and Obika crouched down and began to dig.

'Make it wider,' said the medicine-man. 'Yes, like that.'

The three men were all in a crouching position; the women knelt on both knees with the trunk erect. The light of the oil lamp burnt with vigour now.

'Do not dig any more,' said the medicine-man. 'It is now deep enough. Bring out all the loose soil.'

While Obika was scooping out the red earth with both hands the medicine-man began to bring out the sacrificial objects from his bag. First he brought out four small yams, then four pieces of white chalk and the flower of the wild lily.

'Give me the *omu*.' Edogo passed the tender palm leaves to him. He tore out four leaflets and put away the rest. Then he turned to Obika's mother.

'Let me have *ego nano*.' She untied a bunch of cowries from a corner of her cloth and gave them to him. He counted them carefully on the ground as a woman would before she bought or sold in the market, in groups of six. There were four groups and he nodded his head.

He rose to his feet and positioned Okuata beside the hole so that she faced the direction of her village, kneeling on both knees. Then he took his position opposite her on the other side of the hole, with the sacrificial objects ranged on his right. The others stood a little back.

He took one of the yams and gave it to Okuata. She waved it round her head and put it inside the hole. The medicine-man put in the other three. Then he gave her one of the pieces of white chalk and she did as for the yam. Then came the palm leaves and the flower of the wild lily and last of all he gave her one group of six cowries which she closed in her palm and did as for the others. After this he pronounced the absolution:

'Any evil which you might have seen with your eyes, or spoken with your mouth, or heard with your ears or trodden with your feet; whatever your father might have brought upon you or your mother brought upon you, I cover them all here.'

As he spoke the last words he took the bowl of fired clay and placed it face downwards over the objects in the hole. Then he began to put back the loose earth. Twice he eased up the bowl slightly so that when he finished its curved back showed a little above the surface of the road.

'Where is the water?' he asked.

Obika's mother produced the small pot of water. The bride who had now risen to her feet bent down at the waist and tipping the water into her palm began to wash her face, her hands and arms and her feet and legs up to the knee.

'Do not forget,' said the diviner when she had finished, 'that you are not to pass this way until morning even if the warriors of Abam were to strike this night and you were fleeing for your life.'

'The great god will not let her run for her life, neither today nor tomorrow,' said her mother-in-law.

'We know she will not,' said Aniegboka, 'but we must still do things as they were laid down.' Then turning to Obika he said: 'I have done as you asked me to do. Your wife will bear you nine sons.'

'We thank you,' said Obika and Edogo together.

'This hen will follow me home,' he said as he slung his bag on one shoulder and picked up the hen by the legs tied together with banana rope. He must have noticed how their eyes went again and again to the fowl. 'I alone will eat its flesh. Let none of you pay me a visit in the morning because I shall not share it.' He laughed very loud, like a drunken man. 'Even diviners ought to be rewarded now and again.' He laughed once more. 'Do we not say that the flute player must sometimes stop to wipe his nose?'

'That is what we say,' replied Edogo.

All the way back the medicine-man was full of loud talk. He boasted about the high regard in which, he said, he was held in distant clans. The others listened with one ear and put in a word now and again. The only person who did not open her mouth was Okuata.

When they got to Ilo Agbasioso the diviner parted with them and took a turning to the right. As soon as he was out of earshot Obika asked if it was the custom for the diviner to take the hen home.

'I have heard that some of them do,' said his mother. 'But I have never seen it until today. My own hen was buried with the rest of the sacrifice.'

'I have never heard of it,' said Edogo. 'It seems to me that the man does not get enough custom and is grabbing whatever he sees.'

'Our part was to provide the hen,' said Obika's mother, 'and we have done it.'

'I wanted to put a question to him.'

'No, my son. It is better that you did not. This is not the time to quarrel and dispute.'

Before Obika and his wife, Okuata, retired to their own compound they went first to salute Ezeulu.

'Father, is it the custom for the diviner to take home the hen bought for the sacrifice?' asked Obika.

'No, my son. Did Aniegboka do so?'

'He did. I wanted to speak to him but my mother made a sign to me not to talk.'

'It is not the custom. You must know that there are more people with greedy, long throats in the pursuit of medicine than anywhere else.' He noticed the look of concern on Obika's face. 'Take your wife home and do not allow this to trouble you. If a diviner wants to eat the entrails of sacrifice like a vulture the matter lies between him and his *chi*. You have done your part by providing the animal.'

When they left him Ezeulu felt his heart warm with pleasure as it had not done for many days. Was Obika already a changed person? It was not like him to come to his father and ask questions with so much care on his face. Akuebue had always said that once Obika had a woman to provide for he would change his ways. Perhaps it was going to be so. Another thought came to Ezeulu to confirm it: in the past Obika would have stood over the diviner and made him bury the hen. He smiled.

Chapter Twelve

Although Okuata emerged at dawn feeling awkward and bashful in her unaccustomed loincloth it was a very proud bashfulness. She could go without shame to salute her husband's parents because she had been 'found at home'. Her husband was even now arranging to send the goat and other presents to her mother in Umuezeani for giving him an unspoilt bride. She felt greatly relieved for although she had always known she was a virgin she had had a secret fear which some-times whispered in her ear and made her start. It was the thought of the moonlight play when Obiora had put his penis between her thighs. True, he had only succeeded in playing at the entrance but she could not be too sure.

She had not slept very much, not as much as her husband; but she had been happy. Sometimes she tried to forget her happiness and to think how she would have felt had things turned out differently. For many years to come she would have walked like one afraid the earth might bite her. Every girl knew of Ogbanje Omenyi whose husband was said to have sent to her parents for a matchet to cut the bush on either side of the highway which she carried between her thighs.

Every child in Ezeulu's compound wanted to go to the stream and draw water that morning because their new wife was going. Even little Obiageli who hated the stream because of the sharp stones on the way was very quick in bringing out her water pot. For once she cried when her mother told her to stay back and look after Amoge's child.

Obika's younger sister, Ojiugo, rushed up and down with the proprietary air of one who had a special claim on the bride because even the smallest child in a man's compound knew its mother's hut from the others. Ojiugo's mother, Matefi, carried the same air but with studied restraint which made it all the more telling. Needless to say she wanted it to tell on her husband's younger wife and to prove to her that there was greater honour in having a daughter-in-law than in buying ivory anklets and starving your children.

'See that you come back quickly,' she said to her daughter and her son's wife, 'before this spit on the floor dries up.' She spat.

'It is only bathing that could delay us,' said Nwafo. 'If we just draw water now and bathe another time . . .'

'I think you are mad,' said his mother who had so far pretended to ignore her husband's senior wife. 'But let me see you come back from the stream with yesterday's body and we shall see whose madness is greater, yours or mine.' The vehemence with which she said this seemed so much greater than the cause of her annoyance. In fact she was angry with her son not for what he had proposed but for his disloyalty in joining the excited flurry of the other hut.

'What are you still crawling about like a millipede for?' Matefi asked her daughter. 'Will going to the stream be your day's work?'

Oduche wore his loincloth of striped towelling and white singlet which he normally put on only for church or school. This made his mother even more angry than had Nwafo's proposal, but she succeeded in remaining silent.

Soon after the water party left Obiageli came into Ezeulu's hut carrying Amoge's child on her back. The child was clearly too big for her; one of his legs almost trailed the ground.

'These people are mad,' said Ezeulu. 'Who left a sick child in your hands? Take him back to his mother at once.'

'I can carry him,' said Obiageli.

'Who is carrying the other? Take him to his mother, I say.'

'She has gone to the stream,' replied Obiageli bouncing up on her toes in an effort to keep the child from slipping down her back. 'But I can carry him. See.'

'I know you can,' said Ezeulu, 'but he is sick and should not be shaken about. Take him to your mother.'

Obiageli nodded and went into the inner compound, but Ezeulu

knew she still carried the child (who had now begun to cry). Obiageli's tiny voice was striving valiantly to drown the crying and sing
him to sleep:

> *Tell the mother her child is crying*
> *Tell the mother her child is crying*
> *And then prepare a stew of úzízá*
> *And also a stew of úzìzà*
> *Make a watery pepper-soup*
> *So the little birds who drink it*
> *Will all perish from the hiccup*
> *Mother's goat is in the barn*
> *And the yams will not be safe*
> *Father's goat is in the barn*
> *And the yams will all be eaten*
> *Can you see that deer approaching*
> *Look! he's dipped one foot in water*
> *Snake has struck him!*
> *He withdraws!*
> *Ja – ja . ja kulo kulo!*
> *Traveller Hawk*
> *You're welcome home*
> *Ja – ja . ja kulo kulo!*
> *But where's the length*
> *Of cloth you brought*
> *Ja – ja . ja kulo kulo!*

'Nwafo! . . . Nwafo!' called Ezeulu.

'Nwafo has gone to the stream!' replied his mother from her hut.

'Nwafo has what?' Ezeulu shouted back.

Ugoye decided to go into the *obi* in person and explain that Nwafo
had gone on his own account.

'Nobody asked him to go,' she said.

'Nobody asked him to go?' retorted Ezeulu parodying a child's
talk. 'Did you say that nobody asked him to go? Do you not know
that he sweeps my hut every morning? Or do you expect me to break

kolanut or receive people in an unswept hut? Did your father break his morning kolanut over yesterday's wood ash? The abomination all you people commit in this house will lie on your own heads. If Nwafo has become too strong to listen to you why did you not ask Oduche to come and sweep my hut?'

'Oduche went with the rest.'

Ezeulu chose not to speak any more. His wife went away but soon returned with two brooms. She swept the hut with the palm-leaf broom and the immediate frontage of the *obi* with the longer and stronger bundle of *okeakpa*.

Obika came from his hut while she swept the outside and asked: 'Do you sweep the *iru-ezi* nowadays? Where is Nwafo?'

'No one is born with a broom in his hand,' she replied testily and increased the volume of her singing. Because of the length of the broom she held and wielded it like a paddle. Ezeulu smiled to himself. When she had finished she gathered the sweepings into one heap and carried them into the plot of land on the right where she was going to plant cocoyams that season.

Akuebue planned to visit Ezeulu soon after the morning meal, to rejoice with him for his son's new wife. But he had other important things to talk over with him and that was why he chose to go so early – before other visitors in search of palm wine filled the place. What Akuebue wanted to talk about was not new. They had talked about it many times before. But in the past few days Akuebue had begun to hear things which worried him greatly. It was all about Ezeulu's third son, Oduche, whom he had sent to learn the secrets of the white man's magic. Akuebue had doubted the sense in Ezeulu's action from the very first but Ezeulu had persuaded him of its wisdom. But now it was being used by Ezeulu's enemies to harm his name. People were asking: 'If the Chief Priest of Ulu could send his son among people who kill and eat the sacred python and commit other evils what did he expect ordinary men and women to do? The lizard who threw confusion into his mother's funeral rite did he expect outsiders to carry the burden of honouring his dead?'

And now Ezeulu's first son had joined, albeit surreptitiously, his father's opponents. He had gone to Akuebue on the previous day and asked him to go as Ezeulu's best friend and speak to him without biting the words.

'What is wrong?'

'A man should hold his compound together, not plant dissension among his children.' Whenever Edogo felt deeply he stammered agonizingly. He did so now.

'I am listening.'

Edogo told him that the reason why Ezeulu sent Oduche to the new religion was to leave the way clear for Nwafo to become Chief Priest.

'Who said so?' asked Akuebue. But before Edogo could answer he added: 'You speak about Nwafo and Oduche, what about you and Obika?'

'Obika's mind is not on such things – neither is mine.'

'But Ulu does not ask if a man's mind is on something or not. If he wants you he will get you. Even the one who has gone to the new religion, if Ulu wants him he will take him.'

'That is true,' said Edogo. 'But what worries me is that my father makes Nwafo think he will be chosen. If tomorrow as you say Ulu chooses another person there will be strife in the family. My father will not be there then and it will all rattle around my own head.'

'What you say is very true and I do not blame you for wanting to bale that water before it rises above the ankle.' He thought about it for a while and added: 'But I do not think there will be strife. Nwafo and Oduche come from the same woman. It is fortunate that you and Obika have not set your minds on it.'

'But you know what Obika is,' said Edogo. 'He might wake up tomorrow morning and want it.'

The old man and his friend's son talked for a long time. When Edogo finally rose to go (he had announced his intention to go three or four times before without getting up) Akuebue promised to talk to Ezeulu. He felt pity and a little contempt for the young man. Why could he not open his mouth like a man and say that he wanted to be priest instead of hiding behind Oduche and Obika? That was why Ezeulu never counted him among people. So he had hopes that the *afa* oracle would call his name when the day came? The fellow does not fall where his body might be picked up, he thought. It does not require an oracle to see that he is not the man for Chief Priest. A ripe maize can be told by merely looking at it.

And yet Akuebue felt sorry for Edogo. He knew how a man's first son must feel to be pushed back so that the younger ones might come forward to receive favour. No doubt that was why in the first days of Umuaro, Ulu chose to give only one son to his Chief Priests, for seven generations.

On the way to the stream that morning the bride who had not seen many white singlets in her life was inclined to take too much interest in Oduche and the new religion which provided such marvels. To curb her enthusiasm jealous Ojiugo whispered into her ear that devotees of this new cult killed and ate the python. The bride who, like any other person in Umuaro, had heard of Oduche's adventure with the python asked anxiously:

'Did he kill it? We were told he only put it in his box.'

Unfortunately Ojiugo was one of those people who could never whisper, and what she said reached Oduche's ears. He immediately rushed at Ojiugo and, in the words of Nwafo when he recounted the incident later, gave her thunder on the face. Whereupon Ojiugo virtually threw down her pot and attacked Oduche using the metal bangle on her wrists to give edge to her blows. Oduche replied with even more fiery slaps and a final, vicious blow with his knee on Ojiugo's belly. This brought great criticism and even abuse on Oduche from many of the people who had gathered to help separate them. But Ojiugo clung to her half-brother crying: 'Kill me today. You must kill me. Do you hear me, Eater of python? You must kill me.' She bit one of the people trying to hold her back and scratched another.

'Leave her alone,' said one of the women in exasperation. 'If she wants to be killed then let her.'

'Don't talk like that. Were you not here when he nearly killed her with a kick in the belly?'

'Hasn't she hit him enough for it already?' asked a third.

'No, she hasn't,' said the second woman. 'I think he is one of those who become brave when they see a woman.'

The crowd was immediately divided between supporters of Ojiugo and those who thought she had already revenged herself sufficiently. These latter now urged Oduche to hurry away to the stream and not listen any more to Ojiugo's abuse or try to answer back.

'The offspring of a hawk cannot fail to devour chicks,' said Oyilidie, whom Ojiugo had bitten. 'This one resembles her mother in stubbornness.'

'Should she have resembled your mother then?' This came from Ojinika a broad-looking woman who had an old quarrel with Oyilidie. People said that in spite of Ojinika's tough appearance and the speed with which she flew into quarrels her strength was only in her mouth and a child of two could knock her down with its breath.

'Don't open your rotten mouth near me, do you hear?' said Oyilidie. 'Or I shall beat okro seeds out of your mouth. Perhaps you have forgotten . . .'

'Go and eat shit,' shouted Ojinika. The two were already measuring themselves against each other, standing on tiptoe and chests thrust out.

'What is wrong with these two?' asked another woman. 'Give way and let me pass.'

Ojiugo was still sobbing when she reached home. Nwafo and Oduche had returned earlier but Ojiugo's mother had disdained asking them about the others. When she saw Ojiugo coming in she wanted to ask her if they had had to wait for the stream to return from a journey or wake up from sleep. But the words dried in her mouth.

'What is wrong?' she asked instead. Ojiugo increased her snivelling. Her mother helped her put down her water pot and asked again what was wrong. Before she said anything Ojiugo first went inside their hut, sat down on the floor and wiped her eyes. Then she told her story. Matefi examined her daughter's face and saw what looked like the weal left by Oduche's five fingers. She immediately raised her voice in protest and lamentation so that all the neighbourhood might hear.

Ezeulu walked as unhurriedly as he could into the inner compound and asked what all the noise was about. Matefi wailed louder.

'Shut your mouth,' Ezeulu commanded.

'You tell me to shut my mouth,' screamed Matefi, 'when Oduche takes my daughter to the stream and beats her to death. How can I shut my mouth when they bring back a corpse to me. Go and look at her face; the fellow's five fingers . . .' Her voice had risen till it reverberated in the brain.

'I say shut your mouth! Are you mad?'

Matefi stopped her screaming. She moaned resignedly: 'I have shut my mouth. Why should I not shut my mouth? After all Oduche is Ugoye's son. Yes, Matefi must shut her mouth.'

'Let nobody call my name there!' shouted the other wife as she came out from her hut where she had sat as though all the noise in the compound came from a distant clan. 'I say let nobody mention my name at all.'

'You, shut your mouth,' said Ezeulu, turning to her; 'nobody has called your name.'

'Did you not hear her calling my name?'

'And if she did? . . . Go and jump on her back if you can.'

Ugoye grumbled and returned to her hut.

'Oduche!'

'E-e-h.'

'Come out here!'

Oduche came out from his mother's hut.

'What is all this noise about?' asked Ezeulu.

'Ask Ojiugo and her mother.'

'I am asking you. And don't you tell me to ask another or a dog will lick your eyes this morning. When did you people learn to fling words in my face?' He looked round at them all, his manner changed to that of a crouching leopard. 'Let one of you open his mouth and make *fim* again and I will teach him that a man does not talk when masked spirits speak.' He looked round again, daring anyone to open his mouth. There was silence all round and he turned and went back to his *obi*, anger having smothered his interest in the cause of the affray.

Akuebue's haste in plunging into the subject of Oduche proved to be ill-judged. He was anxious to finish with it before more people arrived, for there could be no doubt that quite soon the three compounds would be filled. Many of the people who came last night would come again, and many more would be coming for the first time because at this hungry season when most barns were empty of all but seed-yams no one would miss the chance of biting a morsel and drinking a horn in the house of a wealthy man. Akuebue knew that as soon as the first man arrived he could no longer talk with Ezeulu; so he wasted no time. Had he known how much Ezeulu had just been annoyed perhaps he would have waited for another day.

Ezeulu listened silently to him, holding back with both hands the mounting irritation he felt.

'Have you finished?' he asked when Akuebue ceased talking.

'Yes, I have finished.'

'I salute you.' He was not looking at his guest but vaguely at the threshold. 'I cannot say that I blame you; you have said nothing that a man could be blamed for saying to his friend. I am not blind and I am not deaf either. I know that Umuaro is divided and confused and I know that some people are holding secret meetings to persuade others that I am the cause of the trouble. But why should that remove sleep from my eyes? These things are not new and they will follow where the others have gone. When the rain comes it will be five years since this same man told a secret meeting in his house that if Ulu failed to fight in their blameful war they would unseat him. We are still waiting, Ulu and I, for him to come and unseat us. What annoys me is not that an overblown fool dangling empty testicles should forget himself because wealth entered his house by mistake; no, what annoys me is that the cowardly priest of Idemili should hide behind him and urge him on.'

'It is jealousy,' said Akuebue.

'Jealousy for what? I am not the first Ezeulu in Umuaro, he is not the first Ezidemili. If his father and his father's father and all the others before them were not jealous of my fathers why should he be of me? No, it is not jealousy but foolishness; the kind that puts its head into the pot. But if it is jealousy, let him go on. The fly that perches on a mound of dung may strut around as it likes, it cannot move the mound.'

'Everybody knows these two,' said Akuebue. 'We all know that if they knew the way to Ani-Mmo they would go to quarrel with our ancestors for giving the priesthood of Ulu to Umuachala and not to their own village. I am not troubled about them. What troubles me is what the whole clan is saying.'

'Who tells the clan what it says? What does the clan know? Sometimes, Akuebue, you make me laugh. You were here – or had you not been born then – when the clan chose to go to war with Okperi over a piece of land which did not belong to us. Did I not stand up then and tell Umuaro what would happen to them? And who was right in the end? What I said, did it happen or did it not?'

Akuebue did not answer.

'Every word happened as I said it would.'

'I do not doubt that,' said Akuebue and, in a sudden access of impatience and recklessness, added, 'but you forget one thing: that no man however great can win judgement against a clan. You may think you did in that land dispute but you are wrong. Umuaro will always say that you betrayed them before the white man. And they will say that you are betraying them again today by sending your son to join in desecrating the land.'

Ezeulu's reply to this showed Akuebue once again that even to his best friend the priest was unknowable. Even his sons did not know him. Akuebue was not sure what reply he had expected, but it was most certainly not the laugh which he got now. It made him afraid and uneasy like one who encounters a madman laughing on a solitary path. He was given no time to examine this strange feeling of fear closely. But he was to have it again in future and it was only then he saw its meaning.

'Don't make me laugh,' said Ezeulu again. 'So I betrayed Umuaro to the white man? Let me ask you one question. Who brought the white man here? Was it Ezeulu? We went to war against Okperi who are our blood brothers over a piece of land which did not belong to us and you blame the white man for stepping in. Have you not heard that when two brothers fight a stranger reaps the harvest? How many white men went in their party that destroyed Abame? Do you know? Five.' He held his right hand up with the five fingers fanned out. 'Five. Now have you ever heard that five people – even if their heads reached the sky – could overrun a whole clan? Impossible. With all their power and magic white men would not have overrun entire Olu and Igbo if we did not help them. Who showed them the way to Abame? They were not born there; how then did they find the way? We showed them and are still showing them. So let nobody come to me now and complain that the white man did this and did that. The man who brings ant-infested faggots into his hut should not grumble when lizards begin to pay him a visit.'

'I cannot dispute any of the things you say. We did many things wrong in the past, but we should not therefore go on doing the same today. We now know what we did wrong, so we can put it right again. We know where this rain began to fall on us . . .'

'I am not so sure,' said Ezeulu. 'But whether you do or not you must not forget one thing. We have shown the white man the way to our house and given him a stool to sit on. If we now want him to go away again we must either wait until he is tired of his visit or we must drive him away. Do you think you can drive him away by blaming Ezeulu? You may try, and the day I hear that you have succeeded I shall come and shake your hand. I have my own way and I shall follow it. I can see things where other men are blind. That is why I am Known and at the same time I am Unknowable. You are my friend and you know whether I am a thief or a murderer or an honest man. But you cannot know the Thing which beats the drum to which Ezeulu dances. I can see tomorrow; that is why I can tell Umuaro: *come out from this because there is death there* or *do this because there is profit in it.* If they listen to me, o-o; if they refuse to listen, o-o. I have passed the stage of dancing to receive presents. You knew my father who was priest before me. You knew my grandfather too, albeit with the eyes of a little child.' Akuebue nodded in agreement.

'Did not my grandfather put a stop to *ichi* in Umuaro? He stood up in all his awe and said: We shall no longer carve our faces as if they were *ozo* doors.'

'He did it,' said Akuebue.

'What was Umuaro's reply to him? They cursed him; they said their men would look like women. They said: *how is a man's endurance to be tested?* Today who asks such a question?'

Akuebue felt that he had already agreed with Ezeulu sufficiently to be able to dissent again. 'What you say cannot be doubted,' he said, 'but if what we are told is true, your grandfather was not alone in that fight. There were said to be more people against *ichi* in Umuaro than . . .'

'Was that how your father told you the story? I heard differently. Anyhow the important thing was that the Chief Priest led them and they followed. But if there is hearsay in that one, what about events in my father's time? You were not an infant when my father set aside the custom which made any child born to a widow a slave unless . . .'

'I am not the man to dispute any of the things you say, Ezeulu. I am your friend and I can talk to you as I like; but that does not mean I forget that one half of you is man and the other half spirit. And what you say about your father and grandfather is very true. But what happened in their time and what is happening today are not the same; they do not even have resemblance. Your father and grandfather did not do what they did to please a stranger . . .'

This stung Ezeulu sharply but again he kept a firm hold on his anger.

'Do not make me laugh,' he said. 'If someone came to you and said that Ezeulu sent his son to a strange religion so as to please another man what would you tell him? I say don't make me laugh. Shall I tell you why I sent my son? Then listen. A disease that has never been seen before cannot be cured with everyday herbs. When we want to make a charm we look for the animal whose blood can match its power; if a chicken cannot do it we look for a goat or a ram; if that is not sufficient we send for a bull. But sometimes even a bull does not suffice, then we must look for a human. Do you think it is the sound of the death-cry gurgling through blood that we want to hear? No, my friend, we do it because we have reached the very end of things and we know that neither a cock nor a goat nor even a bull will do. And our fathers have told us that it may even happen to an unfortunate generation that they are pushed beyond the end of things, and their back is broken and hung over a fire. When this happens they may sacrifice their own blood. This is what our sages meant when they said that a man who has nowhere else to put his hand for support puts it on his own knee. That was why our ancestors when they were pushed beyond the end of things by the warriors of Abam sacrificed not a stranger but one of themselves and made the great medicine which they called Ulu.'

Akuebue cracked his fingers and moved his head up and down. 'So it is a sacrifice,' he muttered to himself. 'So Edogo was right after all, though he had seemed so foolish at the time.' He paused a while then spoke aloud:

'What happens if this boy you are sacrificing turns out to be the one chosen by Ulu when you are looked for and not found.'

'Leave that to the deity. When the time comes of which you speak Ulu will not seek your advice or help. So do not keep awake at night for that.'

'I don't, why should I? My compound is full of its own troubles, so why should I carry yours home; where would I find space to put them? But I must repeat what I said before and if you don't want to listen you can stop your ears. When you spoke against the war with Okperi you were not alone. I too was against it and so were many others. But if you send your son to join strangers in desecrating the land you will be alone. You may go and mark it on that wall to remind you that I said so.'

'Who is to say when the land of Umuaro has been desecrated, you or I?' Ezeulu's mouth was shaped with haughty indifference. 'As for being alone, do you not think that it should be as familiar to me now as are dead bodies to the earth? My friend, don't make me laugh.'

Nwafo who had come into his father's hut when Akuebue was saying of Ezeulu that he was half-man, half-spirit did not understand the present dispute between the two men. But he had seen equally danger-ous-looking scenes come to nothing before. He was therefore not in the least surprised when his father sent him to get palm oil sprinkled with ground pepper from his mother. When he returned with it Ezeulu had already brought down his round basket. This basket had a close-fitting lid and dangled from the roof directly above the log fire. Dangling with it were Ezeulu's ceremonial raffia skirt, two cala-bashes and a few heads of last season's maize specially chosen, on account of their good quality, for planting. Basket, maize and raffia skirt were all black with smoke.

Ezeulu opened the round basket and brought out a boiled and smoked leg of goat and cut a big piece for Akuebue and a very small one for himself.

'I think I shall need something to wrap this,' said Akuebue. Ezeulu sent Nwafo to cut a piece of banana leaf which he held above the smouldering log fire till it wilted slightly and lost its brittle freshness; then he passed it to Akuebue who divided the meat into two, wrapped the bigger half in the banana leaf and put it away in his bag. Then he began to eat the other half, dipping it in the peppered palm oil.

Ezeulu gave a little strand from his own piece to Nwafo and threw the remainder into his mouth. For a long time they ate in silence and when they began to talk again it was about less weighty things. Ezeulu broke off a toothpick from the broom lying on the floor near him and leaned back on the wall. From that position he easily commanded the approaches to his compound and the compound of his two sons. He was thus the first to notice the arrival of the Court Messenger and his escort.

When the two strangers reached Ezeulu's threshold the escort clapped his hands and said: 'Are the owners of this house at home?' There was a slight pause before Ezeulu answered: 'Enter and you will see.' The escort bent down at the low eaves and entered first; then the other followed. Ezeulu welcomed them and told them to sit down. The Court Messenger sat on the mud-bed but his escort remained standing. The greetings over he saluted Ezeulu and explained that he was the son of Nwodika in Umunneora.

'I thought I saw your father's face as soon as you came in,' said Akuebue.

'Very true,' said Ezeulu. 'Anyone setting eyes on him knows he has seen Nwodika. Your friend seems to have come from far.'

'Yes, we have come from Okperi . . .'

'Do you live in Okperi then?' asked Ezeulu.

'Yes,' replied Akuebue. 'Have you not heard of one of our young men who lives with the white man in Okperi?'

Ezeulu had indeed heard but deliberately feigned ignorance.

'True?' he asked. 'I do not hear many things nowadays. So you have come all the way from Okperi this morning and you are here already?

It is good to be strong and young. How are the people of my mother's land? You know my mother came from Okperi.'

'There was nothing but happiness and laughter when we left; what has happened since I cannot say.'

'And who is your companion?'

'He is the Chief Messenger of the great white man, the Destroyer of Guns.'

Ezeulu cracked his fingers and nodded.

'So this is Wintabota's messenger? Is he a man of Okperi?'

'No,' said the escort. 'His clan is Umuru.'

'Was Wintabota well when you left? We have not seen him in these parts for a long time.'

'Even so. This man here is his eye.'

The Chief Messenger did not seem too pleased with the trend of the conversation. In his mind he was angry with this man in the bush who put on airs and pretended to be familiar with the District Officer. His escort sensed this and made desperate efforts to establish his importance.

'Stranger, you are welcome,' said Ezeulu. 'What is your name?'

'He is called Jekopu,' said the escort. 'As I said, nobody sees the Destroyer of Guns without his consent. There is no one in Okperi who does not know the name of Jekopu. The Destroyer of Guns asked me to accompany him on this journey because he is a stranger to these parts.'

'Yes,' said Ezeulu with a meaningful glance in the direction of Akuebue. 'That is as it should be. The white man sends a man from Umuru and the man from Umuru is shown the way by a man of Umuaro.' He laughed. 'What did I tell you, Akuebue? Our sages were right when they said that no matter how many spirits plotted a man's death it would come to nothing unless his personal god took a hand in the deliberation.'

The two men looked puzzled. Then Nwodika's son said: 'That is so; but we have not come on a mission of death.'

'No. I did not say so. It is only a manner of speaking. We have a saying that a snake is never as long as the stick to which we liken its length. I know that Wintabota will not send a mission of death to

Ezeulu. We are good friends. What I said was that a stranger could not come to Umuaro unless a son of the land showed him the way.'

'That is true,' said the escort. 'We have come . . .'

'My friend,' interrupted the Chief Messenger, 'you have already done what you were sent to do; the rest is for me. So put your tongue into its scabbard.'

'Forgive me. I take my hands off.'

Ezeulu sent Nwafo to bring kola from Matefi. By this time both Obika and Edogo had come in, news having reached them that a messenger of the white man was in their father's hut. When the kolanut came it was shown round and broken.

'Have the people you sent to the market for palm wine returned yet?' asked Ezeulu. Obika said no.

'I knew they would not. A man who means to buy palm wine does not hang about at home until all the wine in the market is sold.' He was still leaning with his back on the wall, holding one leg a little off the ground with hands interlocked on the shin.

The Court Messenger removed his blue fez and planted it on his knee exposing a clean-shaven head shining with sweat. The edge of the cap left a ring round the head. He cleared his throat and spoke, almost for the first time.

'I salute you all.' He brought out a very small book from his breast pocket and opened it in the manner of a white man. 'Which one of you is called Ezeulu?' he asked from the book and then looked up and around the hut. No one spoke; they were all too astonished. Akuebue was the first to recover.

'Look round and count your teeth with your tongue,' he said. 'Sit down, Obika, you must expect foreigners to talk through the nose.'

'You say you are a man of Umuru?' asked Ezeulu. 'Do you have priests and elders there?'

'Do not take my question amiss. The white man has his own way of doing things. Before he does anything to you he will first ask you your name and the answer must come from your own lips.'

'If you have any grain of sense in your belly,' said Obika, 'you will know that you are not in the house of the white man but in Umuaro in the house of the Chief Priest of Ulu.'

'Hold your tongue, Obika. You heard Akuebue say just now that strangers talk through the nose. Do you know whether they have Chief Priests in his land or the land of the white man?'

'Tell that young man to take care how he talks to me. If he has not heard of me he should ask those who have.'

'Go and eat shit.'

'Shut your mouth!' roared Ezeulu. 'This man has come all the way from my mother's land to my house and I forbid anyone to abuse him. Besides he is only a messenger. If we dislike his message our quarrel cannot be with him but with the man who sent him.'

'Very true,' said Akuebue.

'There are no words left,' said the escort.

'You asked me a question,' continued Ezeulu turning again to the messenger. 'I shall now answer you. I am that Ezeulu you spoke of. Are you satisfied?'

'Thank you. We are all men here but when we open our mouths we know the men from the boys. We have spoken many words already; some were words of profit, some were not; some were words of sanity and some words of drunkenness. It is now time to say why I have come, for a toad does not run in the daytime unless something is after it. I have not come all the way from Okperi to stretch my legs. Your own kinsman here has told you how Kaputin Winta-bor-tom has put me in charge of many of his affairs. He is the chief of all the white men in these parts. I have known him for more than ten years and I have yet to see another white man who does not tremble before him. When he sent me here he did not tell me he had a friend in Umuaro.' He smiled in derision. 'But if what you say is true we shall know tomorrow when I take you to see him.'

'What are you talking about?' asked Akuebue in alarm.

The Court Messenger continued to smile menacingly. 'Yes,' he said. 'Your friend Wintabota' (he mouthed the name in the ignorant fashion of his hearers) 'has ordered you to appear before him tomorrow morning.'

'Where?' asked Edogo.

'Where else but in his office in Okperi.'

'The fellow is mad,' said Obika.

'No, my friend. If anyone is mad it's you. Anyhow, Ezeulu must prepare at once. Fortunately the new road makes even a cripple hungry for a walk. We set out this morning at the first cock-crow and before we knew where we were we had got here.'

'I said the fellow is mad. Who . . .'

'He is not mad,' said Ezeulu. 'He is a messenger and he must give the message as it was given to him. Let him finish.'

'I have finished,' said the other. 'But I ask whoever owns this young man to advise him for his own good.'

'You are sure you have given all the message?'

'Yes, the white man is not like black men. He does not waste his words.'

'I salute you,' said Ezeulu, 'and I welcome you again: *Nno!*'

'There is one small thing I forgot,' said the Court Messenger. 'There are many people waiting to see the white man and you may have to wait in Okperi for three or four days before your turn comes. But I know that a man like you would not want to spend many days outside his village. If you do me well I shall arrange for you to see him tomorrow. Everything is in my hands; if I say that the white man will see this person, he will see him. Your kinsman will tell you what I eat.' He smiled and put his fez back on the head.

'That is a small matter,' said Ezeulu. 'It will not cause a quarrel. I do not think that what you will put into that small belly of yours will be beyond me. If it is, my kinsmen are there to help.' He paused and seemed to enjoy the messenger's anger at the mention of his small size. 'You must first return, however, and tell your white man that Ezeulu does not leave his hut. If he wants to see me he must come here. Nwodika's son who showed you the way can also show him.'

'Do you know what you are saying, my friend?' asked the messenger in utter disbelief.

'Are you a messenger or not?' asked Ezeulu. 'Go home and give my message to your master.'

'Let us not quarrel about this,' said Akuebue stepping in quickly to save the situation which his spirit told him was fraught with peril. 'If the white man's messenger gives us some time we shall whisper together.'

'What are you whispering for?' asked Ezeulu indignantly. 'I have given my message.'

'Just give us some time,' said Akuebue to the messenger who complied and went outside. 'You may go out with him,' he told the escort.

Ezeulu took no part in the consultation that followed. When the Court Messenger and his companion returned to the hut it was Akuebue who told them that because of the respect he had for the white man Ezeulu had agreed to send his son, Edogo, to bring back whatever message there was for his father. 'In Umuaro it is not our custom to refuse a call, although we may refuse to do what the caller asks. Ezeulu does not want to refuse the white man's call and so he is sending his son.'

'Is that your answer?' asked the Court Messenger.

'It is,' replied Akuebue.

'I will not take it.'

'Then you can go into that bush there and eat shit,' said Obika. 'Do you see where my finger is pointing? That bush.'

'Nobody will eat shit,' said Akuebue, and turning to the messenger he added: 'I have never heard of a messenger choosing the message he will carry. Go and tell the white man what Ezeulu says. Or are you the white man yourself?'

Ezeulu had turned a little away from the others and begun again to pick his teeth with the broomstick.

Chapter Thirteen

As soon as the messenger and his escort left Ezeulu's hut to return to Okperi the Chief Priest sent word to the old man who beat the giant *ikolo* to summon the elders and *ndichie* to an urgent meeting at sunset. Soon after the *ikolo* began to speak to the six villages. Everywhere elders and men of title heard the signal and got ready for the meeting. Perhaps it was the threat of war. But no one spoke of war any more in these days of the white man. More likely the deity of Umuaro had revealed through divination a grievance that must be speedily removed, or else . . . But whatever it was – a call to prepare for battle or to perform a communal sacrifice – it was urgent. For the *ikolo* was not beaten out of season except in a great emergency – when as the saying was an animal more powerful than *nté* was caught by *nté*'s trap.

The meeting began as fowls went to roost and continued into the night. Had it been a day meeting children who had brought their father's stools would have been playing on the outskirts of the market place, waiting for the end of the meeting to carry the stools home again. But no father took his child to a night meeting. Those who lived near the market place carried their stools themselves; the others carried goatskins rolled up under the arm.

Ezeulu and Akuebue were the first to arrive. But they had hardly sat down before other elders and men of title from all the villages of Umuaro began to come into the Nkwo. At first each man as he came in saluted all those who were there before him but as the crowd increased he only greeted those nearest to him, shaking hands with only three or four.

The meeting took place under the timeless ogbu tree on whose mesh of exposed roots generations of Umuaro elders had sat to take weighty decisions. Before long most of the people expected at the meeting had come and the stream of new arrivals became a mere trickle. Ezeulu held a quick consultation with those sitting nearest to him and they all agreed that the time had come to tell Umuaro why they had been called together. The Chief Priest rose to his feet, adjusted his toga and gave the salutation which was at the same time a call to Umuaro to speak with one voice.

'Umuaro kwenu!'

'Hem!!'

'Kwenu!'

'Hem!!'

'Kwezuenu!'

'Hem!!'

'I thank you all for leaving your different tasks at home to answer my call. Sometimes a man may call and no one answers him. Such a man is like one dreaming a bad dream. I thank you that you have not let me call in vain like one struggling in a bad dream.' Somewhere near him someone was talking into his talk. He looked round and saw that it was Nwaka of Umunneora. Ezeulu stopped talking for a while, and then addressed the man.

'Ogbuefi Nwaka, I salute you,' he said.

Nwaka cleared his throat and stopped whatever it was he had been saying to those near him. Ezeulu continued.

'I was thanking you for what you have done. Our people say that if you thank a man for what he has done he will have strength to do more. But there is one great omission here for which I beg forgiveness. A man does not summon Umuaro and not set before them even a pot of palm wine. But I was taken by surprise and as you know the unexpected beats even the man of valour . . .' Then he told them the story of the Court Messenger's visit to him. 'My kinsmen,' he said in conclusion, 'that was what I woke up this morning and found. Ogbuefi Akuebue was there and saw it with me. I thought about it for a long time and decided that Umuaro should join with me in seeing and hearing what I have seen and heard; for when a man sees a snake all by himself he may wonder whether it is an ordinary snake or the untouchable python. So I said to myself: *Tomorrow I shall summon Umuaro and tell them.* Then one mind said to me: *Do you know what may happen in the night or at dawn?* That is why, although I have no palm wine to place before you I still thought I should call you together. If we have life there will be time enough for palm wine. Unless the penis dies young it will surely eat bearded meat. When hunting day comes we shall hunt in the backyard of the grass-cutter. I salute you all.'

For a long time no one stood up to reply. Instead there was general talking (which sometimes sounded like murmuring) among the assembled rulers of Umuaro. Ezeulu sat down on his stool and fixed his eye on the ground. He did not even reply when Akuebue told him that he had spoken all the words that needed to be said. At last Nwaka of Umunneora stood up.

'Umuaro kwenu!'

'Hem!!'

'Umuaro kwenu!'

'Hem!!'

'Kwekwanu ozo!'

'Hem!!'

He put right his toga which had nearly come undone from his left shoulder.

'We have all heard what Ezeulu said. They were good words and I want to thank him for calling us together and speaking them to us. Do I speak the mind of Umuaro?'

'Speak on,' replied the men.

'When a father calls his children together he should not worry about placing palm wine before them. Rather it is they who should bring palm wine to him. Again I say thank you to the priest of Ulu. That he thought it necessary to call us and tell us these things shows the high regard in which he holds us, for which we give him our thanks.

'But there is one thing which is not clear to me in this summons. Perhaps it is clear to others; if so someone should explain it to me. Ezeulu has told us that the white ruler has asked him to go to Okperi. Now it is not clear to me whether it is wrong for a man to ask his friend to visit him. When we have a feast do we not send for our friends in other clans to come and share it with us, and do they not also ask us to their own celebrations? The white man is Ezeulu's friend and has sent for him. What is so strange about that? He did not send for me. He did not send for Udeozo; he did not send for the priest of Idemili; he did not send for the priest of Eru; he did not send for the priest of Udo nor did he ask the priest of Ogwugwu to come and see him. He has asked Ezeulu. Why? Because they are friends. Or does Ezeulu think that their friendship should stop short of entering each other's houses? Does he want the white man to be his friend only by word of mouth? Did not our elders tell us that as soon as we shake hands with a leper he will want an embrace? It seems to me that Ezeulu has shaken hands with a man of white body.' This brought low murmurs of applause and even some laughter. Like many potent things from which people shrink in fear leprosy is nearly always called by its more polite and appeasing name – *white body*. The applause and laughter was mingled with the salutation: *Owner of words* to Nwaka. He waited for the laughter to die down and said: 'If laughter presses you you can laugh; as for me it does not press me.' Ezeulu sat in the same way as he had sat when he ended his speech.

'What I say is this,' continued Nwaka, 'a man who brings ant-ridden faggots into his hut should expect the visit of lizards. But if Ezeulu is now telling us that he is tired of the white man's friendship our advice to him should be: *You tied the knot, you should also know how to undo it. You passed the shit that is smelling; you should carry it away.* Fortunately the evil charm brought in at the end of a pole is not too difficult to take outside again.

'I have heard one or two voices murmuring that it is against custom for the priest of Ulu to travel far from his hut. I want to ask such people: Is this the first time Ezeulu would be going to Okperi? Who was the white man's witness that year we fought for our land – and lost?' He waited for the general murmuring to die down. 'My words are finished. I salute you all.'

Others spoke. Although none spoke as harshly as Nwaka, only two came out clearly against his line of thinking. Perhaps there were others who did also, but they did not speak. Most of those who spoke said it would be foolhardy to ignore the call of the white man; had they forgotten what happened to clans which fell out with him? Nwokeke Nnabenyi tried to soften the harsh words even more. He said that six elders should be chosen to go with Ezeulu.

'You may go with him if your feet are hungry for a walk,' shouted Nwaka.

'Ogbuefi Nwaka, please do not speak into my words. You stood up here and spoke to your fill and no one answered you back.' He repeated his suggestion that six elders of Umuaro should go with their Chief Priest to Okperi.

Ezeulu stood up then. The big fire which had been lit some distance away shone in his face. There was complete silence when he spoke. His words did not carry the rage in his chest. As always his anger was not caused by open hostility such as Nwaka showed in his speech but by the sweet words of people like Nnabenyi. They looked to him like rats gnawing away at the sole of a sleeper's foot, biting and then blowing air on the wound to soothe it, and lull the victim back to sleep.

He saluted Umuaro and began to speak almost with gaiety in his voice.

'When I called you together it was not because I am lost or because my eyes have seen my ears. All I wanted was to see the way you would take my story. I have now seen it and I am satisfied. Sometimes when we have given a piece of yam to a child we beg him to give us a little from it, not because we really want to eat it but because we want to test our child. We want to know whether he is the kind of person who will give out or whether he will clutch everything to his chest when he grows up.

'You yourselves know whether Ezeulu is the kind of man to run away because the white man has sent a message to him. If I had stolen his goat or killed his brother or fucked his wife then I might plunge into the bush when I heard his voice. But I have not offended him in any way. Now, as for what I shall do I had set my mind on it before I asked Ikolo to summon you. But if I had done anything without first speaking to you you might turn round and say: *Why did he not tell us?* Now I have told you and happiness fills my mind. This is not the time for many words. When the time comes to speak we shall all speak until we are tired and perhaps we shall find then that there are orators in Umuaro besides Nwaka. For the present I salute you for answering my call. Umuaro kwenu!'

'Hem!!'

One of the people who followed Ezeulu home that night and offered to go with him in the morning to Okperi was his younger half-brother, Okeke Onenyi, a famous medicine-man. But Ezeulu refused his offer as he had refused all the others, among them his friend, Akuebue's. He had taken the decision to go alone and he was not going to change.

As soon as he had made his offer and it was refused Okeke Onenyi rose to go although the first sporadic drops of a heavy rain had started to fall.

'Won't you wait and watch the face of the sky awhile?' asked Edogo.

'No, my son,' replied Okeke Onenyi and, feigning lightheartedness, added: 'Only those who carry evil medicine on their body should fear the rain.' He walked out into the coming storm. The darkness was lit up at short, irregular intervals by lightning; sometimes it was a strong, steady light, sometimes it flickered before it went out as if the rushing wind shook its flame.

Okeke Onenyi's voice rose powerfully against the wind and thunder as he sang and whistled a song to keep him company in the dark.

Ezeulu had said nothing to persuade him not to go in the rain. But then he rarely had anything to say to him. It was difficult to think of them as brothers. But even if they had been closer together Ezeulu might still have said nothing because his mind was not there in the hut with them. In fact all he had said for a long time was that this rain was the harbinger of a new moon. But no one took his meaning.

Ezeulu and his half-brother were not enemies, but neither were they friends. Ezeulu was known to harbour an ill-will against all medicine-men most of whom he said were greedy charlatans. True medicine, he said, had died with his father's generation. Practitioners of today were mere dwarfs.

Ezeulu's father had indeed been a great medicine-man and magician. He performed countless marvels but the one that people talked about most was his ability to make himself invisible. There was a time when war was raging between Umuaro and Aninta and no one from the one clan dared set foot in the other. But the Chief Priest passed through Aninta as often as he wished. He always went with his son, Okeke Onenyi, who was then a little boy. He gave the boy a short broom to hold in his left hand and told him not to speak or salute any passer-by but walk close to the right edge of the path. The boy went in front and the Chief Priest followed at a distance behind, always keeping the boy in sight. Any passer-by who approached them suddenly stopped before they reached him and began to peer into the bush on the other side of the path like a hunter who had heard the rustle of game. He would be peering thus until the boy and his father passed behind him and only then would he turn again and continue on his way. Sometimes a passer-by would turn right round on their approach and go back the way he was coming.

Okeke Onenyi learnt many herbs and much *anwansi* or magic from his father. But he never learnt this particular magic whose name was *Oti-anya afu-uzo.*

There were few priests in the history of Umuaro in whose body priesthood met with medicine and magic as they did in the body of the last Ezeulu. When it happened the man's power was boundless.

Okeke Onenyi always said that the cause of the coolness between him and the present Ezeulu, his half-brother, was the latter's resentment at the splitting of the powers between them. 'He forgets,' says Okeke Onenyi, 'that the knowledge of herbs and *anwansi* is something inscribed in the lines of a man's palm. He thinks that our father deliberately took it from him and gave to me. Has he heard me complaining that the priesthood went to him?'

As was to be expected this was how people who did not like Ezeulu saw his estrangement from Okeke Onenyi. They were quick to point out that it was Ezeulu's pride and jealousy that made him so disdainful of his brother's renown in medicine. They pointed to the recent Covering-up Sacrifice for Obika's wife when, rather than ask his brother, Ezeulu had sent for a worthless medicine-man who could not even eat three meals a day from his doctoring.

But there were others like Akuebue who knew Ezeulu better who retorted that there was something which Okeke Onenyi did to Ezeulu. It was not very clear what this thing was. All that was known was that it was not a thing which a brother should do to a brother; that it was unforgivable. The trouble was that Ezeulu would never unburden himself even to his friends on this matter. So his defenders had nothing but conjectures to put forward. Some said that Okeke Onenyi had tied up the womb of Ezeulu's first wife after she had borne him only three children.

'But that cannot be,' was the usual reply to this. 'We know all the evil medicine-men in Umuaro and Okeke Onenyi is not among them. He is not the kind of man to inflict a curse on a woman who has done him no harm, least of all his brother's wife.'

'But you forget that Okeke Onenyi has a big grudge against Ezeulu,' the others might say. 'You forget that in their childhood their father led Okeke to think that he was going to succeed to the priesthood and that on the old man's death Okeke all but questioned the decision of the oracle.'

'That may be so,' the other side might say. 'But we know all our medicine-men and we say again that Okeke Onenyi has never yet been accused by anyone of sealing up his wife's womb. Besides, medicine-men who carry on such vile practices, like men who relish human flesh, never prosper with children. But just look at Okeke Onenyi's compound flowing with sons and daughters!'

This final argument was unanswerable especially when it was pointed out that Okeke Onenyi's best friend in Ezeulu's compound was Edogo, the son of the very women he was said to have afflicted! In fact this relationship between Edogo and his uncle was known to give Ezeulu great dissatisfaction. Perhaps it was out of pique that he had said that the carving done by the one was about as good as the medicine practised by the other.

'Those two?' he once asked, 'a derelict mortar and rotten palm nuts!'

For two or three days now Captain Winterbottom had been feeling unduly tired and run down. The rains did not seem to bring the expected respite. His gums looked paler than ever and his feet felt cold. He would not be due for another bout of fever for yet awhile; but these were the signs all right. Of course he was not afraid as a new boy might be. Fever to an old coaster was no more than an inconvenience; it laid one off for a few days that was all.

Tony Clarke was suitably impressed. 'You should go and see a doctor,' he said, knowing that this was the kind of stuff expected of new boys.

'Doctor? Good Lord! For a fever? No my boy. It's the first time you want to be careful. Poor Macmillan wasn't careful enough in spite of my warning. I've had a fever every single year for ten years and when you've had it so often you stop taking any notice. No, all I need is a change of air for a week and you'll see me back as sound as a bell. The trip to Enugu will do it.'

He was planning a visit to Headquarters in two days' time. For obvious reasons he wanted to tidy up the business of a Warrant Chief for Umuaro before he met the headquarters' chaps. He could not possibly conclude the matter in two days but he wanted to be able to say that he had taken the first steps. He was a great believer in leaving the house in order as he expected to find it on his return. So he wrote copious handing-over notes for Tony Clarke. He put down in black and white what he proposed to do on the subject of the Paramount Chief. 'I have today sent messengers to Umuaro to bring Ezeulu here for a preliminary discussion. Arising out of this discussion I shall fix an appropriate date in the future when the warrant of office will be given to him in the presence of the elders and *ndichie* of his clan.' Captain Winterbottom enjoyed mystifying other Europeans with words from the Ibo language which he claimed to speak fluently.

Having made these detailed arrangements for the benefit of Ezeulu Captain Winterbottom was understandably enraged when the messenger came back with the insulting reply from the self-important fetish priest. He immediately signed a warrant of arrest in his capacity as magistrate for the apprehension of the priest and gave instructions for two policemen to go to Umuaro first thing in the morning and bring the fellow in.

'As soon as he comes,' he told Clarke, 'you are to lock him up in the guardroom. I do not wish to see him until after my return from Enugu. By that time he should have learnt good manners. I won't have my natives thinking they can treat the Administration with contempt.'

Perhaps it was Captain Winterbottom's rage and frenzy that brought it on; perhaps his steward was right about its cause. But on that very morning when two policemen set out to arrest Ezeulu in Umuaro Captain Winterbottom suddenly collapsed and went into a delirium. The only intelligible thing he kept saying was: *My feet are cold; put the hot water bottle there!* His steward heated some water, put it in the rubber bottle and placed it on the man's feet. Winterbottom screamed that it was not hot enough. The steward poured in boiling water but even that was still not hot enough. He kept changing the water every few minutes and still the Captain complained. By the time Tony Clarke (who could not drive a car) found Wade to take the Captain in his old Ford to the hospital six miles away his feet had been badly scalded. But this was not discovered until the following day in the hospital.

Clarke and Wade were amazed and not a little embarrassed to see Dr Mary Savage, the severe and unfeminine missionary doctor in charge of the hospital, collapse into tears and panic as Captain Winterbottom was brought in. She kept calling, 'Tom, Tom,' and behaving generally as though her doctoring had deserted her. But her panic lasted only a short time; she was soon mistress of herself and the situation. However, it had lasted long enough to have been noticed by a few native nurses and ward attendants who spread it not only in the hospital but in the small village of Nkisa. Both in the hospital and outside in the village Dr Savage was known as Omesike, One Who Acts With Power, and it was not expected that she would ever cry for a patient, not even when the patient happened to be Captain Winterbottom whom they mischievously called her husband.

Winterbottom's delirium lasted three days and in all that time Dr Savage rarely left his bedside. She even postponed the operations which she performed every Wednesday for which that day was known throughout the village as *Day of the Cutting Open of Bowels*. It was always a sad day and the little daily market which had sprung up outside the gates of the hospital to supply the needs of patients from distant clans attracted fewer market women on Wednesdays than on any other day of the week. It was also noticed that even the sky knew that day of death and mourned in gloom.

Dr Savage checked through her list of operation cases and was satisfied that there was none that could be called very urgent and decided to postpone them till Friday. Captain Winterbottom's condition had improved very slightly and there was a little hope. The next day or two would be decisive and a lot would depend on skilled nursing to help him over the critical threshold. He was in a special ward all by himself and nobody was allowed in there except Dr Savage and her only European Sister.

Captain Winterbottom's steward, John Nwodika, was told to escort the two policemen to Umuaro as he had done for the messenger. But in his mind he had sworn never again to take a representative of 'gorment' to his home clan. His resolve was strengthened in this case when he got to know that the two policemen would be armed with a warrant of arrest and handcuffs for the Chief Priest of Ulu. But since he could not turn round and say to his master: *No, I shall not go*, he agreed to go but made other plans. Consequently when the two policemen came for him before the crow of the first cock they found him shivering from a sudden attack of *iba*. Wrapped up in an old blanket which Captain Winterbottom had given him for the child his wife delivered four months ago John managed with great effort to whisper a few directions to the men. Once they were in Umuaro, he said, any suckling child could show them Ezeulu's house. This turned out to be literally true.

The two men entered Umuaro at the time of the morning meal. Soon they met a man carrying a pot of palm wine and stopped him.

'Where is Ezeulu's house?' asked the leader, Corporal Matthew Nweke. The man looked suspiciously at the uniformed strangers.

'Ezeulu,' he said after a long time in which he had seemed to search his memory. 'Which Ezeulu?'

'How many Ezeulus do you know?' asked the corporal irritably.

'How many Ezeulus do I know?' repeated the man after him. 'I don't know any Ezeulus.'

'Why did you ask me which Ezeulu if you don't know any?'

'Why did I ask you—'

'Shut up! Bloody fool!' shouted the policeman in English.

'I say I don't know any Ezeulu. I am a stranger here.'

Two other people they stopped spoke in more or less the same fashion. One of them even said that the only Ezeulu he knew was a man of Umuofia, a whole day's journey in the direction of the sunrise.

The two policemen were not in the least surprised. The only way to make people talk was by frightening them. But they had been warned by the European officer against using violence and threats and in particular they were not to use the handcuffs unless the fellow resisted. This was why they had shown so much restraint. But now they were convinced that unless they did something drastic they might wander around Umuaro till sunset without finding Ezeulu's house. So they slapped the next man they saw when he tried to be evasive. To drive the point home they also showed him the handcuffs. This brought the desired result. He asked the men to follow him. He took them to the approaches of the compound they were looking for and pointed at it.

'It is not our custom,' he told the policemen, 'to show our neighbour's creditors the way to his hut. So I cannot enter with you.' This was a reasonable request and the policemen released him. He ran away as fast as he could so that the inmates of the compound might not catch as much as a glimpse of his escaping back.

The policemen marched into the hut and found an old woman chewing her toothless gums. She peered at them in obvious fright and did not seem to understand any of the questions they put to her. She did not even seem to remember her own name.

Fortunately a little boy came in at that moment with a small piece of potsherd to take burning coals to his mother for making a fire. It was this boy who took the men around the bend of the footpath to Ezeulu's compound. As soon as he went out with them the old woman picked up her stick and hobbled over at an amazing speed to his mother's hut to report his behaviour. Then she returned to her hut – much more slowly, curved behind her straight stick. Her name was Nwanyieke, a childless widow. Soon after she got back she heard the boy, Obielue, crying.

Meanwhile the policemen arrived at Ezeulu's hut. They were then no longer in the mood for playing. They spoke sharply, baring all their weapons at once.

'Which one of you is called Ezeulu?' asked the corporal.

'Which Ezeulu?' asked Edogo.

'Don't ask me which Ezeulu again or I shall slap okro seeds out of your mouth. I say who is called Ezeulu here?'

'And I say which Ezeulu? Or don't you know who you are looking for?' The four other men in the hut said nothing. Women and children thronged the door leading from the hut into the inner compound. There was fear and anxiety in the faces.

'All right,' said the corporal in English. 'Jus now you go sabby which Ezeulu. Gi me dat ting.' This last sentence was directed to his companion who immediately produced the handcuffs from his pocket.

In the eyes of the villager handcuffs or *iga* were the most deadly of the white man's weapons. The sight of a fighting man reduced to impotence and helplessness with an iron lock was the final humiliation. It was a treatment given only to violent lunatics.

So when the fierce-looking policeman showed his handcuffs and moved towards Edogo with them Akuebue came forward as the elder in the house and spoke reasonably. He appealed to the policemen not to be angry with Edogo. 'He only spoke as a young man would. As you know, the language of young men is always *pull down and destroy*; but an old man speaks of conciliation.' He told them that Ezeulu and his son had set out for Okperi early in the morning to answer the white man's call. The policemen looked at each other. They had indeed met a man with another who looked like his son. They remembered them because they were the first people they had met going in the opposite direction but also because the man and his son looked very distinguished.

'What does he look like?' asked the corporal.

'He is as tall as an iroko tree and his skin is white like the sun. In his youth he was called Nwa-anyanwu.'

'And his son?'

'Like him. No difference.'

The two policemen conferred in the white man's tongue to the great admiration of the villagers.

'Sometine na dat two porson we cross for road,' said the corporal.

'Sometine na dem,' said his companion. 'But we no go return back jus like dat. All dis waka wey we waka come here no fit go for nating.'

The corporal thought about it. The other continued:

'Sometine na lie dem de lie. I no wan make dem put trouble for we head.'

The corporal still thought about it. He was convinced that the men spoke the truth but it was necessary to frighten them a little, if only to coax a sizeable 'kola' out of them. He addressed them in Ibo:

'We think that you may be telling us a lie and so we must make quite sure otherwise the white man will punish us. What we shall do then is to take two of you – handcuffed – to Okperi. If we find Ezeulu there we shall set you free; if not . . .' He completed with a sideways movement of the head which spoke more clearly than words. 'Which two shall we take?'

The others conferred anxiously and Akuebue spoke again begging the representatives of 'gorment' to believe their story. 'What would be the wisdom of deceiving messengers of the white man?' he asked. 'Where shall we run afterwards? If you go back to Okperi and Ezeulu is not there you can come back and take not two but all of us.'

The corporal thought about it and agreed. 'But we cannot come and go for nothing. When a masked spirit visits you you have to appease its footprints with presents. The white man is the masked spirit of today.'

'Very true,' said Akuebue, 'the masked spirit of our day is the white man and his messengers.'

Ezeulu's head wife was asked to prepare yam pottage with chicken for the two men. When it was ready they ate and drank palm wine. Then they rested awhile and prepared to go. Akuebue thanked them for their visit and told them that if they had met the owner of the house at home he would have given them more hospitality. Anyhow would they accept this small 'kola' on his behalf?' He placed two live cocks before them and Edogo placed beside the cocks a wooden bowl containing two shillings. The corporal thanked them but at the same time repeated his warning that if it turned out that they had been telling lies about Ezeulu, 'gorment' would make them see their ears with their own eyes.

The sudden collapse of Captain Winterbottom on the very day he sent policemen to arrest the Chief Priest of Umuaro was clearly quite significant. The first man to point the connection was John Nwodika, Second Steward to Captain Winterbottom himself. He said it was just as he feared; the priest had hit him with a potent charm. In spite of everything then, power still resided in its accustomed place.

'Did I not say so?' he asked the other servants after their master had been removed to hospital. 'Was it for nothing I refused to follow the policemen? I told them that the Chief Priest of Umuaro is not a soup you can lick in a hurry.' His voice carried a note of pride. 'Our master thinks that because he is a white man our medicine cannot touch him.' He switched over to English for the benefit of Clarke's steward who came in just then and who did not speak Ibo.

'I use to tellam say blackman juju no be someting wey man fit take play. But when I tellam na so so laugh im de laugh. When he finish laugh he call me John and I say Massa. He say You too talk bush talk. I tellam say O-o, one day go be one day. You no see now?'

The story of Ezeulu's magical powers spread through Government Hill hand in hand with the story of Captain Winterbottom's mysterious collapse. When Mr Clarke returned from hospital his steward asked how the big master was. He shook his head and said: 'He's pretty bad, I'm afraid.'

'Sorry sah,' said the steward, looking very worried. 'Dey say na dat bad juju man for yonda wey . . .'

'Go and get my bath ready, will you?' Clarke was so exhausted that he was in no mood for stewards' chit-chat. So he lost the opportunity of hearing the reason for the Captain's illness which was circulating not just through Government Hill but very soon throughout Okperi. It was only two days later that Wright told him about it.

Other servants on Government Hill were waiting in his kitchen to hear the latest news from his steward. He went to get ready the bath and whispered to them that there was no hope, that Clarke had told him he was afraid.

Later in the evening Clarke and Wade drove to the hospital again. They did not see the patient or the doctor; but Sister Warner told them there was no change. For the first time since it all started Tony Clarke felt anxious. They drove back in silence.

There was a Court Messenger outside his bungalow when he got home.

''Deven sah,' said the man.

'Good evening,' replied Clarke.

'De witch-doctor from Umuaro don come.' There was fear in his voice as though he was reporting the arrival of smallpox in the village.

'I beg your pardon.'

The man gave more details and it was only then that Clarke understood he was talking about Ezeulu.

'Lock him up in the guardroom till morning.' Clarke made to enter the bungalow.

'Massa say make I putam for gaddaloom?'

'That's what I said,' shouted Clarke. 'Are you deaf?'

'No be say I deaf sah but . . .'

'Get out!'

The messenger sent people to sweep the guardroom and spread a new mat in it so that it might be taken for a guest-room. Then he went to Ezeulu who had been sitting in the Courtroom with Obika since their arrival and spoke nicely to him.

'The big white man is sick but the other one says welcome to you,' he said. 'He says it is dark now and he will see you in the morning.'

Ezeulu said nothing to him. He followed him into the dark guardroom and sat on the mat. Obika also sat down. Ezeulu brought out his snuff bottle.

'We shall send a lamp to you,' said the messenger.

Soon afterwards John Nwodika came in with his wife who had a small load on her head. She set it down and it proved to be an enormous mound of pounded cassava and a bowl of bitter-leaf soup. John Nwodika made a ball of foofoo, dipped it in the soup and swallowed to show that there was no poison in it. Ezeulu thanked him and his wife (who turned out to be the daughter of his friend in Umuagu) but refused to eat.

'Food is not my care now,' he said.

'Pray, eat a little – just one ball,' said the son of Nwodika. But the old man would not be persuaded.

'Obika will eat for both of us.'

'A fowl does not eat into the belly of a goat,' said the other, but the old man still refused.

The messenger came in again with a palm-oil lamp and Ezeulu thanked him.

Corporal Matthew Nweke who had gone to Umuaro with another policeman returned to find his wives weeping quietly and a large crowd in his one-room lodging. He was alarmed, his mind going to his little son who had measles. He rushed to the mat where he lay and touched him; he was wide awake.

'What is the matter?' he asked then.

No one spoke. The corporal who was called 'Couple' then turned to one of the policemen in the room and put the question specifically to him. The man cleared his voice and told him that they did not expect to see him and his companion back alive, especially when the man he had gone to arrest arrived on his own. 'Couple' wanted to explain how they had crossed each other but the man did not let him. He pressed on with a full account of all that had happened since morning and ended with the latest news from Nkisa Hospital to the effect that Captain Winterbottom would not see the dawn.

At that point John Nwodika came in.

'But you were not well in the morning?' asked Couple.

'That is what I have come to tell you. The illness was a warning from the Chief Priest. I am happy I listened to it; otherwise we would be telling another story now.' John then told them how the Chief Priest knew all about Winterbottom's sickness before anyone told him about it.

'What did he say?' asked one or two people together.

'He said: *If he is ill he will also be well*. I don't know what he meant, but it seemed to me that there was mockery in his voice.'

At first 'Couple' Matthew Nweke was not too worried. He had a strong personal protection which a great *dibia* in his village made for him during his last leave. But as he heard more and more about Ezeulu his faith in his safety began to weaken. In the end he held a quick consultation with the policeman who had accompanied him to

Umuaro and they decided that to be on the safe side they should go and see a local *dibia* straight away. It was past ten o'clock at night when they arrived at the man's house. He was called throughout the village *The Bow that shoots at the Sky*.

As soon as they came in he told them the object of their mission. 'You have done right to come straight to me because you indeed walked into the mouth of a leopard. But there is something bigger than a leopard. That is why I say welcome to you because you have reached the final refuge.' He told them that they must not eat anything which they had taken from Umuaro. They must bring the two cocks and the money for sacrifice which they would carry and deposit on the highway. For what they had already eaten he gave them a preparation to drink and also to mix into their bath water.

Chapter Fourteen

As he ate the pounded cassava and bitter-leaf soup Obika watched his father with the tail of his eye and caught a certain restlessness in him. He knew it would be useless asking him questions in his present mood. Even at the best of times Ezeulu only spoke when he wanted to and not when people asked him.

He got up and made towards the narrow door, then seemed to change his mind or else to remember something he should have taken with him. He came back to his goatskin bag and searched for his snuff bottle. When he found it he made towards the door again and this time went outside saying from the doorway that he was going to urinate.

He had resolved that as long as he was in Okperi he would never look for the new moon. But the eye is very greedy and will steal a look at something its owner has no wish to see. So as Ezeulu urinated outside the guardroom his eyes looked for the new moon. But the sky had an unfamiliar face. It was impossible to put one's finger anywhere on it and say that the moon would come out there. A momentary alarm struck Ezeulu but on thinking again he saw no cause for alarm. Why should the sky of Okperi be familiar to him? Every land had its own sky; it was as it should be.

That night Ezeulu saw in a dream a big assembly of Umuaro elders, the same people he had spoken to a few days earlier. But instead of himself it was his grandfather who rose up to speak to them. They refused to listen. They shouted together: *He shall not speak; we will not listen to him.* The Chief Priest raised his voice and pleaded with them to listen but they refused saying that they must bale the water while it was still only ankle-deep. 'Why should we rely on him to tell us the season of the year?' asked Nwaka. 'Is there anybody here who cannot see the moon in his own compound? And anyhow what is the power of Ulu today? He saved our fathers from the warriors of Abam but he cannot save us from the white man. Let us drive him away as our neighbours of Aninta drove out and burnt Ogba when he left what he was called to do and did other things, when he turned round to kill the people of Aninta instead of their enemies.' Then the people seized the Chief Priest who had changed from Ezeulu's grandfather to himself and began to push him from one group to another. Some spat on his face and called him the priest of a dead god.

Ezeulu woke up with a start as though he had fallen from a great height.

'What is it?' asked Obika in the darkness.

'Nothing. Did I say anything?'

'You were quarrelling with someone and saying you would see who would drive the other away.'

'I think there must be spiders on the rafters.'

He was now sitting up on his mat. What he had just seen was not a dream but a vision. It had all taken place not in the halflight of a dream but in the clarity of the middle day. His grandfather whom he had known with the eyes of a child had emerged again very clearly across a whole lifetime in which his image had grown weak and indistinct.

Ezeulu took out his ground tobacco and put a little in each nostril to help his thinking. Now that Obika was asleep again he felt free to consider things by himself. He thought once more of his fruitless, albeit cursory, search for the door of the new moon. So even in his mother's village which he used to visit regularly as a boy and a young man and which next to Umuaro he knew better than any village – even here he was something of a stranger! It gave him a feeling of loss which was both painful and pleasant. He had temporarily lost his status as Chief Priest which was painful; but after eighteen years it was a relief to be without it for a while. Away from Ulu he felt like a child whose stern parent had gone on a journey. But his greatest pleasure came from the thought of his revenge which had suddenly formed in his mind as he had sat listening to Nwaka in the market place.

These thoughts were a deliberate diversion. At the end of them

Ezeulu had steadied himself from his dizzy nightmare. Now he looked at it again more closely and one thing stood out. His quarrel with the white man was insignificant beside the matter he must settle with his own people. For years he had been warning Umuaro not to allow a few jealous men to lead them into the bush. But they had stopped both ears with fingers. They had gone on taking one danger-ous step after another and now they had gone too far. They had taken away too much for the owner not to notice. Now the fight must take place, for until a man wrestles with one of those who make a path across his homestead the others will not stop. Ezeulu's muscles tingled for the fight. Let the white man detain him not for one day but one year so that his deity not seeing him in his place would ask Umuaro questions.

Following Captain Winterbottom's instruction that Ezeulu should be put in his place and taught to be polite to the Administration Mr Clarke refused to see him on the next day as the Head Messenger had promised. In fact he refused to see him for four days.

On the second morning as Clarke and Wade drove again towards the hospital at Nkisa they came upon a sacrifice by the roadside. They often saw roadside sacrifices and would not normally have stopped. But this one struck them by its extraordinary lavishness. Wade pulled up and they went to see. Instead of the usual white chick there were two fully grown cocks. The other objects were normal; young, yellow-ish palm fronds cut from the summit of the tree, a clay bowl with two lobes of kolanut inside it and a piece of white chalk. But the two white men only saw these objects later. What caught their eye immediately on reaching the sacrifice was the English florin.

'Well I never!' said Wade.

'Now this is very strange, a most extravagant sacrifice. I wonder what it's all about.'

'Perhaps it's for the recovery of the King's Representative,' said Wade lightly. Then something seemed to strike him and he spoke seriously. 'I don't like the look of it. I don't mind if they use their cowries and manillas but the head of George the Fifth!'

Clarke chuckled but stopped immediately as Wade put his left hand into the bowl and picked out the piece of silver, cleaned it first with leaves and then on his woollen hose and put it into his pocket.

'Good heavens! What do you think you are doing?'

'I won't have the King of England dragged into a disgusting juju,' replied Wade, laughing.

This incident worried Clarke a great deal. He had convinced himself that he admired people like Wade and Wright who seemed to do an important job without taking themselves too seriously, who were always looking for the lighter side of things. But was this lack of feeling – for it certainly showed a monstrous lack of feeling to desecrate someone else's sacrifice – part of the temperament of look-ing for the lighter side of life? If so would one not finally come down in favour of the seriousness (and its accompanying pomposity) of the Winterbottoms?

Without making any conscious decision Clarke was preparing himself to assume the burden of the Administration in the event of Winterbottom's death. It would fall on him to defend his natives if need be from the thoughtless acts of white people like Wade.

That same morning Ezeulu sent Obika back to Umuaro to tell his family how things stood, and to arrange for his younger wife to come and cook his meals. But their clansman, John Nwodika, would not hear of it.

'It is not necessary,' he said. 'My wife is the daughter of your old friend and she will not allow you to send home for another woman. I know that we cannot give you the kind of food you would eat at home. But if we have two palm kernels to chew we shall give one to you and a cup of water to swallow it with.'

Ezeulu could not refuse the offer when it was put that way. What-ever he might have against Nwodika's son he could not offend the daughter of his friend, Egonwanne, who died three years come next harvest. So he told Obika not to send Ugoye but to arrange for large quantities of yams and other foods to be brought.

Ezeulu had good reasons for disliking the son of Nwodika. He came from the very village in Umuaro which was always poking its finger into Ezeulu's eye; his job was said to comprise licking plates in the white man's kitchen in Okperi which was a great degradation for a son of Umuaro. Worst of all he had brought the white man's insolent messenger to Ezeulu's house. But by the end of his first day in Okperi Ezeulu was beginning to soften towards the man, and to see that even a hostile clansman was a friend in a strange country. For the Okperi of Government Hill was indeed a strange country to Ezeulu. It was not the Okperi he had known as a boy and young man, the village of his mother, Nwanyieke. There must still be parts of that old Okperi left, but Ezeulu could not possibly go out in search of it at this time of his disgrace. Where would he find the eye with which to look at the old sites and old faces? It was fortunate that he felt that way for it saved him the mortification of being told he was a prisoner and could not come and go as he liked.

As he ate his meal that night he heard the voices of children welcoming the new moon. 'Onwa atu-o-o-o! Onwa atu-o-o-o!' went up on all sides of Government Hill. But Ezeulu's sharp ear picked out a few voices that sang in a curious dialect. Except for the word moon he could not make out what they said. No doubt they were the children of some of these people who spoke a curious kind of Igbo – through the nose.

The first time Ezeulu heard the children's voices his heart flew out. Although he had expected it, when it did come he was not ready. His mind had momentarily forgotten. But he recovered almost at once. Yes, his deity must now be asking: 'Where is he?' and soon Umuaro will have to explain.

There was great anxiety in Ezeulu's compound throughout the first and second days of his absence. Although it was the heart of the planting season nobody went to work. Obika's bride, Okuata, left her lonely hut and moved into her mother-in-law's. Edogo left his own compound and sat in his father's *obi* waiting for news. Neighbours and even passers-by came in and asked: 'Have they returned yet?' After a while the question began to make Edogo angry especially when it came from those whose main interest was gossip.

By the middle of the second day, however, Obika returned. At first no one dared ask any questions; some of the women appeared on the brink of tears. Even at such a serious and anxious moment Obika could not resist the temptation to alarm them further. He had worn a face like a muddied pond as he came up the approaches to the hut; now he slumped down on the floor as though he had run all the way from Okperi. He called for cold water which his sister brought him. When he had drunk and set the calabash down Edogo put the first question to him.

'Where is the person with whom you went?' he asked, skirting the dreaded finality of a name. Not even Obika could dare to joke after that. He allowed a short pause and said: 'He was well when I left him.'

The tightening fear in the faces broke.

'Why did the white man send for him?'

'Where did you leave him?'

'When is he coming home?'

'Which one shall I answer?' Obika tried to recover the earlier tension again but it was too late. 'I haven't got seven mouths. When I left him this morning the white man had not told us anything. We did not even see him because they said he was at the mouth of death.' This piece of news caused a little stir. From the stories told of the white man it had not occurred to them that he could be sick like ordinary people. 'Yes, he is already half dead. But he has a younger brother to whom he had given the message to give to Ezeulu. But this one was so troubled by his brother's sickness that he forgot to see us. So Ezeulu said to me: *Prepare and go home or they will think we have come to harm.* That is why I returned.'

'Who gives him food?' asked Ugoye.

'You remember the son of Nwodika who brought the white man's first messenger here,' Obika replied, though not to Ugoye but the men. 'It turned out that his wife is the daughter of Ezeulu's old friend in Umuagu. She has been cooking for us since yesterday and she says that as long as she is alive Ezeulu will not send home for another woman.'

'Did I hear you well?' asked Akuebue, who had so far said very little. 'Did you say that the wife of a man of Umunneora is giving food to Ezeulu?'

'Yes.'

'Please do not tell me such a story again. Edogo, get ready now, we are going to Okperi.'

'Ezeulu is not a small child,' said Anosi, their neighbour. 'He cannot be taught those with whom he may eat.'

'Do you hear what I say, Edogo? Get ready now; I am going home to get my things.'

'I do not want to stop you from going,' said Obika, 'but do not talk as if you alone have sense. Ezeulu and I did not simply open our mouths while our eyes were shut. Last night Ezeulu refused food even though Nwodika's son tasted it for us. But by this morning Ezeulu had seen enough of the man's mind to know that he had no ill-will.'

Akuebue was not impressed by anything the others said. He knew enough about the men of Umunneora. As for those who said that Ezeulu was not a child they could not know the bitterness in his mind. Akuebue knew the man better than his children or his wives. He knew that it was not beyond him to die abroad so as to plague his enemies at home. It was possible that the hands of Nwodika's son were clean, but one must make quite sure even at the risk of offending him. Who would swallow phlegm for fear of offending others? How much less swallow poison?

Ezeulu's neighbour, Anosi, whose opinion had gone unheeded earlier on in the discussion and who had kept quiet since then surfaced again with an opposite view.

'I think that Akuebue is right in what he says. Let him go with Edogo to satisfy himself that all is well. But let Ugoye also go with them, taking yams and other things; in that way the visit will not offend anyone.'

'But what is this fear of causing offence?' asked Akuebue impatiently. 'I am not a small boy; I know how to cut without drawing blood. But I shall not be afraid to offend a man of Umunneora if Ezeulu's life hangs on it.'

'True,' agreed Anosi. 'Very true. My father used to say that it is the fear of causing offence that makes men swallow poison. You enter the house of a bad man and he brings out a kolanut. You do not like the way he has brought it out and your mind tells you not to eat it. But you are afraid to offend your host and you swallow *ukwalanta*. I agree with Akuebue.'

*

Perhaps no one felt Ezeulu's absence as keenly as Nwafo. And now his mother was going too. But this second blow was greatly softened by the thought that Edogo was going as well.

Ezeulu's absence had given Edogo an opportunity to show his resentment against the old man's favourite. As the first son Edogo had taken temporary possession of his father's hut to await his return. Nwafo who rarely left the hut now began to feel his half-brother's hostility pushing him out. Although he was only a little boy he had the mind of an adult; he could tell when someone looked at him with a good eye or with a bad. Even if Edogo had said nothing Nwafo would still have known that he was not wanted. But Edogo had told him yesterday to go to his mother's hut and not sit around the *obi* gazing into the eyes of people older than himself. Nwafo went out and cried; for the first time in his life he had been told that he was not welcome in his father's hut.

Throughout today he had kept away until Obika's return when everyone in the compound and even neighbours had come in to hear the news. He took his accustomed position defiantly; but Edogo said nothing to him – he did not even appear to have noticed him.

Nwafo's sister Obiageli cried for a long time after their mother and the others left for Okperi. Oduche's promise to pick her *icheku* and *udala* did not console her. In the end Obika threatened to go and call out the fearsome masked spirit called Ichele. This produced an immediate result. Obiageli sat in one corner of the *obi* sniffling quietly.

As night drew near Nwafo's mind returned to the thought which had been troubling him since yesterday. What would happen to the new moon? He knew his father had been expecting it before he went away. Would it follow him to Okperi or would it wait for his return? If it appeared in Okperi with what metal gong would Ezeulu receive it? Nwafo looked at the *ogene* which lay by the wall, the stick with which it was beaten showing at its mouth. The best solution was for the new moon to wait for his return tomorrow.

However as dusk came down Nwafo took his position where his father always sat. He did not wait very long before he saw the young thin moon. It looked very thin and reluctant. Nwafo reached for the *ogene* and made to beat it but fear stopped his hand.

*

Ezeulu was still hearing in his mind the voices of the children of Government Hill when Nwodika's son and his wife brought him his supper. As usual Nwodika's son took a ball of foofoo, dipped it in the soup and swallowed. Ezeulu ate with a good appetite. Although he would not eat *egusi* soup out of choice this one was so well prepared that one hardly knew it was *egusi*. The fish in it was either *asa* or something equally good, and it had been smoked half dry which was the beauty of that type of fish. The foofoo had a very good texture, neither too light nor too heavy; no doubt the cassava had been lightened with green bananas.

He was half-way through his meal when his son, his wife and his friend arrived. They were shown in by the Head Messenger whose duty it was to look after prisoners detained in the guardroom. At first Ezeulu feared that something bad had happened at home. But when he saw the yams they brought his mind returned again.

'Why did you not wait till morning?'

'We did not know whether you would be setting out for home in the morning,' said Akuebue.

'Home?' Ezeulu laughed. It was the laughter of those who do not cry. 'Who talks of home? I have not seen the white man who sent for me. They say he is in the mouth of death. Perhaps he wants a Chief Priest to be sacrificed at his funeral.'

'The earth of Umuaro forbid!' said Akuebue, and the others joined in.

'Are we at Umuaro now?' asked Ezeulu.

'If the man is sick and he has not left a message for you then you should go home and come again when he is well,' said Edogo, who did not think that this was the place for his father and his friend to engage in their battle of words.

'This is not a journey I want to do twice. No, I shall sit here until I have seen the head and the tail of this matter.'

'Do you know how long he will be sick? You may be here . . .'

'If he is sick till palm fruits ripen at the tip of the frond I shall wait . . . How are the people at home, Ugoye?'

'They were well when we left them.' Her neck looked shorter from carrying the load.

'The children, Obika's wife and all the others?'

'Everybody was well.'

'And what about the people of your household?' he asked Akuebue.

'They were quiet when I left them. There was no sickness only hunger.'

'That is a small matter,' said Nwodika's son. 'Hunger is better than sickness.' As he said this he went outside and blew his nose. He came back rubbing the nose with the back of his hand.

'Nwego, you need not wait to collect the utensils. I shall bring them home. Go and find something for these people to eat.'

His wife took Ugoye's head-load and the two women went to prepare another meal.

There was no time to waste and as soon as the women left Akuebue spoke.

'Obika has told us how Nwodika's son and his wife have been taking care of you.'

'You have seen with your eyes.' Ezeulu's mouth was full of fish.

'Thank you,' said Akuebue to John Nwodika.

'Thank you,' said Edogo.

'We have done nothing that calls for thanks. What can a poor man and his wife do? We know that Ezeulu has meat and fish in his own house but while he is here we will share the palm kernel we eat with him. A woman cannot place more than the length of her leg on her husband.'

'When Obika told us about it I said to myself that there was nothing like travelling.'

'True,' said Ezeulu. 'The young he-goat said that but for his sojourn in his mother's clan he would not have learnt to stick up his upper lip.' He laughed to himself. 'I should have travelled more often in my mother's country.'

'It has certainly taken away your heavy face of yesterday,' said Akuebue. 'When they told me that a man of Umunneora was looking after you I told them it was a lie. How could it be seeing the war we wage at home?'

'That is for the people at home,' said Nwodika's son. 'I do not carry it with me when I travel. Our wise men have said that a traveller to distant places should make no enemies. I stand by it.'

'Very true,' said Akuebue, wondering how best to lead on to the object of his coming. After a short pause he decided to split it open with one blow of the matchet as the people of Nsugbe were said to split their coconut. 'Our journey has two aims. We brought Ugoye to relieve Nwodika's wife of her burden and to thank Nwodika himself and tell him that whatever his kinsmen may be doing at home he is today a brother to Ezeulu and his family.' As he said this Akuebue was already searching arm-deep in his goatskin bag for his little razor and kolanut. The tying of the blood-knot between Edogo and John Nwodika was over in the short silence that followed. Ezeulu and Akuebue watched in silence as the two young men ate a lobe of kolanut smeared with each other's blood.

'How did you come to work for the white man?' asked Akuebue when they resumed ordinary talking. Nwodika's son cleared his throat.

'How did I come to work for the white man? I should say that my *chi* planned that it should be so. I did not know anything about the white man at the time; I had not learnt his language or his custom. It will be three years next dry season. My age mates and I came from Umunneora to Okperi to learn a new dance as we had done for many years in the dry season after the harvest. To my great astonishment I found that my friend called Ekemezie in whose house I always lodged during these visits and who came and lodged with me whenever our village played host to his village, I found that he was no longer among the dancers of Okperi. I searched in vain for him among the crowd that came out to welcome us. Another friend called Ofodile took me to his house instead and it was from him I heard that Ekemezie had gone to work for the white man. I do not know how I felt when I heard that news. It was almost as if I had been told that my friend had died. I tried to find out more from Ofodile about this white man's work but Ofodile is not the kind of person who can sit down and tell a story to the end. But the next day Ekemezie came to see me and brought me to this *Gorment Heel*. He called me by name and I answered. He said everything was good in its season; dancing in the season of dancing. But, he said, a man of sense does not go on hunting little bush rodents when his age mates are after big game. He told me to leave dancing and join in the race for the white man's money. I was all eyes. Ekemezie called me Nwabueze and I said yes it was my name. He said the race for the white man's money would not wait till tomorrow or till we were ready to join; if the rat could not run fast enough it must make way for the tortoise. He said other people from every small clan – some people we used to despise – they were all now in high favour when our own people did not even know that day had broken.'

The three men listened in silence. In his mind Akuebue was flicking his fingers and saying: *I now understand why Ezeulu has taken such a sudden liking for him. Their thoughts are brothers.* But Ezeulu was actually hearing Nwodika's opinion of the white man for the first time and glowing with justification. Only he concealed his satisfaction, for once he had taken a stand on any matter he did not want to appear eager for others' support; it was not his concern but theirs.

'So my brothers,' continued Nwodika's son, 'that was how your brother came to work for the white man. At first he put me to weed his compound, but after one year he called me and said that my handi-work was good and took me to work inside his house. He asked me my name and I told him my name was Nwabueze; but he could not call it so he said he would call me Johnu.' This brought a smile to his face, but it was short-lived. 'I know that some people at home have been spreading the story that I cook for the white man. Your brother does not see even the smoke from his fire; I just put things in order in his house. You know the white man is not like us; if he puts this plate here he will be angry if you have it there. So I go round every day and see that everything is in its right place. But I can tell you that I do not aim to die a servant. My eye is on starting a small trade in tobacco as soon as I have collected a little money. People from other places are gathering much wealth in this trade and in the trade for cloth. People from Elumelu, Aninta, Umuofia, Mbaino, they control the great new market. They decide what goes on in it. Is there one Umuaro man among the wealthy people here? Not one. Sometimes I feel shame when others ask me where I come from. We have no share in the market; we have no share in the white man's office; we have no share anywhere. That was why I rejoiced when the white man called me the other day and told me that there was a wise man in my village and that his name was Ezeulu. I told him yes. He asked if he was still alive and I said yes. He said: *Go with the Head Messenger and tell him that I have a few questions I want to ask him about the custom of his people because I know he is a wise man.* I said to myself: *This is our chance to bring our clan in front of the white man.* I did not know that it would turn out like this.' He bent his head forward and looked at the ground in sorrow.

'It is not your fault,' said Akuebue. 'Things are always like that. Our eye sees something; we take a stone and aim at it. But the stone rarely succeeds like the eye in hitting the mark.'

'I blame myself,' said Nwodika's son sadly.

'You are a suspicious one,' said Ezeulu. The others had gone to pass the night at the place of Nwodika's son leaving Akuebue and Ezeulu in the small guardroom.

'I stand for a man dying when his *chi* says so.'

'But this man is not a poisoner although he comes from Umunneora.'

'I don't know,' said Akuebue, shaking his head. 'Every lizard lies on its belly, so we cannot tell which has a bellyache.'

'No. But I tell you Nwodika's son has a straight mind towards me. I can smell a poisoner as clearly as I can a leper.'

Akuebue still shook his head. Ezeulu could just make out the movement in the weak light of the palm-oil lamp.

'Did you not watch him when you brought up the question of the blood-tie?' Ezeulu continued. 'If he had had an evil thought you would have seen it in the middle of his forehead. No, the man is not dangerous. Rather he acts like a man of olden times, when people liked themselves. Today there are too many wise people; and it is not good wisdom they have but the kind that blackens the nose.'

'How does a man get any sleep with all these mosquitoes?' asked Akuebue, waving his fly-whisk wildly around.

'You have not seen them yet; wait till we have blown this lamp out. I was meaning to ask Nwodika's son to get me a bunch of arigbe leaves to try and smoke them out. But your coming took everything off my mind. Last night they almost carved us up.' He too waved his horse-tail. 'Did you say your people were all well?' he asked, trying to shift the conversation from himself.

'They were all quiet,' replied Akuebue, yawning with head thrown backwards.

'What was Udenkwo's story? You know you did not have the chance to tell me all of it.'

'That is so,' said Akuebue with revived interest. 'If I told you I was happy with Udenkwo I would be deceiving myself. She is my daughter but I can tell you she takes entirely after her mother. I have told her many times that a woman who carries her head on a rigid neck as if she is carrying a pot of water will never live for long with any husband. I have not heard my in-law's story but from what Udenkwo told me I can say that the cause of the quarrel was very small. My in-law was told to bring a cock for sacrifice. When he got home he pointed at one cock and told the children to catch it and tie it up for him. It turned out to be Udenkwo's cock and she started a quarrel. This is what she told me. I asked her did she want her husband to go to the market for a cock when his wives kept fowls. She said: *Why should it always be my cock; what about the other wife, or did the spirits say they only ate Udenkwo's chicken?* I said to her: *How many times has he taken your cock and how is a man to know which cock belongs to who?* She did not answer. All that she knew was that whenever my in-law wanted a cock for a sacrifice he remembered her.'

'That was all?'

'That was all.'

Ezeulu smiled. 'One would think our in-law made a sacrifice every market.'

'Exactly what I told her. But as I said Udenkwo is like her mother. Her real anger was that my in-law did not put his forehead on the ground to beg her.'

Ezeulu did not speak immediately. He seemed to be reconsidering the matter.

'Every man has his own way of ruling his household,' he said at last. 'What I do myself if I need something like that is to call one of my wives and say to her: *I need such and such a thing for a sacrifice, go and get it for me.* I know I can take it but I ask her to go and bring it herself. I never forget what my father told his friend when I was a boy. He said: *In our custom a man is not expected to go down on his knees and knock his forehead on the ground to his wife to ask her forgiveness or beg a favour. But, a wise man knows that between him and his wife there may arise the need for him to say to her in secret: "I beg you." When such a thing happens nobody else must know it, and that woman if she has any sense will never boast about it or even open her mouth and speak of it. If she does it the earth on which the man brought himself low will destroy her entirely.* That was what my father told his friend who held that a man was never wrong in his own house. I have never forgotten those words of my father's. My wife's cock belongs to me because the owner of a person is also owner of whatever that person has. But there are more ways than one of killing a dog.'

'That is true,' Akuebue admitted. 'But such words should be kept for the ears of my in-law. As for my daughter I do not want her to go on thinking that whenever her husband says yah! to her she must tie her little baby on her back, take the older one by the hand and return to me. My mother did not behave like that. Udenkwo learnt it from her mother, my wife, and she is going to pass it on to her children, for when mother-cow is cropping giant grass her calves watch her mouth.'

It was on his fourth day in Okperi that Ezeulu received a sudden summons to see Mr Clarke. He followed the messenger who brought the order to the corridor of the white man's office. There were many other people there, some of them sitting on a long bench and the rest on the cement floor. The messenger left Ezeulu in the corridor and went into an adjoining room where many people worked at various tables for the white man. Ezeulu saw the messenger through a window as he talked to a man who seemed to be the leader of all these workers. The messenger pointed in his direction and the other man followed with his eye and saw Ezeulu. But he only nodded and continued to write in his big book. When he finished what he was writing he opened a connecting door and disappeared into another room. He did not stay long there; when he came out again he beckoned at Ezeulu, and showed him into the white man's presence. He too was writing, but with his left hand. The first thought that came to Ezeulu on seeing him was to wonder whether any black man could ever achieve the same mastery over book as to write it with the left hand.

'Your name is Ezeulu?' asked the interpreter after the white man had spoken.

This repeated insult was nearly too much for Ezeulu but he managed to keep calm.

'Did you not hear me? The white man wants to know if your name is Ezeulu.'

'Tell the white man to go and ask his father and his mother their names.'

There followed an exchange between the white man and his interpreter. The white man frowned his face and then smiled and explained something to the interpreter who then told Ezeulu that there was no insult in the question. 'It is the way the white man does his own things.' The white man watched Ezeulu with something like amusement on his face. When the interpreter finished he tightened up his face and began again. He rebuked Ezeulu for showing disrespect for the orders of the government and warned him that if he showed such disrespect again he would be very severely punished.

'Tell him,' said Ezeulu, 'that I am still waiting to hear his message.' But this was not interpreted. The white man waved his hand angrily and raised his voice. Ezeulu did not need to be told that the white man said he did not want to be interrupted again. After that he calmed down and spoke about the benefits of the British Administration. Clarke had not wanted to deliver this lecture which he would have called complacent if somebody else had spoken it. But he could not help himself. Confronted with the proud inattention of this fetish priest whom they were about to do a great favour by elevating him above his fellows and who, instead of gratitude, returned scorn, Clarke did not know what else to say. The more he spoke the more he became angry.

In the end thanks to his considerable self-discipline and the breathing space afforded by talking through an interpreter Clarke was able to rally and rescue himself. Then he made the proposal to Ezeulu.

The expression on the priest's face did not change when the news was broken to him. He remained silent. Clarke knew it would take a little time for the proposal to strike him with its full weight.

'Well, are you accepting the offer or not?' Clarke glowed with the I-know-this-will-knock-you-over feeling of a benefactor.

'Tell the white man that Ezeulu will not be anybody's chief, except Ulu.'

'What!' shouted Clarke. 'Is the fellow mad?'

'I tink so sah,' said the interpreter.

'In that case he goes back to prison.' Clarke was now really angry. What cheek! A witch-doctor making a fool of the British Administration in public!

Chapter Fifteen

Ezeulu's reputation at Government Hill had suffered a sharp decline when the first day passed and the second and the third and still no news came that Captain Winterbottom had died. Now it rose again in a different way with his refusal to be a white man's chief. Such an action had no parallel anywhere in Igboland. It might be thought foolish for a man to spit out a morsel which fortune had placed in his mouth but in certain circumstances such a man compelled respect.

Ezeulu himself was full of satisfaction at the way things had gone. He had settled his little score with the white man and could forget him for the moment. But it was not easy to forget and as he went over the events of the past few days he almost persuaded himself that the white man, Wintabota, had meant well but that his good intentions had been frustrated in action by all the intermediaries like the Head Messenger and this ill-mannered, young white pup. After all, he reminded himself, it was Wintabota who a few years ago proclaimed him a man of truth from all the witnesses of Okperi and Umuaro. It was he also who later advised him to send one of his sons to learn the wisdom of his race. All this would suggest that the white man had goodwill towards Ezeulu. But what was the value of the goodwill which brought him to this shame and indignity? The wife who had seen the emptiness of life had cried: *Let my husband hate me as long as he provides yams for me every afternoon.*

In any case, Ezeulu said to himself, Wintabota must answer for the actions of his messengers. A man might pick his way with the utmost care through a crowded market but find that the hem of his cloth had upset and broken another's wares; in such a case the man, not his cloth, was held to repair the damage.

But in spite of all this Ezeulu's dominant feeling was that more or less he was now even with the white man. He had not yet said the last word to him, but for the moment his real struggle was with his own people and the white man was, without knowing it, his ally. The longer he was kept in Okperi the greater his grievance and his resources for the fight.

At first few people in Umuaro believed the story that Ezeulu had rejected the white man's offer to be a Warrant Chief. How could he refuse the very thing he had been planning and scheming for all these years, his enemies asked? But Akuebue and others undertook to spread the story to every quarter of Umuaro and very soon it was known also in all the neighbouring villages.

Nwaka of Umunneora treated the story with contempt. When he could no longer disbelieve it he explained it away.

'The man is as proud as a lunatic,' he said. 'This proves what I have always told people, that he inherited his mother's madness.'

Like every other thing Nwaka said from malice this one had its foundation in truth. Ezeulu's mother, Nwanyieke, had indeed suffered from severe but spasmodic attacks of madness. It was said that had her husband not been such a powerful man with herbs she might have raved continuously.

But despite Nwaka and other implacable enemies of Ezeulu the number of people who were beginning to think that he had been used very badly grew every day in Umuaro. More and more people began to visit him at Okperi; on one day alone he received nine visitors, some of whom brought him yams and other presents.

Two weeks after he was first admitted into the Nkisa Mission Hospital Captain Winterbottom had recovered sufficiently for Tony Clarke to be allowed to see him – for five minutes. Dr Savage stood at the door with a pocket watch.

He was incredibly white, almost a smiling corpse.

'How's life with you?' he asked.

Clarke could hardly wait to answer. He rushed in with the story of Ezeulu's refusal to be chief as though he wanted to extract an answer before Winterbottom's mouth was closed for ever.

'Leave him inside until he learns to co-operate with the Administration.'

'I did say you were not to talk,' said Dr Savage, coming quickly between them wearing a false smile. Captain Winterbottom had shut his eyes and was already looking worse. Tony Clarke felt guilty and left immediately but with a big weight taken off his mind. On his way back to Government Hill he thought with admiration of the facility with which Captain Winterbottom even in sickness could hit on the right word. Refusing to co-operate with the Administration.

After Ezeulu's refusal to be chief Clarke had made one more attempt through the Chief Clerk to persuade him to change his mind, and had failed. The situation thus became quite intolerable. Should he keep the man in prison or set him loose? If he let him go the reputation of the Administration would sag to the ground especially in Umuaro where things were only now beginning to look up after a long period of hostility to the Administration and Christianity. According to what Clarke had read Umuaro had put up more resistance to change than any other clan in the whole province. Their first school was only a year or so old and a tottering Christian mission had been set up after a series of failures. What would be the effect on such a district of the triumphant return of a witch-doctor who had defied the Administration?

But Clarke was not the person to lock a man up without fully satisfying his own conscience that justice had not only been done but appeared to have been done. Now that he had been given the answer his earlier scruples sounded a little silly; but they had been very real. What had worried him was this: if he kept the fellow in jail what would he say was his offence? What would he put down in the log? For making an ass of the Administration? For refusing to be a chief? This apparently small point vexed Clarke like a fly at siesta. He realized it was insignificant but that did not help matters; if anything it made them worse. He could not just clap an old man (yes, a very old man) into jail without reasonable explanation. All very silly really, he thought, now that Winterbottom had given him the answer. The moral of all this was that if older coasters like Winterbottom were no wiser than younger ones they at least had finesse, and this was not to be dismissed lightly.

*

Captain Winterbottom had a setback in his recovery and for another fortnight no one was allowed to see him. Among the servants and African staff on Government Hill the rumour spread first that he was insane and then that he was paralysed. Ezeulu's reputation continued to rise with these rumours. Now that the cause of his imprisonment was generally known it was impossible not to have sympathy for him. He had done no harm to the white man and could justifiably hold up his *ofo* against him. In that position whatever Ezeulu did in retaliation was not only justified, it was bound by its merit to have potency. John Nwodika explained that Ezeulu was like a puff-adder which never struck until it had first unlocked its seven deadly fangs one after the other. If while it did this its tormentor did not have the good sense to run for its life it would have only itself to blame. Ezeulu had given enough warning to the white man during the four markets he had been locked in prison. So he could not be blamed if he now hit back by destroying his enemy's sense or killing one side of his body leaving the other side to squirm in half life, which was worse than total death.

Ezeulu had now been held for thirty-two days. The white man had sent emissaries to beg him to change his mind but had not had the face to see him again in person – at least so the story went in Okperi. Then one morning, on the eighth Eke market since his arrest he was suddenly told he was free to go home. To the amazement of the Head Messenger and the Chief Clerk who brought him the message he broke into his rare belly-deep laugh.

'So the white man is tired?'

The two men smiled their agreement.

'I thought he had more fight than that inside him.'

'The white man is like that,' said the Chief Clerk.

'I prefer to deal with a man who throws up a stone and puts his head to receive it, not one who shouts for a fight but when it comes he trembles and passes premature shit.'

The two men seemed by the look on their faces to agree with this too.

'Do you know what my enemies at home call me?' Ezeulu asked. At this point John Nwodika came in to express his joy at what had happened.

'Ask him; he will tell you. They call me the friend of the white man. They say Ezeulu brought the white man to Umuaro. Is that not so, Son of Nwodika?'

'It is true,' said the other, looking a little confused from being asked to confirm the end of a story whose beginning he had not heard.

Ezeulu killed a fly that had perched on his shin. It fell down on the floor and he looked at the palm with which he killed it: then he rubbed the palm on the mat to remove the stain and examined it again.

'They say I betrayed them to the white man.' He was still looking at his palm. Then he seemed to ask himself: Why am I telling these things to strangers? and stopped.

'You should not give too much thought to that,' said John Nwodika. 'How many of those who deride you at home can wrestle with the white man as you have done and press his back to the ground?'

Ezeulu laughed. 'You call this wrestling? No, my clansman. We have not wrestled; we have merely studied each other's hand. I shall come again, but before that I want to wrestle with my own people whose hand I know and who know my hand. I am going home to challenge all those who have been poking their fingers into my face to come outside their gate and meet me in combat and whoever throws the other will strip him of his anklet.'

'The challenge of Eneke Ntulukpa to man, bird and beast,' said John Nwodika with childlike excitement.

'You know it?' said Ezeulu happily.

John Nwodika broke into the taunting song with which the bird, Eneke, once challenged the whole world. The two strangers laughed; it was just like Nwodika.

'Whoever puts the other down,' said Ezeulu when the song was ended, 'will strip him of his anklet.'

Ezeulu's sudden release was the first major decision Clarke had taken on his own. It was exactly one week since his visit to Nkisa to obtain a satisfactory definition of the man's offence and in that time he had already developed considerable self-confidence. In letters he had written home to his father and his fiancée after the incident he had made fun of his earlier amateurishness – a certain sign of present self-assurance. No doubt his new confidence had been helped by the letter from the Resident authorizing him to take day to day decisions and to open confidential correspondence not addressed personally to Winterbottom.

The mail runner brought in two letters. One looked formidable with red wax and seal – the type junior Political Officers referred to lightly as *Top Secret: Burn Before You Open*. He examined it carefully and saw it was not personal to Winterbottom. He felt like a man who had just been initiated into an important secret society. He put the packet aside for the moment to read the smaller one first. It turned out to be no more than the weekly Reuter's telegram sent as an ordinary letter from the nearest telegraphic office fifty miles away. It carried the news that Russian peasants in revolt against the new régime had refused to grow crops. 'Serve them right,' he said, and put it aside; he would take it at the close of day to the notice board in the Regimental Mess. He sat up and took the other packet.

It was a report by the Secretary for Native Affairs on Indirect Rule in Eastern Nigeria. The accompanying note from the Lieutenant-Governor said that the report had been discussed fully at the recent meeting of Senior Political Officers at Enugu which Captain Winterbottom had unfortunately been too ill to attend. It went on to say that in spite of the very adverse report attached he had not been given any directive for a change of policy. That was a matter for the Governor. But as a decision might be taken one way or another soon it was clearly inadvisable to extend the appointment of Warrant Chiefs to new areas. It was significant that the Warrant Chief for Okperi was singled out in the report for criticism. The letter concluded by asking Winterbottom to handle the matter with tact so that the Administration did not confuse the minds of the natives or create the impression of indecision or lack of direction as such an impression would do untold harm.

When days later Clarke was able to tell Winterbottom about the Report and the Lieutenant-Governor's letter he showed an amazing lack of interest, no doubt the result of the fever. He only muttered under his breath something like: *Shit on the Lieutenant-Governor!*

Chapter Sixteen

Although it was now the heart of the wet season Ezeulu and his companion had set out for home in dry, hopeful, morning weather. His companion was John Nwodika who would not hear of his plan to do the long journey alone. Ezeulu begged him not to trouble himself but it was all in vain.

'It is not a journey which a man of your station can take alone,' he said. 'If you are bent on returning today I must come with you. Otherwise stay till tomorrow when Obika is due to visit.'

'I cannot stay another day,' said Ezeulu. 'I am the tortoise who was trapped in a pit of excrement for two whole markets; but when helpers came to haul him out on the eighth day he cried! Quick, quick: I cannot stand the stench.'

So they set out. Ezeulu wore his shimmering, yellow loincloth underneath and a thick, coarse, white toga over it; this outer cloth was passed under the right armpit and its two ends thrown across the left shoulder. Over the same shoulder he carried his long-strapped goatskin bag. On his right hand he held his *alo* – a long, iron, walking-staff with a sharp, spear-like lower end which every titled man carried on important occasions. On his head was a red *ozo* cap girdled with a leather band from which an eagle feather pointed slightly backwards.

John Nwodika wore a thick brown shirt over khaki trousers.

The weather held until they were about half-way between Okperi and Umuaro. Then the rain seemed to say: *Now is the time; there are no houses on the way where they can seek shelter*. It took both hands off its support and fell down with immense, smothering abandon.

John Nwodika said: 'Let us shelter under a tree for a while to see if it will diminish.'

'It is dangerous to stand under a tree in a storm like this. Let us go on. We are not salt and we are not carrying evil medicine on our body. At least I am not.'

So they pressed on, the cloth clinging as if terrified to their bodies. Ezeulu's goatskin bag was full of water and he knew his snuff was already ruined. The red cap too never liked water and would be the worse for it. But Ezeulu was not depressed; if anything he felt a certain elation which torrential rain sometimes gave – the heady feeling which sent children naked into the rain singing:

> *Mili zobe ezobe!*
> *Ka mgbaba ogwogwo!*

But Ezeulu's elation had an edge of bitterness to it. This rain was part of the suffering to which he had been exposed and for which he must exact the fullest redress. The more he suffered now the greater would be the joy of revenge. His mind sought out new grievances to pile upon all the others.

He crooked the first finger of his left hand and drew it across his brow and over his eyes to clear the water that blinded him. The broad, new road was like an agitated, red swamp. Ezeulu's staff no longer hit the earth with a hard thud; its pointed end sank in with a swish up to the length of a finger before it met hard soil. Occasionally the rain subsided suddenly as if to listen. Only then was it possible to see separately the giant trees and the undergrowth with limp, dripping leaves. But such lulls were very short-lived; they were immediately overrun by new waves of thick rain.

Rain was good on the body only if it lasted so long and stopped clean. If it went on longer the body began to run cold. This rain did not know the boundary. It went on and on until Ezeulu's fingers held on to his staff like iron claws.

'This is what you have earned for your trouble,' he said to John Nwodika. His voice was thick and he cleared his throat.

'It is you I am worried about.'

'Me? Why should anyone worry about an old man whose eyes have spent all their sleep? No, my son. The journey in front of me is very small beside what I have put behind. Whenever the flame goes out now I shall put the torch away.'

Another gust of rain came and smothered John Nwodika's reply.

Ezeulu's people were greatly worried when he came in numb and shivering. They made a big fire for him while his wife, Ugoye, quickly prepared camwood ointment. But first of all he needed some water to wash his feet which were covered with red mud right up to his *ozo* anklet. Then he took the camwood paste from the coconut shell and rubbed his chest while Edogo rubbed his back. Matefi whose turn it was to cook for Ezeulu that night (they had kept count even in his absence) had already started preparing utazi soup. Ezeulu drank it hot and his body began gradually to return to him.

The rain was already spent when Ezeulu got home and soon stopped altogether. The first thing he did after he had drunk his utazi soup was to send Nwafo to tell Akuebue of his return.

Akuebue was grinding his snuff when Nwafo brought him the news. He did not wait to finish his grinding. He transferred the half-ground snuff into a small bottle using a special thin knife-blade. Then he swept the finer particles to the middle of the grinding-stone with a feather and transferred them also to the bottle. He used the feather again on the big and the small stones until all the powder had gone into the bottle. He put the two stones away and called one of his wives to tell her where he was going.

'If Osenigwe comes to borrow the stones,' he said as he threw his cloth over his shoulder, 'tell him I have not finished.'

There were already a handful of people in Ezeulu's hut when Akuebue arrived. All the neighbours were there and every passer-by who heard of his return interrupted his errand to greet him. Ezeulu said very little, accepting most of the greeting with his eye and a nod. The time had not come to speak or to act. He must first suffer to the limit because the man to fear in action is the one who first submits to suffer to the limit. That was the terror of the puff-adder; it would suffer every provocation, it would even let its enemy step on its trunk; it must wait and unlock its seven fangs one after the other. Then it would say to its tormentor: *Here I am!*

All efforts to draw Ezeulu into the conversation failed or achieved only limited success. When his visitors spoke about his refusal to be white man's chief he only smiled. It was not that he disliked the people around him or the subject about which they spoke. He enjoyed it all and even wished that Nwodika's son had stayed on to tell them about all the things that had happened; but he had only stopped for a short while and then gone on to his own village to pass the night before returning to Okperi in the morning. He had even refused to wash the mud off his feet.

'I am going out in the rain again,' he had said. 'Washing my feet now would be like cleaning the anus before passing excrement.'

As if he knew what Ezeulu was thinking about at that moment one of his visitors said: 'The white man has met his match in you. But there is one side to this story which I do not understand – the rôle played by the son of Nwodika in Umunneora. When the matter has cooled down he must answer one or two questions.'

'I stand with you,' said Anosi.

'Nwodika's son has already explained,' said Akuebue, who had been acting as Ezeulu's mouth. 'What he did was done in the belief that he was helping Ezeulu'.

The other man laughed. 'He did? What an innocent man! I suppose he puts his bowl of foofoo into his nostrils. Tell me another story!'

'Never trust a man of Umunneora. That is what I say.' This was Ezeulu's neighbour, Anosi. 'If a man of Umunneora tells me to stop I will run, and if he tells me to run, I shall stand where I am.'

'This one is different,' said Akuebue. 'Travelling has changed him.'

'Hi-hi-hi-hi,' laughed Ifeme. 'He will only add foreign tricks to the ones his mother taught him. You are talking like a small boy, Akuebue.'

'Do you know why it has rained all afternoon today?' asked Anosi. 'It is because Udendu's daughter is going on *uri*. So the rain-makers of Umunneora chose to spoil their kinsman's feast. They not only hate others, they hate themselves more. Their badness wears a hat.'

'True. It is pregnant and nursing a baby at the same time.'

'Very true. They are my mother's people but all I do is peep fearfully at them.'

Ifeme rose to go. He was a short, stoutly built man who always spoke at the top of his voice as though every conversation was a quarrel.

'I must go, Ezeulu,' he shouted so loud that those in the women's huts heard him. 'We thank the great god and we thank Ulu that no bad story has accompanied your travel. Perhaps you were saying to yourself there: *Ifeme has not come to visit me, I wonder whether there is a quarrel between us.* There is no quarrel between Ezeulu and Ifeme. I was thinking all the time that I must visit Ezeulu; my eyes reached you but my feet lagged behind. I kept saying: *Tomorrow I shall go,* but every day gave me a different order. As I said before: *Nno.*'

'It was the same with me,' said Anosi. 'I kept saying: *Tomorrow I shall go, tomorrow I shall go,* like the toad which lost the chance of growing a tail because of *I am coming, I am coming.*'

Ezeulu moved his back from against the wall where it had rested and appeared to be giving all his attention to his grandson, Amechi, who was trying in vain to open the old man's clenched fist. But his mind was still on the conversation around him, and he spoke a word or two when he had to. He looked up momentarily and thanked Ifeme for his visit.

Amechi's restlessness increased and soon turned to crying even though Ezeulu had allowed him to open his fist.

'Nwafo, come and take him to his mother. I think sleep is coming.'

Nwafo came, bent down on both knees and presented his back to Amechi. But instead of climbing on he stopped crying, clenched his little fist and landed a blow in the middle of Nwafo's back. This caused general laughter, and he looked round the company with streaks of recent tears under his eyes.

'All right, you go away, Nwafo; he doesn't like you – you are not a good person. He wants Obiageli.'

And truly Amechi climbed on to Obiageli's back without any trouble.

'You see,' said two or three voices together.

Obiageli raised herself to her feet with difficulty, bent slightly and made a sudden jerk with the waist. This threw the child further up her back and she walked away.

'Softly,' said Ezeulu.

'Don't worry yourself,' said Anosi. 'She knows what to do.'
Obiageli went out in the direction of Edogo's compound singing:

> *Tell the mother her child is crying*
> *Tell the mother her child is crying*
> *And then prepare a stew of úzízá*
> *And also a stew of úzízá*
> *Make a watery pepper-soup*
> *So the little birds who drink it*
> *Will all perish from the hiccup*
> *Mother's goat is in the barn*
> *And the yams will not be safe*
> *Father's goat is in the barn*
> *And the yams will all be eaten*
> *Can you see that deer approaching*
> *Look! he's dipped one foot in water*
> *Snake has struck him!*
> *He withdraws!*
> *Ja – ja . ja kulo kulo!*
> *Traveller Hawk*
> *You're welcome home*
> *Ja – ja . ja kulo kulo!*
> *But where's the length*
> *Of cloth you brought*
> *Ja – ja . ja kulo kulo!*

As long as he was in exile it was easy for Ezeulu to think of Umuaro
as one hostile entity. But back in his hut he could no longer see the
matter as simply as that. All these people who had left what they were
doing or where they were going to say welcome to him could not be
called enemies. Some of them – like Anosi – might be people of little
consequence, ineffectual, perhaps fond of gossip and sometimes given
to malice; but they were different from the enemy he had seen in his
dream at Okperi.

In the course of the second day he counted fifty-seven visitors
excluding the women. Six of them had brought palm wine; his son-

in-law, Ibe, and his people had brought two big pots of excellent wine and a cock. Throughout that day Ezeulu's hut had the appearance of a festival. Two or three people had even come from Umunneora, the enemy village. Again, at the end of the day, Ezeulu continued his division of Umuaro into ordinary people who had nothing but good will for him and those others whose ambition sought to destroy the central unity of the six villages. From the moment he made this division thoughts of reconciliation began, albeit timidly, to visit him. He knew he could say with justice that if one finger brought oil it messed up the others; but was it right that he should stretch his hand against all these people who had shown so much concern for him during his exile and since his return?

The conflict in his mind was finally resolved for him on the third day from a very unexpected quarter. His last visitor that day had been Ogbuefi Ofoka, one of the worthiest men in Umuaro but not a frequent visitor to Ezeulu's house. Ofoka was well known for speaking his mind. He was not one of those who would praise a man because he had offered him palm wine. Rather than let palm wine blind him Ofoka would throw it away, put his horn back in his goatskin bag and speak his mind.

'I have come to say *Nno* to you and to thank Ulu and thank Chukwu for seeing that you did not stub your foot against a rock,' he said. 'I want to tell you that all Umuaro heaved a sigh of relief the day you set foot in your hut once again. Nobody sent me to deliver this message to you but I think you should know it. Why do I say so? Because I know the frame of mind in which you went away.' He paused and then stretched his neck out towards Ezeulu in some kind of defiance. 'I am one of those who stood behind Nwaka of Umunneora when he said that you should go and speak to the white man.'

Ezeulu's face did not show any change.

'Do you hear me well?' continued Ofoka. 'I am one of those who said that we shall not come between you and the white man. If you like you may ask me never to set foot in your house again when I have spoken. I want you to know if you do not already know it that the elders of Umuaro did not take sides with Nwaka against you. We all know him and the man behind him; we are not deceived. Why then did we agree with him? It was because we were confused. Do you hear me? The elders of Umuaro are confused. You can say that Ofoka told you so. We are confused. We are like the puppy in the proverb which attempted to answer two calls at once and broke its jaw. First you, Ezeulu, told us five years ago that it was foolish to defy the white man. We did not listen to you. We went out against him and he took our gun from us and broke it across his knee. So we know you were right. But just as we were beginning to learn our lesson you turn round and tell us to go and challenge the same white man. What did you expect us to do?' He paused for Ezeulu to answer but he did not.

'If my enemy speaks the truth I will not say because it is spoken by my enemy I will not listen. What Nwaka said was the truth. He said: *Go and talk to the white man because he knows you*. Was that not the truth? He spoke in malice but he spoke truth. Who else among us could have gone out and wrestled with him as you have done? Once again, *Nno*. If you do not like what I have said you may send me a message not to come to your house again. I am going.'

This summed up all the argument that had been going on in Ezeulu's mind for the past three days. Perhaps if Akuebue had spoken the same words they might not have had equal power. But coming from a man who was neither a friend nor an enemy they caught Ezeulu unprepared and struck home.

Yes, it was right that the Chief Priest should go ahead and confront danger before it reached his people. That was the responsibility of his priesthood. It had been like that from the first day when the six harassed villages got together and said to Ezeulu's ancestor: *You will carry this deity for us*. At first he was afraid. What power had he in his body to carry such potent danger? But his people sang their support behind him and the flute man turned his head. So he went down on both knees and they put the deity on his head. He rose up and was transformed into a spirit. His people kept up their song behind him and he stepped forward on his first and decisive journey, compelling even the four days in the sky to give way to him.

The thought became too intense for Ezeulu and he put it aside to cool. He called his son, Oduche.

'What are you doing?'

'I am weaving a basket.'

'Sit down.'

Oduche sat on the mud-bed and faced his father. After a short pause Ezeulu spoke direct and to the point. He reminded Oduche of the importance of knowing what the white man knew. 'I have sent you to be my eyes there. Do not listen to what people say – people who do not know their right from their left. No man speaks a lie to his son; I have told you that before. If anyone asks you why you should be sent to learn these new things tell him that a man must dance the dance prevalent in his time.' He scratched his head and continued in a relaxed voice. 'When I was in Okperi I saw a young white man who was able to write his book with the left hand. From his actions I could see that he had very little sense. But he had power; he could shout in my face; he could do what he liked. Why? Because he could write with his left hand. That is why I have called you. I want you to learn and master this man's knowledge so much that if you are suddenly woken up from sleep and asked what it is you will reply. You must learn it until you can write it with your left hand. That is all I want to tell you.'

As the excitement over Ezeulu's return died down life in his compound gradually went back to its accustomed ways. The children in particular rejoiced at the end of the half-mourning under which they had lived for more than a whole moon. 'Tell us a story,' said Obiageli to her mother, Ugoye. Actually it was Nwafo who had put her up to it.

'Tell you a story with these unwashed utensils scattered around?'

Nwafo and Obiageli immediately went to work. They moved away the little mortar for grinding pepper and turned it over and put the smaller vessels on the bamboo ledge. Ugoye herself changed the nearly-burnt-out taper on the tripod with a new one from the palm-oil-soaked bunch in a potsherd.

Ezeulu had eaten every morsel of the supper Ugoye prepared for him. This should have made any woman very happy. But in a big compound there was always something to spoil one's happiness. For Ugoye it was her husband's senior wife, Matefi. No matter what Ugoye did Matefi's jealousy never let her rest. If she cooked a modest meal in her own hut Matefi said she was starving her children so that she could buy ivory bracelets; if she killed a cock as she did this evening Matefi said she was seeking favour from her husband. Of course she never said any of these things to Ugoye's face, but all her gossip eventually got back to Ugoye. This evening as Oduche was dressing the chicken in an open fire Matefi had gone up and down clearing her throat.

After the room had been tidied up Nwafo and Obiageli spread a mat and sat by their mother's low stool.

'Which story do you want to hear?'

'Onwuero,' said Obiageli.

'No,' said Nwafo, 'we have heard it too often. Tell us about—'

'All right,' cut in Obiageli. 'Tell us about Eneke Ntulukpa.'

Ugoye searched her memory for a while and found what she looked for.

Once upon a time there was a man who had two wives. The senior wife had many children but the younger one had only one son. But the senior wife was wicked and envious. One day the man and his family went to work on their farm. This farm was at the boundary between the land of men and the land of spirits . . .

Ugoye, Nwafo and Obiageli sat in a close group near the cooking place. Oduche sat apart near the entrance to the one sleeping-room holding his new book, *Azu Ndu*, to the yellow light of the taper. His lips moved silently as he spelt out and formed the first words of the reader:

a b a	aba
e g o	ego
i r o	iro
a z u	azu
ọ m u	ọmu

Meanwhile Ezeulu had pursued again his thoughts on the coming struggle and began to probe with the sensitiveness of a snail's horns the possibility of reconciliation or, if that was too much, of narrowing down the area of conflict. Behind his thinking was of course the knowledge that the fight would not begin until the time of harvest, after three moons more. So there was plenty of time. Perhaps it was this knowledge that there was no hurry which gave him confidence to play with alternatives – to dissolve his resolution and at the right time form it again. Why should a man be in a hurry to lick his fingers; was he going to put them away in the rafter? Or perhaps the thoughts of reconciliation were from a true source. But whatever it was, Ezeulu was not to be allowed to remain in two minds much longer.

'Ta! Nwanu!' barked Ulu in his ear, as a spirit would in the ear of an impertinent human child. 'Who told you that this was your own fight?'

Ezeulu trembled and said nothing, his gaze lowered to the floor.

'I say who told you that this was your own fight to arrange the way it suits you? You want to save your friends who brought you palm wine he-he-he-he-he!' Only the insane could sometimes approach the menace and mockery in the laughter of deities – a dry, skeletal laugh. 'Beware you do not come between me and my victim or you may receive blows not meant for you! Do you not know what happens when two elephants fight? Go home and sleep and leave me to settle my quarrel with Idemili, whose envy seeks to destroy me that his python may again come to power. Now you tell me how it concerns you. I say go home and sleep. As for me and Idemili we shall fight to the finish; and whoever throws the other down will strip him of his anklet!'

After that there was no more to be said. Who was Ezeulu to tell his deity how to fight the jealous cult of the sacred python? It was a fight of the gods. He was no more than an arrow in the bow of his god. This thought intoxicated Ezeulu like palm wine. New thoughts tumbled over themselves and past events took on new, exciting significance. Why had Oduche imprisoned a python in his box? It had been blamed on the white man's religion; but was that the true cause? What if the boy was also an arrow in the hand of Ulu?

And what about the white man's religion and even the white man himself? This was close on profanity but Ezeulu was now in a mood to follow things through. Yes, what about the white man himself? After all he had once taken sides with Ezeulu and, in a way, had taken sides with him again lately by exiling him, thus giving him a weapon with which to fight his enemies.

If Ulu had spotted the white man as an ally from the very beginning, it would explain many things. It would explain Ezeulu's decision to send Oduche to learn the ways of the white man. It was true Ezeulu had given other explanations for his decision but those were the thoughts that had come into his head at the time. One half of him was man and the other half *mmo* – the half that was painted over with white chalk at important religious moments. And half of the things he ever did were done by this spirit side.

Chapter Seventeen

The people of Umuaro had a saying that the noise even of the loudest events must begin to die down by the second market week. It was so with Ezeulu's exile and return. For a while people talked about nothing else; but gradually it became just another story in the life of the six villages, or so they imagined.

Even in Ezeulu's compound the daily rounds established themselves again. Obika's new wife had become pregnant; Ugoye and Matefi carried on like any two jealous wives; Edogo went back to his carving which he had put aside at the height of the planting season; Oduche made more progress in his new faith and in his reading and writing; Obika, after a short break, returned to palm wine in full force. His temporary restraint had been largely due to the knowledge that too much palm wine was harmful to a man going in to his wife – it made him pant on top of her like a lizard fallen from an iroko tree – and reduced him in her esteem. But now that Okuata had become pregnant he no longer went in to her.

Even Ezeulu himself seemed to have put away all his grievance. No hint of it came into his daily offering of kolanut and palm wine to his fathers or into the simple ritual he performed at every new moon. It was also time for his younger wife to be pregnant again having rested for over a year since the death of her last child. So she began to answer his call to sleep some nights in his hut. This did not improve her relations with Matefi who was past child-bearing.

The minor feasts and festivals of the year took place in their proper season. Some of them were observed by all six villages together and some belonged to individual ones. Umuagu celebrated their *Mgba Agbogho* or the Wrestling of the Maidens; Umunneora observed their annual feast in honour of Idemili, Owner of the python. Together the six villages held the quiet retreat called *Oso Nwanadi* to placate the resentful spirits of kinsmen killed in war or in other ways made to suffer death in the cause of Umuaro.

The heavy rains stopped as usual for a spell of dry weather without which yams could not produce big tubers despite luxuriant leaves. In short, life went on as though nothing had happened or was ever going to happen.

There was one minor feast which Ezeulu's village, Umuachala, celebrated towards the end of the wet season and before the big festival of the year – the New Yam Feast. This minor celebration was called *Akwu Nro*. It had little ritual and was no more than a memorial offering by widows to their departed husbands. Every widow in Umuachala prepared foofoo and palm-nut soup on the night of *Akwu Nro* and put it outside her hut. In the morning the bowls were empty because her husband had come up from Ani-Mmo and eaten the food.

This year's *Akwu Nro* was to have an added interest because Obika's age group would present a new ancestral Mask to the village. The coming of a new Mask was always an important occasion especially when as now it was a Mask of high rank. In the last few days there had been a lot of coming and going among members of the Otakagu age group. Those of them who had leading roles to play at the ceremony would naturally be targets of malevolence and envy and must therefore he 'hardboiled' in protective magic. But even the others had to have some defensive preparation rubbed into shallow cuts on the arm.

All the arrangements were made secretly in keeping with the mystery of ancestral spirits. In recent years new thinking had gone into the need for strengthening the defences around this mystery in Umuaro. It had become clear to the elders that although no woman dared speak openly when she saw a Mask it was not too difficult for her to guess the man behind it. All that was necessary was to look at all the people around the Mask and see who was absent. To overcome this difficulty the elders had recently ruled that whenever a group or a village wished to bring out a Mask they must go outside their group or village for their man. So the Otakagu age group in Umuachala had gone all the way to Umuogwugwu to select the man to wear the mask. The man they chose was called Amumegbu; he was in Umuach-ala during all the preparations but his presence was kept very secret.

Both Edogo and Obika were intimately concerned with the Mask that was to come. It belonged to Obika's age group, but more than that he had been selected as one of the two people to slaughter rams in its presence. Edogo came into it because he had carved the mask.

It was a little past midday. Obika sat on the floor of his hut, his feet astride the stone on which he sharpened his matchet. Trickles of sweat ran down his face and he held his lower lip with the upper teeth as he worked. He had already used a whole head of salt to give greater edge to the stone; and now and again he squeezed a little lime juice on to the blade. Two emptied fruits lay near the stone with three or four uncut ones. Obika had been working on his new matchet at intervals during the past three days and it was now sharp enough to shave the hair. He rose and went outside to see it well in the light. He held it up before him and by twisting his wrist made it flash like a mirror in the sun. He seemed satisfied, went back into his hut and put it away. Then he passed through to the inner compound and saw his wife turning water from the big pot outside the hut into a bowl. She stood up wearily and spat as she always did nowadays.

'Old woman,' Obika teased her.

'I have said if you know what you did to me you should come and undo it,' she said, smiling.

Not very long after that the first sounds of the coming event were heard in the village. Half a dozen young men ran up and down the different quarters beating their *ogene* and searching for the Mask; for no one knew which of the million ant holes in Umuachala it would come through. They kept up their search for a very long time and the sound of their metal gong and of their feet when they were near kept the whole village on edge. As soon as the sun's heat began to soften the village emptied itself on to the *ilo*.

The *ilo* of Umuachala was among the biggest in Umuaro and the best kept. It was sometimes called Ilo Agbasioso because its length cowed even the best runners. At one of its four corners stood the *okwolo* house from where those initiated into the mystery of ancestral spirits watched the display on the *ilo*. The *okwolo* was a tall, unusual hut having only two side and back walls. Looking at it from the open front one saw tiers of steps running the whole breath of the hut and rising from the ground almost to the roof. The elders of the village sat on the lowest rungs which had the best view and the others sat on the back and higher rungs. Behind the *okwolo* stood a big udala tree which like all udala trees in Umuaro was sacred to ancestral spirits. Even now many children were playing under it waiting for the occasional fall of a ripe, light-brown fruit – the prize for the fastest runner or the luckiest child nearest whom it fell. The tree was full of the tempting fruit but no one, young or old, was allowed to pick from the tree. If anyone broke this rule he would be visited by all the Masked spirits in Umuaro and he would have to wipe off their foot-steps with heavy fines and sacrifice.

Although Ezeulu and Akuebue were early there were already immense crowds on the *ilo* when they arrived. Everybody in Umuach-ala seemed to be either there or on his way, and many people came from all the other villages of Umuaro. Women and girls, young men and boys had already formed a big ring on the *ilo*; as more and more people poured in from every quarter the ring became thicker and the noise greater. There were no young men with whips trying to keep the crowd clear of the centre; this would take care of itself as soon as the Mask arrived.

A big stir and commotion developed in one part of the crowd and spread right round. People asked those nearest them what it was and they pointed at something. Thousands of fingers were soon pointed in the same direction. There, in a fairly quiet corner of the *ilo*, sat Otakekpeli. This man was known throughout Umuaro as a wicked medicine-man. More than twice he had had to take kolanut from the palm of a dead man to swear he had no hand in the death. Of course he had survived each oath which could mean he was innocent. But people did not believe it; they said he had immediately rushed home and drunk powerful, counteracting potions.

From what was known of him and by the way he sat away from other people it was clear he had not come merely to watch a new Mask. An occasion such as this was often used by wicked men to try out the potency of their magic or to match their power against that of others.

There were stories of Masks which had come out unprepared and been transfixed to a spot for days or even felled to the ground.

Perhaps the most suspicious thing about Otakekpeli was his posture. He sat like a lame man with legs folded under him. They said it was the fighting posture of a boar when a leopard was about: it dug a shallow hole in the earth, sat with its testicles hidden away in it and waited with standing bristles on its head of iron. As a rule, the leopard would go its way, in search of goats and sheep.

The crowd watched Otakekpeli with disapproval; but no one challenged him because it was dangerous to do so but even more because most people in their hearts looked forward to the spectacle of two potent forces grappling with each other. If the Otakagu age group chose to bring out a new Mask without first boiling themselves hard it was their own fault. In fact most of these encounters produced no visible results at all because the powers were equally matched or the target was stronger than the assailant.

The approach of the Mask caused a massive stampede. The women and children scattered and fled in the opposite direction, screaming with the enjoyment of danger. Soon they were all back again because the Mask had not even come into sight; only the *ogene* and singing of its followers had been heard. The metal gong and voices became louder and louder and the crowd looked around them to be sure that the line of flight was clear.

There was another stampede when the first harbingers of the Mask burst into the *ilo* from the narrow footpath by which it was expected to arrive. These young men wore raffia and their matchets caught the light as they threw them up or clashed them in salute of each other from left to right and then back from right to left. They ran here and there, and sometimes one would charge at full speed in one direction. The crowd at that point would scatter and the man would brake all of a sudden and tremble on all toes.

The gong and the voices were now quite near but they were almost lost in the uproar of the crowd. It was likely that the Mask had stopped for a while or it would have appeared by now. Its attendants kept up their song.

The first spectacle of the day came with the arrival of Obika and a flute man at his heels singing of his exploits. The crowd cheered, especially the women because Obika was the handsomest young man in Umuachala and perhaps in all Umuaro. They called him Ugonachomma.

No sooner was Obika in the *ilo* than he caught sight of Otakekpeli sitting on his haunches. Without second thoughts he made straight for him at full speed, then stopped dead. He shouted at the medicine-man to get up at once and go home. The other merely smiled. The crowd forgot all about the Mask. Okuata had taken a position away from the thickest press because of her pregnancy. Her heart had swollen when the crowd greeted her husband; now she shut her eyes and the ground reeled round her.

Obika was now pointing at Otakekpeli and then pointing at his own chest. He was telling the man that if he wanted to do something useful with his life he should get up. The other man continued to laugh at him. Obika renewed his progress but not with the former speed. He prowled like a leopard, his matchet in his right hand and a leather band of amulets on his left arm. Ezeulu was biting his lips. It would be Obika, he thought, the rash, foolish Obika. Did not all the other young men see Otakekpeli and look away? But his son could never look away. Obika—

Ezeulu stopped in mid-thought. With the flash of lightning Obika had dropped his matchet, rushed forward and in one movement lifted Otakekpeli off the ground and thrown him into the near-by bush in a shower of sand. The crowd burst out in one great high-vaulting cheer as Otakekpeli struggled powerlessly to his feet pointing an impotent finger at Obika who had already turned his back on him. Okuata opened her eyes again and heaved a sigh.

The Mask arrived appropriately on the crest of the excitement. The crowd scattered in real or half-real terror. It approached a few steps at a time, each one accompanied by the sound of bells and rattles on its waist and ankles. Its body was covered in bright new cloths mostly red and yellow. The face held power and terror; each exposed tooth was the size of a big man's thumb, the eyes were large sockets as big as a fist, two gnarled horns pointed upwards and inwards above its head nearly touching at the tip. It carried a shield of skin in the left hand and a huge matchet in the right.

'Ko-ko-ko-ko-ko-ko-oh!' it sang like cracked metal and its attendants replied with a deep monotone like a groan:

'Hum-hum-hum.'

'Ko-ko-ko-ko-ko-ko-oh.'

'Oh-oyoyo-oyoyo-oyoyo-oh: oh-oyoyo-oh. Hum-hum.'

There was not much of a song in it. But then an Agaba was not a Mask of song and dance. It stood for the power and aggressiveness of youth. It continued its progress and its song, such as it was. As it got near the centre of the *ilo* it changed into the song called *Onye ebuna uzo cho ayi okwu*. It was an appeal to all and sundry not to be the first to provoke the ancestral Mask; and it gave minute details of what would befall anyone who ignored this advice. He would become an outcast, with no fingers and no toes, living all by himself in a solitary hut, a beggar's satchel hanging down his shoulder; in other words, a leper.

Whenever it tried to move too fast or too dangerously two sweating attendants gave a violent tugging at the strong rope round its waist. This was a very necessary, if somewhat hazardous, task. On one occasion the Mask became so enraged by this restraint that it turned on the two men with raised matchet. They instantly dropped the rope and fled for their lives. This time the cry of the scattering crowd carried real terror. But the two men did not leave the Mask free too long. As soon as it gave up chasing them they returned once more to their task.

A very small incident happened now which would not have been remembered had it not been followed by something more serious. One of the young men had thrown up his matchet and failed to catch it in the air. The crowd always on the look-out for such failures sent up a big boo. The man, Obikwelu, picked up his matchet again and tried to cover up by a show of excessive agility; but this only brought more laughter.

Meanwhile the Mask had proceeded to the *okwolo* to salute some of the elders.

'Ezeulu de-de-de-de-dei,' it said.

'Our father, my hand is on the ground,' replied the Chief Priest.

'Ezeulu, do you know me?'

'How can a man know you who are beyond human knowledge?'

'Ezeulu, our Mask salutes you,' it sang.

'Eje-ya-mma-mma-mma-mma-mma-mma-eje-ya-mma!' sang its followers.

'Ora-obodo, Agaba salutes you!'

'Eje-ya-mma-mma-mma-mma-mma-mma-eje-ya-mma!'

'Have you heard the song of the Spider?'

'Eje-ya-mma-mma-mma-mma-mma-mma-eje-ya-mma!'

It broke off suddenly, turned round and ran straight ahead. The crowd in that direction broke up and scattered.

Although Edogo could have taken one of the back seats in the *okwolo* he chose to stand with the crowd so as to see the Mask from different positions. When he had finished carving the face and head he had been a little disappointed. There was something about the nose which did not please him – a certain fineness which belonged not to an Agaba but to a Maiden Spirit. But the owners of the work had not complained; in fact they had praised it very highly. Edogo knew, however, that he must see the Mask in action to know whether it was good or bad. So he stood with the crowd.

Looking at it now that it had come to life the weakness seemed to disappear. It even seemed to make the rest of the face more fierce. Edogo went from one part of the crowd to another in the hope that someone would make the comparison he wanted to hear, but no one did. Many people praised the new Mask but no one thought of comparing it with the famous Agaba of Umuagu, if only to say that this one was not as good as that. If Edogo had heard anyone say so he might have been happy. He had not after all set out to excel the greatest carver in Umuaro but he had hoped that someone would link their two names. He began to blame himself for not sitting in the *okwolo*. There, among the elders, was a more likely place to hear the kind of conversation he was listening for. But it was too late now.

The climax of the evening came with the slaughtering of the rams. As a chair was set in the middle of the *ilo* and the Mask sat down there was comparative silence. Two attendants took up positions on either side of the seated Mask and fanned it. The first ram was led forward and the Mask touched the neck with its matchet. Then it was taken a short distance away but still in full view of the presiding spirit. There was now complete silence except for the flute which, in place of its usual thin and delicate tone, produced broad, broken sounds. Obika came forward, threw up his matchet with a twirl so that it revolved and caught the light of the evening on its blade. He did this twice and each time caught it perfectly in mid-air. Then he stepped forward and with one precise blow severed the ram's head. The crowd cheered tumultuously as one of the attendants picked up the head which had rolled in the sand and held it up. The Mask looked on with the same unchanging countenance.

When the noisy excitement went down the second ram was brought forward and the Mask again touched its neck. Obikwelu stepped forward. He was nervous because he had dropped his matchet earlier on. He threw it up thrice and caught it perfectly. He stepped forward, raised it and struck. It was as if he had hit a rock; the ram struggled to escape; the crowd booed and laughed. Obikwelu was very unlucky that day. The ram had moved its head at the last moment and he had struck the horn. The Mask looked on unperturbed. Obikwelu tried again and succeeded but it was too late; the laughter of the crowd drowned the few belated cheers.

Chapter Eighteen

After a long period of silent preparation Ezeulu finally revealed that he intended to hit Umuaro at its most vulnerable point – the Feast of the New Yam.

This feast was the end of the old year and the beginning of the new. Before it a man might dig up a few yams around his house to ward off hunger in his family but no one would begin the harvesting of the big farms. And, in any case, no man of title would taste new yam from whatever source before the festival. It reminded the six villages of their coming together in ancient times and of their continuing debt to Ulu who saved them from the ravages of the Abam. At every New Yam Feast the coming together of the villages was re-enacted and every grown man in Umuaro took a good-sized seed-yam to the shrine of Ulu and placed it in the heap from his village after circling it round his head; then he took the lump of chalk lying beside the heap and marked his face. It was from these heaps that the elders knew the number of men in each village. If there was an increase over the previous year a sacrifice of gratitude was made to Ulu; but if the number had declined the reason was sought from diviners and a sacrifice of appeasement was ordered. It was also from these yams that Ezeulu selected thirteen with which to reckon the new year.

If the festival meant no more than this it would still be the most important ceremony in Umuaro. But it was also the day for all the minor deities in the six villages who did not have their own special feasts. On that day each of these gods was brought by its custodian and stood in a line outside the shrine of Ulu so that any man or woman who had received a favour from it could make a small present in return. This was the one public appearance these smaller gods were allowed in the year. They rode into the market place on the heads or shoulders of their custodians, danced round and then stood side by side at the entrance to the shrine of Ulu. Some of them would be very old, nearing the time when their power would be transferred to new carvings and they would be cast aside; and some would have been made only the other day. The very old ones carried face marks like the men who made them, in the days before Ezeulu's grandfather proscribed the custom. At last year's festival only three of these ancients were left. Perhaps this year one or two more would disappear, following the men who made them in their own image and departed long ago.

The festival thus brought gods and men together in one crowd. It was the only assembly in Umuaro in which a man might look to his right and find his neighbour and look to his left and see a god standing there – perhaps Agwu whose mother also gave birth to madness or Ngene, owner of a stream.

Ezeulu had gone out to visit Akuebue when his six assistants came to see him. Matefi told them where he had gone and they decided to wait for him in his *obi*. It was approaching evening when he returned. Although he knew what must have brought them he feigned surprise.

'Is it well?' he asked after the initial salutations.

'It is well.'

An awkward silence followed. Then Nwosisi who represented the village of Umuogwugwu spoke. It was not his custom to waste words.

'You have asked if all is well and we said yes; but a toad does not run in the daytime unless something is after it. There is a little matter which we have decided to bring to you. It is now four days since the new moon appeared in the sky; it is already grown big. And yet you have not called us together to tell us the day of the New Yam Feast—'

'By our reckoning,' Obiesili took up, 'the present moon is the twelfth since the last feast.'

There was silence. Obiesili was always a tactless speaker and no one had asked him to put his mouth into such a delicate matter. Ezeulu cleared his throat and welcomed the people again – to show that he was neither in a hurry nor excited.

'You have done what you should do,' he said. 'If anyone says you have failed in your duty he is telling a lie. A man who asks questions does not lose his way; that is what our fathers taught us. You have done well to come and ask me about this matter which troubles you. But there is something I did not fully understand. You said, Obiesili, just now that according to your reckoning I should have announced the next New Yam Feast at the last new moon.'

'I said so.'

'I see. I thought perhaps I did not hear you well. Since when did you begin to reckon the year for Umuaro?'

'Obiesili did not use his words well,' said Chukwulobe. 'We do not reckon the year for Umuaro; we are not Chief Priest. But we thought that perhaps you have lost count because of your recent absence—'

'What! Are you out of your senses, young man?' Ezeulu shouted. 'There is nothing that a man will not hear these days. Lost count! Did your father tell you that the Chief Priest of Ulu can lose count of the moons? No, my son,' he continued in a surprisingly mild tone, 'no Ezeulu can lose count. Rather it is you who count with your fingers who are likely to make a mistake, to forget which finger you counted at the last moon. But as I said at the beginning you have done well to come and ask. Go back to your villages now and wait for my message. I have never needed to be told the duties of the priesthood.'

If anyone had come into Ezeulu's hut after the men had left he would have been surprised. The old priest's face glowed with happiness and some of his youth and handsomeness returned temporarily from across the years. His lips moved, letting through an occasional faint whisper. But soon the outside world broke in on him. He stopped whispering and listened more carefully. Nwafo and Obiageli were reciting something just outside his *obi*.

'Eke nekwọ onye uka!' they said over and over again. Ezeulu listened even more carefully. He was not mistaken.

'Eke nekwọ onye uka! Eke nekwọ onye uka! Eke nekwọ onye uka!'

'Look it's running away!' cried Obiageli and the two laughed excitedly.

'Eke nekwọ onye uka! Nekwọ onye uka! Nekwọ onye uka!'

'Nwafo!' shouted Ezeulu.

'Nna,' replied the other fearfully.

'Come here.'

Nwafo came in with a tread that would not have killed an ant. Sweat was running down his head and face. Obiageli had melted away the moment Ezeulu called.

'What were you saying?'

Nwafo said nothing. His eyelids blinked almost audibly.

'Are you deaf? I asked you what you were saying.'

'They said that was how to scare away a python.'

'I did not ask you what anybody said. I asked what you were saying. Or do you want me to get up from here before you answer?'

'We were saying: Python, run! There is a Christian here.'

'And what does it mean?'

'Akwuba told us that a python runs away as soon as it hears that.'

Ezeulu broke into a long, loud laughter. Nwafo's relief beamed all over his grimy face.

'Did it run away when you said it?'

'It ran away *fiam* like an ordinary snake.'

The news of Ezeulu's refusal to call the New Yam Feast spread through Umuaro as rapidly as if it had been beaten out on the *ikolo*. At first people were completely stunned by it; they only began to grasp its full meaning slowly because its like had never happened before.

Two days later ten men of high title came to see him. None of the ten had taken fewer than three titles, and one of them – Ezekwesili Ezukanma – had taken the fourth and highest. Only two other men in the entire six villages had this distinction. One of them was too old to be present and the other was Nwaka of Umunneora. His absence from this delegation showed how desperate they all were to appease Ezeulu.

They came in together, giving the impression that they had already met elsewhere. Before he entered Ezeulu's hut each of them planted his iron staff outside and transferred his red cap on to its head.

Throughout their deliberation no one came within hearing distance of the hut. Anosi who had wanted to take scraps of gossip to Ezeulu and pick up what he could on the crisis came out of his hut carrying snuff in his left hand and then saw all the red-capped *alo* staffs outside his neighbour's hut. He turned away to visit another neighbour.

Ezeulu presented a lump of chalk to his visitors and each of them drew his personal emblem of upright and horizontal lines on the floor. Some painted their big toe and others marked their face. Then he brought them three kolanuts in a wooden bowl. A short formal argument began and ended. Ezeulu took one kolanut, Ezekwesili took the second and Onenyi Nnanyelugo took the third. Each of them offered a short prayer and broke his nut. Nwafo carried the bowl to them in turn and they first put in all the lobes before selecting one. Nwafo carried the bowl round and the rest took a lobe each.

After they had all chewed and swallowed their kola Ezekwesili spoke.

'Ezeulu, the leaders of Umuaro assembled here have asked me to tell you that they are thankful for the kola you gave them. Thank you again and again and may your stock be replenished.'

The others joined in to say: 'Thank you, may your stock be replenished.'

'Perhaps you can guess why we have come. It is because of certain stories that have reached our ears; and we thought the best thing was to find out what is true and what is not from the only man who can tell us. The story we have heard is that there is a little disagreement about the next New Yam Festival. As I said we do not know if it is true or not, but we do know that there is fear and anxiety in Umuaro which if allowed to spread might spoil something. We cannot wait for that to happen; an adult does not sit and watch while the she-goat suffers the pain of childbirth tied to a post. Leaders of Umuaro, have I spoken according to your wish?'

'You have delivered our message.'

'Ezekwesili,' called Ezeulu.

'Eei,' answered the man who had just spoken.

'I welcome you. Your words have entered my ears. Egonwanne.'

'Eei.'

'Nnanyelugo.'

'Eei.'

Ezeulu called each one by his salutation name.

'I welcome you all. Your mission is a good one and I thank you. But I have not heard that there is a disagreement about the New Yam Feast. My assistants came here two days ago and said it was time to announce the day of the next festival and I told them that it was not their place to remind me.'

Ezekwesili's head was slightly bowed and he was rubbing his hairless dome. Ofoka had taken his snuff bottle from his pure white goatskin bag and was tipping some of the stuff into his left palm. Nnanyelugo who sat nearest to him rubbed his own palms together to clean them and then presented the left to Ofoka without saying a word. Ofoka turned the snuff from his own hand into Nnanyelugo's and tipped out some more for himself.

'But with you,' continued Ezeulu, 'I need not speak in riddles. You all know what our custom is. I only call a new festival when there is only one yam left from the last. Today I have three yams and so I know that the time has not come.'

Three or four of the visitors tried to speak at once but the others gave way to Onenyi Nnanyelugo. He saluted everyone by name before he started.

'I think that Ezeulu has spoken well. Everything he has said entered my ears. We all know the custom and no one can say that Ezeulu has offended against it. But the harvest is ripe in the soil and must be gathered now or it will be eaten by the sun and the weevils. At the same time Ezeulu has just told us that he still has three sacred yams to eat from last year. What then do we do? How do you carry a man with a broken waist? We know why the sacred yams are still not finished; it was the work of the white man. But he is not here now to breathe with us the air he has fouled. We cannot go to Okperi and ask him to come and eat the yams that now stand between us and the harvest. Shall we then sit down and watch our harvest ruined and our children and wives die of hunger? No! Although I am not the priest of Ulu I can say that the deity does not want Umuaro to perish. We call him the saver. Therefore you must find a way out, Ezeulu. If I could I would go now and eat the remaining yams. But I am not the priest of Ulu. It is for you, Ezeulu, to save our harvest.'

The others murmured their approval.

'Nnanyelugo.'

'Eei.'

'You have spoken well. But what you ask me to do is not done. Those yams are not food and a man does not eat them because he is hungry. You are asking me to eat death.'

'Ezeulu,' said Anichebe Udeozo. 'We know that such a thing has never been done before but never before has the white man taken the Chief Priest away. These are not the times we used to know and we must meet them as they come or be rolled in the dust. I want you to look round this room and tell me what you see. Do you think there is another Umuaro outside this hut now?'

'No, you are Umuaro,' said Ezeulu.

'Yes, we are Umuaro. Therefore listen to what I am going to say. Umuaro is now asking you to go and eat those remaining yams today and name the day of the next harvest. Do you hear me well? I said go and eat those yams today, not tomorrow; and if Ulu says we have committed an abomination let it be on the heads of the ten of us here. You will be free because we have set you to it, and the person who sets a child to catch a shrew should also find him water to wash the odour from his hand. We shall find you the water. Umuaro, have I spoken well?'

'You have said everything. We shall take the punishment.'

'Leaders of Umuaro, do not say that I am treating your words with contempt; it is not my wish to do so. But you cannot say: *do what is not done and we shall take the blame*. I am the Chief Priest of Ulu and what I have told you is his will not mine. Do not forget that I too have yam-fields and that my children, my kinsmen and my friends – yourselves among them – have also planted yams. It could not be my wish to ruin all these people. It could not be my wish to make the smallest man in Umuaro suffer. But this is not my doing. The gods sometimes use us as a whip.'

'Did Ulu tell you what his annoyance was? Is there no sacrifice that would appease him?'

'I will not hide anything from you. Ulu did say that two new moons came and went and there was no one to break kolanut to him and Umuaro kept silent.'

'What did he expect us to say?' asked Ofoka, a little hotly.

'I don't know what he expected you to say, Ofoka. Nnanyelugo asked me a question and I answered.'

'But if Ulu—'

'Let us not quarrel about that, Ofoka. We asked Ezeulu what was Ulu's grievance and he has told us. Our concern now should be how to appease him. Let us ask Ezeulu to go back and tell the deity that we have heard his grievance and we are prepared to make amends. Every offence has its sacrifice, from a few cowries to a cow or a human being. Let us wait for an answer.'

'If you ask me to go back to Ulu I shall do so. But I must warn you that a god who demands the sacrifice of a chick might raise it to a goat if you went to ask a second time.'

'Do not say that I am fond of questions,' said Ofoka. 'But I should like to know on whose side you are, Ezeulu. I think you have just said that you have become the whip with which Ulu flogs Umuaro . . .'

'If you will listen to me, Ofoka, let us not quarrel about that,' said Ezekwesili. 'We have come to the end of our present mission. Our duty now is to watch Ezeulu's mouth for a message from Ulu. We have planted our yams in the farm of Anaba-nti.'

The others agreed and Nnanyelugo deftly steered the conversation to the subject of change. He gave numerous examples of customs that had been altered in the past when they began to work hardship on the people. They all talked at length about these customs which had either died in full bloom or had been stillborn. Nnanyelugo reminded them that even in the matter of taking titles there had been a change. Long, long ago there had been a fifth title in Umuaro – the title of king. But the conditions for its attainment had been so severe that no man had ever taken it, one of the conditions being that the man aspiring to be king must first pay the debts of every man and every woman in Umuaro. Ezeulu said nothing throughout this discussion.

As he promised the leaders of Umuaro Ezeulu returned to the shrine of Ulu in the morning. He entered the bare, outer room and looked round vacantly. Then he placed his back against the door of the inner room which not even his assistants dared enter. The door gave under the pressure of his body and he walked in backwards. He guided himself by running his left hand along one of the side walls. When he got to the end of it he moved a few steps to the right and stood directly in front of the earth mound which represented Ulu. From the rafters right round the room the skulls of all past chief priests looked down on the mound and on their descendant and successor. Even in the hottest day a damp chill always possessed the shrine because of the giant trees outside which put their heads together to cut off the sun, but more especially because of the great, cold, underground river flowing under the earth mound. Even the approaches to the shrine were cold and, all year round, there was always some *ntu-nanya-mili* dropping tears from the top of the ancient trees.

As Ezeulu cast his string of cowries the bell of Oduche's people began to ring. For one brief moment he was distracted by its sad, measured monotone and he thought how strange it was that it should sound so near – much nearer than it did in his compound.

Ezeulu's announcement that his consultation with the deity had produced no result and that the six villages would be locked in the old year for two moons longer spread such alarm as had not been known in Umuaro in living memory.

Meanwhile the rains thinned out. There was one last heavy downpour to usher in a new moon. It brought down the harmattan as well, and each new day made the earth harder so that the eventual task of digging up whatever remained of the harvest grew daily.

Disagreement was not new in Umuaro. The rulers of the clan had often quarrelled about one thing or another. There was a long-drawn-out dispute before face marks were finally abolished and there had been other disagreements of more or less weight before it and since. But none of them had quite filtered down to the ground – to the women and even the children – like the present crisis. It was not a remote argument which could end one way or the other and still leave the ground untouched. Even children in their mother's belly took sides in this one.

Yesterday Nwafo had had to wrestle with his friend, Obielue. It had all started from the moment they went to inspect the bird-snare they had set with resin on the top of two icheku trees. Obielue's trap held a very small nza while Nwafo's was empty. This had happened before, and Obielue began to boast about his skill. In exasperation Nwafo called him 'Never-a-dry-season-in-the-nose'. Now, Obielue did not care for this name because his nose ran constantly and left the precincts of his nostrils red and sore. He called Nwafo 'Anthill-nose'; but it was not nearly as appropriate as the other and could not be turned into a song as readily. So he put Ezeulu's name in the song children sang whenever they saw an Udo ram, one of those fierce animals that belong to the shrine of Udo and could come and go as they wished. Children enjoyed teasing them from a good distance. The song, which was accompanied by the clapping of hands, implored the ram to remove the ugly lumps in its scrotum. To which the singers answered (on behalf of the ram): How does one remove yam tubers? The request and the response were sung in time with the swinging of the tubers. In place of *ebunu* Obielue sang *Ezeulu*. Nwafo could not stand this and gave his friend a blow in the mouth which brought blood to his front teeth.

Almost overnight Ezeulu had become something of a public enemy in the eyes of all and, as was to be expected, his entire family shared in his guilt. His children came up against it on their way to the stream and his wives suffered hostility in the market. The other day at the Nkwo Matefi had gone to buy a small basket of prepared cassava from Ojinika, wife of Ndulue. She knew Ojinika quite well and had bought from her and sold to her countless times. But on this day Ojinika spoke to her as if she was a stranger from another clan.

'I shall pay *ego nato*,' said Matefi.

'I have told you the price is *ego nese*.'

'I think *ego nato* suits it well; it's only a tiny basket.' She picked up the basket to show that it was small. Ojinika seemed to have forgotten all about her and was engrossed in arranging her okro in little lots on the mat.

'What do you say?'

'Put that basket down at once!' Then she changed her tone and sneered. 'You want to take it for nothing. You wait till the yams are ruined and come and buy a basket of cassava for eighteen cowries.'

Matefi was not the kind of person another woman could tie into her lappa and carry away. She gave Ojinika more than she got – told her the bride-price they paid for her mother. But when she got home she began to think about the hostility that was visibly encircling them all in Ezeulu's compound. Something told her that someone was going to pay a big price for it and she was afraid.

'Go and call me Obika,' she told her daughter, Ojiugo.

She was preparing some cocoyams for thickening soup when Obika came in and sat on the bare floor with his back on the wooden post in the middle of the entrance. He wore a very thin strip of cloth which was passed between the legs and between the buttocks and wound around the waist. He sat down heavily like a tired man. His mother went on with her work of dressing the cocoyams.

'Ojiugo says you called me.'

'Yes.' She went on with what she was doing.

'To watch you prepare cocoyams?'

She went on with her work.

'What is it?'

'I want you to go and talk to your father.'

'About what?'

'About what? About his . . . Are you a stranger in Umuaro? Do you not see the trouble that is coming?'

'What do you expect him to do? To disobey Ulu?'

'I knew you would not listen to me.' She managed to hang all her sorrows and disappointments on those words.

'How can I listen to you when you join outsiders in urging your husband to put his head in a cooking pot?'

'Sometimes I want to agree with those who say the man has caught his mother's madness,' said Ogbuefi Ofoka. 'When he came back from Okperi I went to his house and he talked like a sane man. I reminded him of his saying that a man must dance the dance prevailing in his time and told him that we had come – too late – to accept its wisdom. But today he would rather see the six villages ruined than eat two yams.'

'I have had the same thoughts myself,' said Akuebue who was visiting his in-law. 'I know Ezeulu better than most people. He is a proud man and the most stubborn person you know is only his messenger; but he would not falsify the decision of Ulu. If he did it Ulu would not spare him to begin with. So, I don't know.'

'I have not said that Ezeulu is telling a lie with the name of Ulu or that he is not. What we told him was to go and eat the yams and we would take the consequences. But he would not do it. Why? Because the six villages allowed the white man to take him away. That is the reason. He has been trying to see how he could punish Umuaro and now he has the chance. The house he has been planning to pull down has caught fire and saved him the labour.'

'I do not doubt that he has had a grievance for a long time, but I do not think it goes as deep as this. Remember he has his own yam-fields like the rest of us . . .'

'That was what he told us. But, my friend, when a man as proud as this wants to fight he does not care if his own head rolls as well in the conflict. And besides he forgot to mention that whether our harvest is ruined or not we would still take one yam each to Ulu.'

'I don't know.'

'Let me tell you one thing. A priest like Ezeulu leads a god to ruin himself. It has happened before.'

'Or perhaps a god like Ulu leads a priest to ruin himself.'

There was one man who saw the mounting crisis in Umuaro as a blessing and an opportunity sent by God. His name was John Jaja Goodcountry, Catechist of St Mark's C.M.S. Church, Umuaro. His home was in the Niger Delta which had been in contact with Europe and the world for hundreds of years. Although he had been in Umuaro only a year he could show as much progress in his church and school as many other teachers and pastors would have been proud to record after five or more years. His catechumen class had grown from a mere fourteen to nearly thirty – mostly young men and boys who also went to school. There had been one baptism in St Mark's Church itself and three in the parish church at Okperi. Altogether Mr Goodcountry's young church presented nine candidates for these occasions. He had not been able to field any candidates for confirmation, but that was hardly surprising in a new church among some of the most difficult people in the Ibo country.

The progress of St Mark's came about in a somewhat unusual way. Mr Goodcountry with his background of the Niger Delta Pastorate which could already count native martyrs like Joshua Hart to its credit was not prepared to compromise with the heathen over such things as sacred animals. Within weeks of his sojourn in Umuaro he was ready for a little war against the royal python in the same spirit as his own people had fought and conquered the sacred iguana. Unfortunately he came up against a local stumbling block in Moses Unachukwu, the most important Christian in Umuaro.

From the beginning Mr Goodcountry had taken exception to Unachukwu's know-all airs which the last catechist, Mr Molokwu, had done nothing to curb. Goodcountry had seen elsewhere how easy it was for a half-educated and half-converted Christian to mislead a whole congregation when the pastor or catechist was weak; so he wanted to establish his leadership from the very beginning. His intention was not originally to antagonize Unachukwu more than was necessary for making his point; after all he was a strong pillar in the church and could not be easily replaced. But Unachukwu did not give Mr Goodcountry a chance; he challenged him openly on the question of the python and so deserved the public rebuke and humiliation he got.

Having made his point Mr Goodcountry was prepared to forget the whole thing. He had no idea what kind of person he was dealing with. Unachukwu got a clerk in Okperi to write a petition on behalf of the priest of Idemili to the Bishop on the Niger. Although it was called a petition it was more of a threat. It warned the bishop that unless his followers in Umuaro left the royal python alone they would regret the day they ever set foot on the soil of the clan. Being the work of one of the knowledgeable clerks on Government Hill the petition made allusions to such potent words as law and order and the King's peace.

The bishop had just had a very serious situation in another part of his diocese on this same matter of the python. A young, energetic ordinand had led his people on a shrine-burning adventure and had killed a python in the process, whereupon the villagers had chased out all the Christians among them and burnt their houses. Things might have got out of hand had the Administration not stepped in with troops for a show of force. After this incident the Lieutenant-

Governor had written a sharp letter to the bishop to apply the reins on his boys.

For this reason, but also because he did not himself approve of such excess of zeal, the bishop had written a firm letter to Goodcountry. He had also replied to Ezidemili's petition assuring him that the catechist would not interfere with the python but at the same time praying that the day would not be far when the priest and all his people would turn away from the worship of snakes and idols to the true religion.

This letter from the big, white priest far away reinforced the view which had been gaining ground that the best way to deal with the white man was to have a few people like Moses Unachukwu around who knew what the white man knew. As a result many people – some of them very important – began to send their children to school. Even Nwaka sent a son – the one who seemed least likely among his children to become a good farmer.

Mr Goodcountry not knowing the full story of the deviousness of the heathen mind behind the growth of his school and church put it down to his effective evangelization which, in a way, it was – a vindication of his work against his bishop's policy of appeasement. He wrote a report on the amazing success of the Gospel in Umuaro for the *West African Church Magazine*, although, as was the custom in such reports, he allowed the credit to go to the Holy Spirit.

Now Mr Goodcountry saw in the present crisis over the New Yam Feast an opportunity for fruitful intervention. He had planned his church's harvest service for the second Sunday in November the proceeds from which would go into the fund for building a place of worship more worthy of God and of Umuaro. His plan was quite simple. The New Yam Feast was the attempt of the misguided heathen to show gratitude to God, the giver of all good things. This was God's hour to save them from their error which was now threatening to ruin them. They must be told that if they made their thank-offering to God they could harvest their crops without fear of Ulu.

'So we can tell our heathen brethren to bring their one yam to church instead of giving it to Ulu?' asked a new member of Goodcountry's church committee.

'That is what I say. But not just one yam. Let them bring as many as they wish according to the benefits they received this year from Almighty God. And not only yams, any crop whatsoever or livestock or money. Anything.'

The man who had asked the question did not seem satisfied. He kept scratching his head.

'Do you still not understand?'

'I understand but I was thinking how we could tell them to bring more than one yam. You see, our custom, or rather their custom, is to take just one yam to Ulu.'

Moses Unachukwu, who had since returned to full favour with Goodcountry, saved the day. 'If Ulu who is a false god can eat one yam the living God who owns the whole world should be entitled to eat more than one.'

So the news spread that anyone who did not want to wait and see all his harvest ruined could take his offering to the god of the Christians who claimed to have power of protection from the anger of Ulu. Such a story at other times might have been treated with laughter. But there was no more laughter left in the people.

Chapter Nineteen

The first serious sufferers from the postponement of the harvest were the family of Ogbuefi Amalu who had died in the rainy season from *aru-mmo*. Amalu was a man of substance and, in normal times, the rites of second burial and funeral feast would have followed two or three days after his death. But it was a bad death which killed a man in the time of famine. Amalu himself knew it and was prepared. Before he died he had called his first son, Aneto, and given him directions for the burial feast.

'I would have said: Do it a day or two after I have been put into the earth. But this is *ugani*; I cannot ask you to arrange my burial feast with your saliva. I must wait until there are yams again.' He spoke with great difficulty, struggling with every breath. Aneto was down on both knees beside the bamboo bed and strained to catch the whispers which were barely audible over the noisy breathing coming from the cavity of the sick man's chest. The many coatings of camwood which had been rubbed on it had caked and cracked like red earth in the dry season. 'But you must not delay it beyond four moons from my death. And do not forget, I want you to slaughter a bull.'

There was a story told of a young man in another clan who was so pestered by trouble that he decided to consult an oracle. The reason, he was told, was that his dead father wanted him to sacrifice a goat to him. The young man said to the oracle: 'Ask my father if he left as much as a fowl for me.' Ogbuefi Amalu was not like that man. Everyone knew he was worth four hundred bulls and that he had not asked his son for more than was justly due.

In anticipation of the New Yam Festival Aneto and his brothers and kinsmen had chosen the day for Amalu's second burial and announced it to all Umuaro and to all their relations and in-laws in the neighbouring clans.

What were they to do now? Should they persist with their plan and give Amalu a poor man's burial feast without yams and risk his ire on their heads or should they put it off beyond the time that Amalu had appointed and again risk his anger? The second choice seemed the better and the less dangerous one. But to be quite sure Aneto went to *afa*, to put the alternatives to his father.

When he got to the oracle he found that there were not two alternatives but only one. He dared not ask his father whether he would accept a poor man's funeral; rather he asked whether he could delay the rites until there were yams in Umuaro. Amalu said no. He had already stood too long in the rain and sun and could not bear it one day longer. A poor man might wander outside for years while his kinsmen scraped their meagre resources together; that was his penalty for lack of success in his life. But a great man who had toiled through two titles must be called indoors by those for whom he had toiled and for whom he left his riches.

Aneto called a kindred meeting and told them what his father had said. No one was surprised. 'Who would blame Amalu?' they asked. 'Has he not stood outside long enough?' No, the fault was Ezeulu's. He had seen to it that Amalu's kinsmen would waste their substance in buying yams from neighbouring clans when their own crop lay locked in the soil. Many of these neighbouring people were already growing fat out of Umuaro's misfortune. Every Nkwo market they brought new yams to Umuaro and sold them like anklets of ivory. At first only men without title, women and children ate these foreign yams. But as the famine grew more harsh and stringent someone pointed out that there was nothing in the custom of Umuaro forbidding a man of title from eating new yams grown on foreign earth; and in any case who was there when they were dug out to swear that they were new yams? This made people laugh with one side of their face. But if there was any man of title who took this advice and ate these yams he made sure that no one saw him. What many of them did do was to harvest the yams planted around their homestead to feed their wives and children. From ancient usage it had always been possible for a man to dig up a few homestead yams in times of severe famine. But today it was not just a few yams and, what was more, the homestead area crept farther and farther afield as the days passed.

The plight of Umuaro lay more heavily on Ezeulu and his family than other people knew. In the Chief Priest's compound nobody could think of indulging in the many old and new evasions which allowed others to eat an occasional new yam be it local or foreign. Because they were more prosperous than most families they had a larger stock of old yams. But these had long shrivelled into tasteless fibre. Before cooking they had to be beaten with a heavy pestle to separate the wiry strands. Soon even these were finished.

But the heaviest load was on Ezeulu's mind. He was used to loneliness. As Chief Priest he had often walked alone in front of Umuaro. But without looking back he had always been able to hear their flute and song which shook the earth because it came from a multitude of voices and the stamping of countless feet. There had been moments when the voices were divided as in the land dispute with Okperi. But never until now had he known them to die away altogether. Few people came to his hut now and those who came said nothing. Ezeulu wanted to hear what Umuaro was saying but nobody offered to tell and he would not make anyone think he was curious. So with every passing day Umuaro became more and more an alien silence – the kind of silence which burnt a man's inside like the blue, quiet, razor-edge flame of burning palmnut shells. Ezeulu writhed in the pain which grew and grew until he wanted to get outside his compound or even into the Nkwo market place and shout at Umuaro.

Because no one came near enough to him to see his anguish – and if they had seen it they would not have understood – they imagined that he sat in his hut gloating over the distress of Umuaro. But although he would not for any reason now see the present trend reversed he carried more punishment and more suffering than all his fellows. What troubled him most – and he alone seemed to be aware of it at present – was that the punishment was not for now alone but for all time. It would afflict Umuaro like an *ogulu-aro* disease which counts a year and returns to its victim. Beneath all anger in his mind lay a deeper compassion for Umuaro, the clan which long, long ago when lizards were in ones and twos chose his ancestor to carry their deity and go before them challenging every obstacle and confronting every danger on their behalf.

Perhaps if the silence in which Ezeulu was trapped had been complete he would have got used to it in time. But it had cracks through which now and again a teasing driblet of news managed to reach him: this had the effect of deepening the silence, like a pebble thrown in a cave.

Today Akuebue threw such a pebble. He was the only man among Ezeulu's friends and kinsmen who still came now and again to see him. But when he came he sat in silence or spoke about unimportant things. Today, however, he could not but touch on a new development in the crisis which troubled him. Perhaps Akuebue was the only man in Umuaro who knew that Ezeulu was not deliberately punishing the six villages. He knew that the Chief Priest was helpless; that a thing greater than *nte* had been caught in *nte*'s trap. So whenever he came to visit Ezeulu he kept clear of the things nearest to their thoughts because they were past talking. But today he could not keep silence over the present move of the Christians to reap the harvest of Umuaro.

'It troubles me,' he said, 'because it looks like the saying of our ancestors that when brothers fight to death a stranger inherits their father's estate.'

'What do you expect me to do?' Ezeulu opened both palms towards his friend. 'If any man in Umuaro forgets himself so far as to join them let him carry on.'

Akuebue shook his head in despair.

As soon as he left Ezeulu called Oduche and asked him if it was true that his people were offering sanctuary to those who wished to escape the vengeance of Ulu. Oduche said he did not understand.

'You do not understand? Are your people saying to Umuaro that if anyone brings his sacrifice to your shrine he will be safe to harvest his yams? Now do you understand?'

'Yes. Our teacher told them so.'

'Your teacher told them so? Did you report it to me?'

'No.'

'Why?'

Silence.

'I said why did you not report it to me?'

For a long time father and son looked steadily at each other in silence. When Ezeulu spoke again his tone was calm and full of grief.

'Do you remember, Oduche, what I told you when I sent you among those people?'

Oduche shifted his eyes to the big toe of his right foot which he placed a little forward.

'Since you have become dumb let me remind you. I called you as a father calls his son and told you to go and be my eye and ear among those people. I did not send Obika or Edogo; I did not send Nwafo, your mother's son. I called you by name and you came here – in this *obi* – and I sent you to see and hear for me. I did not know at that time that I was sending a goat's skull. Go away, go back to your mother's hut. I have no spirit for talking now. When I am ready to talk I shall tell you what I think. Go away and rejoice that your father cannot count on you. I say, go away from here, lizard that ruined his mother's funeral.'

Oduche went out at the brink of tears. Ezeulu felt a slight touch of comfort.

At last another new moon came and he ate the twelfth yam. The next morning he sent word to his assistants to announce that the New Yam Feast would be eaten in twenty-eight days.

Throughout that day the drums beat in Amalu's compound because the funeral feast was tomorrow. The sound reached every village in Umuaro to remind them; not that anyone needed reminding at such a time when men were as hungry as locusts.

In the night Ezeulu dreamt one of those strange dreams which were more than ordinary dreams. When he woke up everything stood out with the detail and clarity of daylight, like the one he had dreamt in Okperi.

He was sitting in his *obi*. From the sound of the voices the mourners seemed to be passing behind his compound, beyond the tall, red walls. This worried him a good deal because there was no path there. Who were these people then who made a path behind his compound?

He told himself that he must go out and challenge them because it was said that unless a man wrestled with those who walked behind his compound the path never closed. But he lacked resolution and stood where he was. Meanwhile the voices and the drums and the flutes grew louder. They sang the song with which a man was carried to the bush for burial:

> Look! a python
> Look! a python
> Yes, it lies across the way.

As usual the song came in different waves like gusts of storm following on each other's heels. The mourners in front sang a little ahead of those in the middle near the corpse and these were again ahead of those at the rear. The drums came with this last wave.

Ezeulu raised his voice to summon his family to join him in challenging the trespassers but his compound was deserted. His irresolution turned into alarm. He ran into Matefi's hut but all he saw were the ashes of a long-dead fire. He rushed out and ran into Ugoye's hut calling her and her children but her hut was already falling in and a few blades of green grass had sprouted on the thatch. He was running towards Obika's hut when a new voice behind the compound brought him to a sudden halt. The noise of the burial party had since disappeared in the distance. But beside the sorrow of the solitary voice that now wailed after them they might have been returning with a bride. The sweet agony of the solitary singer settled like dew on the head.

> I was born when lizards were in ones and twos
> A child of Idemili. The difficult tear-drops
> Of Sky's first weeping drew my spots. Being
> Sky-born I walked the earth with royal gait
> And mourners saw me coiled across their path.
> But of late
> A strange bell
> Has been ringing a song of desolation:
> > Leave your yams and cocoyams

And come to school.
And I must scuttle away in haste
When children in play or in earnest cry:
      Look! a Christian is on the way.
Ha ha ha ha ha ha ha ha ha ha ha ha ha . . .

The singer's sudden, demented laughter filled Ezeulu's compound and he woke up. In spite of the cold harmattan he was sweating. But he felt an enormous relief to be awake and know that it had been a dream. The blind alarm and the life-and-death urgency fell away from it at the threshold of waking. But a vague fear remained because the voice of the python had ended as the voice of Ezeulu's mother when she was seized with madness. Nwanyi Okperi, as they called her in Umuaro, had been a great singer in her youth, making songs for her village as easily as some people talked. In later life when her madness came on her these old songs and others she might have made forced themselves out in eccentric spurts through the cracks in her mind. Ezeulu in his childhood lived in fear of these moments when his mother's feet were put in stocks, at the new moon.

The passage of Ogbazulobodo at that moment helped in establishing Ezeulu in the present. Perhaps it was the effect of the dream, but in all his life he had never heard a night spirit pass with this fury. It was like a legion of runners each covered from neck to ankle with strings of rattling *ekpili*. It came from the direction of the *ilo* and disappeared towards Nkwo. It must have seen signs of light in someone's compound for it seemed to stop and cry: *Ewo okuo! Ewo okuo!* The offender whoever it was must have quickly put out the light, and the pacified spirit continued its flight and soon disappeared in the night.

Ezeulu wondered why it had not saluted him when it passed near his compound. Or perhaps it did before he woke up.

After the dream and the commotion of Ogbazulobodo's passage he tried in vain to sleep again. Then they began to fire the cannon in Amalu's place. Ezeulu counted nine claps separated by the beating of *ekwe*. By that time sleep had completely left his eyes. He got up and groped for the latch of his carved door and opened it. Then he took his matchet and his bottle of snuff from the head of the bed and groped his way to the outer room. There he felt the dry chill of the harmattan. Fortunately the fire had not died from the two big ukwa logs. He stoked it and produced a small flame.

No other person in the village could carry the *ogbazulobodo* as well as Obika. Whenever somebody else tried there was a big difference: either the speed was too slow or the words stuck in his throat. For the power of *ike-agwu-ani*, great though it was, could not change a crawling millipede into an antelope nor a dumb man into an orator. That was why in spite of the great grievance which Amalu's family nursed against Ezeulu and his family Aneto still came to beg Obika to run as *ogbazulobodo* on the night before his father's second burial.

'I do not want to say no to you,' said Obika after Aneto had spoken, 'but this is not something a man can do when his body is not all his. Since yesterday I have been having a little fever.'

'I do not know what it is but everybody you see nowadays sounds like a broken pot,' said Aneto.

'Why not ask Nweke Ukpaka to run for you?'

'I knew about Nweke Ukpaka when I came to you. I even passed by his house.'

Obika considered the matter.

'There are many people who can do it,' said Aneto. 'But he whose name is called again and again by those trying in vain to catch a wild bull has something he alone can do to bulls.'

'True,' said Obika. 'I agree but I am agreeing in cowardice.'

'If I say no,' Obika told himself, 'they will say that Ezeulu and his family have revealed a second time their determination to wreck the burial of their village man who did no harm to them.'

He did not tell his wife that he would be going out that night until he had eaten his evening meal. Obika always went into his wife's hut to eat his meals. His friends teased him about it and said the woman had spoilt his head. Okuata was polishing off the soup in her bowl when Obika spoke. She crooked her first finger once more, wiped the bowl with it, stretched it again and ran it down her tongue.

'Going out with this fever?' she asked. 'Obika, have pity on yourself.

The funeral is tomorrow. What is there they cannot do without you until morning?'

'I shall not stay long. Aneto is my age mate and I must go and see how he is preparing.'

Okuata maintained a sullen silence.

'Bar the door well. Nobody will carry you away. I shall not stay long.'

The *ekwe-ogbazulobodo* sounded *kome kome kokome kome kokome* and continued for a while warning anyone still awake to hurry up to bed and put out every light because light and *ogbazulobodo* were mortal enemies. When it had beaten long enough for all to hear it stopped. Silence and the shrill call of insects seized the night again. Obika and the others who would carry the *ayaka* spirit-chorus sat on the lowest rung of the *okwolo* steps talking and laughing. The man who beat the *ekwe* joined them, leaving his drum in the half-light of the palm-oil torch.

When the *ekwe* began to beat out the second and final warning Obika was still talking with the others as though it did not concern him. The old man, Ozumba, who kept the regalia of the night spirits took a position near the drummer. Then he raised his cracked voice and called *ugoli* four or five times as if to clear the cobweb from it. Then he asked if Obika was there. Obika looked in his direction and saw him vaguely in the weak light. Slowly and deliberately he got up and went to Ozumba, and stood before him. Ozumba bent down and took up a skirt made of a network of rope and heavily studded with rattling *ekpili*. Obika raised both arms above his head so that Ozumba could tie the skirt round his waist without hindrance. When this was done Ozumba waved his arms about like a blind man until they struck the iron staff. He pulled it out of the ground and placed it in Obika's right hand. The *ekwe* continued to beat in the half-light of the palm-oil torch. Obika closed his hand tight on the staff and clenched his teeth. Ozumba allowed him a little time to prepare himself fully. Then very slowly he lifted the *ike-agwu-ani* necklace. The *ekwe* beat faster and faster. Obika held his head forward and Ozumba put the *ike-agwu-ani* round his neck. As he did so he said:

Tun-tun gem-gem
Ọsọ mgbada bu nugwu.
The speed of the deer
Is seen on the hill.

As soon as these words left his mouth Ogbazulobodo swung round and cried: *Ewo ọkuo! Ewo ọkuo!* The drummer threw down his sticks and hastily blew out the offending light. The spirit planted the staff into the earth and it reverberated. He pulled it out again and vanished like the wind in the direction of Nkwo leaving potent words in the air behind.

'*The fly that struts around on a mound of excrement wastes his time; the mound will always be greater than the fly. The thing that beats the drum for ngwesi is inside the ground. Darkness is so great it gives horns to a dog. He who builds a homestead before another can boast more broken pots. It is ofo that gives rain-water power to cut dry earth. The man who walks ahead of his fellows spots spirits on the way. Bat said he knew his ugliness and chose to fly by night. When the air is fouled by a man on top of a palm tree the fly is confused. An ill-fated man drinks water and it catches in his teeth . . .*'

He was at once blind and full of sight. He did not see any of the landmarks like trees and huts but his feet knew perfectly where they were going; he did not leave out even one small path from the accustomed route. He knew it without the use of eyes. He only stopped once when he smelt light . . . '*Even while people are still talking about the man Rat bit to death Lizard takes money to have his teeth filed. He who sees an old hag squatting should leave her alone; who knows how she breathes? White Ant chews igbegulu because it is lying on the ground; let him climb the palm tree and chew. He who will swallow udala seeds must consider the size of his anus. The fly that has no one to advise him follows the corpse into the ground . . .*'

A fire began to rage inside his chest and to push a dry bitterness up his mouth. But he tasted it from a distance or from a mouth within his mouth. He felt like two separate persons, one running above the other.

'*. . . When a handshake passes the elbow it becomes another thing. The sleep that lasts from one market day to another has become death. The man*

*who likes the meat of the funeral ram, why does he recover when sickness
visits him? The mighty tree falls and the little birds scatter in the bush . . .
The little bird which hops off the ground and lands on an ant-hill may not
know it but is still on the ground . . . A common snake which a man sees all
alone may become a python in his eyes . . . The very Thing which kills Mother
Rat is always there to make sure that its young ones never open their eyes
. . . The boy who persists in asking what happened to his father before he has
enough strength to avenge him is asking for his father's fate . . . The man
who belittles the sickness which Monkey has suffered should ask to see the
eyes which his nurse got from blowing the sick fire . . . When death wants to
take a little dog it prevents it from smelling even excrement . . .'*

The eight men who would sing the *ayaka* chorus were still talking
where Obika left them. Ozumba had come to sit with them to await
his return. They were talking about the big bull which Amalu's children had bought for his funeral when they heard the voice already
coming back. The *ayaka* men scrambled to their feet and got ready
to break into song as soon as Ogbazulobodo re-entered the *ilo*. They
were all amazed that he was already returning. Had he left out any
of the paths?

'Not Obika,' said Ozumba proudly. 'He is a sharp one. Give me a
sharp boy even though he breaks utensils in his haste.'

This was hardly out of his mouth when Ogbazulobodo raced in
and fell down at the foot of the *okwolo*. Ozumba removed the necklace
from his neck and called his name. But Obika did not answer. He
called again and touched his chest.

They poured some of the cold water which was always kept handy
over his face and body. The song of the *ayaka* had stopped as abruptly
as it had started. They all stood around unable yet to talk.

The first cock had not crowed. Ezeulu was still in his *obi*. The fire still
glowed on the big logs but the flame had long gone out. Were those
footsteps he was hearing? He listened carefully. Yes, they were getting
louder, and voices too. He felt for his matchet. What could this be?

'Who?' he called. The footsteps stopped, and the voices. For a
moment there was silence, heavy with the presence of the strangers
outside in the dark.

'People,' said a voice.

'Who is called people? My gun is loaded, let me warn people.'

'Ezeulu, it is me, Ozumba.'

'Ozumba.'

'Eh.'

'What brings you out at this time?'

'An abomination has overtaken us. Goat has eaten palm leaves from off my head.'

Ezeulu merely cleared his throat and began slowly to stoke the fire. 'Let me build a fire to see your faces.' One of the sticks of firewood was too long and he broke it across his knee. He blew the fire a few times and it broke into a flame.

'Come in and let me hear what you are saying.'

As soon as he saw Obika's body coming in under the low eaves he sprang to his feet and took up his matchet.

'What happened to him? Who did this? I said who?'

Ozumba began to explain but Ezeulu did not hear. The matchet fell from his hand and he slumped down on both knees beside the body. 'My son,' he cried. 'Ulu, were you there when this happened to me?' He hid his face on Obika's chest.

When the first light came nearly every arrangement had been made for the announcement of the death. The village death-drums were leaning against a wall. A bottle of gunpowder had been found and put aside. Ezeulu wandered up and down among the busy people trying to help. At one point he found the long broom they used paddle-wise to sweep the compound, took it up and began to sweep. But someone took it from him and led him by the hand back to his hut.

'People will soon be here,' he said weakly, 'and the place is still unswept.'

'Leave it to me. I shall find somebody to do it straight away.'

Obika's death shook Umuaro to the roots; a man like him did not come into the world too often. As for Ezeulu it was as though he had died.

Some people expected Ezidemili to be jubilant. Such people did not know him. He was not that kind of man and besides he knew too well the danger of such exultation. All he was heard to say quietly was: 'This should teach him how far he could dare next time.'

But for Ezeulu there was no next time. Think of a man who, unlike lesser men, always goes to battle without a shield because he knows that bullets and matchet strokes will glance off his medicine-boiled skin; think of him discovering in the thick of battle that the power has suddenly, without warning, deserted him. What next time can there be? Will he say to the guns and the arrows and the matchets: *Hold! I want to return quickly to my medicine-hut and stir the pot and find out what has gone wrong; perhaps someone in my household – a child, maybe – has unwittingly violated my medicine's taboo?* No.

Ezeulu sank to the ground in utter amazement. It was not simply the blow of Obika's death, great though it was. Men had taken greater blows: that was what made a man a man. For did they not say that a man is like a funeral ram which must take whatever beating comes to it without opening its mouth; that the silent tremor of pain down its body alone must tell of its suffering?

At any other time Ezeulu would have been more than a match to his grief. He would have been equal to any pain not compounded with humiliation. But why, he asked himself again and again, why had Ulu chosen to deal thus with him, to strike him down and then cover him with mud? What was his offence? Had he not divined the god's will and obeyed it? When was it ever heard that a child was scalded by the piece of yam its own mother put in its palm? What man would send his son with a potsherd to bring fire from a neighbour's hut and then unleash rain on him? Who ever sent his son up the palm to gather nuts and then took an axe and felled the tree? But today such a thing had happened before the eyes of all. What could it point to but the collapse and ruin of all things? Then a god, finding himself powerless, might take flight and in one final, backward glance at his abandoned worshippers cry:

If the rat cannot flee fast enough
Let him make way for the tortoise!

Perhaps it was the constant, futile throbbing of these thoughts that finally left a crack in Ezeulu's mind. Or perhaps his implacable assailant having stood over him for a little while stepped on him as on an insect and crushed him under the heel in the dust. But this final act of malevolence proved merciful. It allowed Ezeulu, in his last days, to live in the haughty splendour of a demented high priest and spared him knowledge of the final outcome.

Meanwhile Winterbottom, after a recuperative leave in England had returned to his seat and married the doctor. He did not ever hear of Ezeulu again. The only man who might have carried the story to Government Hill was John Nwodika, his steward. But John had since left Winterbottom's service to set up a small trade in tobacco. It looked as though the gods and the powers of event finding Winterbottom handy had used him and left him again in order as they found him.

So in the end only Umuaro and its leaders saw the final outcome. To them the issue was simple. Their god had taken sides with them against his headstrong and ambitious priest and thus upheld the wisdom of their ancestors – that no man however great was greater than his people; that no one ever won judgement against his clan.

If this was so, then Ulu had chosen a dangerous time to uphold that truth for in destroying his priest he had also brought disaster on himself, like the lizard in the fable who ruined his mother's funeral by his own hand. For a deity who chose a moment such as this to chastise his priest or abandon him before his enemies was inciting people to take liberties; and Umuaro was just ripe to do so. The Christian harvest which took place a few days after Obika's death saw more people than even Goodcountry could have dreamed. In his extremity many a man sent his son with a yam or two to offer to the new religion and to bring back the promised immunity. Thereafter any yam harvested in his fields was harvested in the name of the son.